King of
the Dead

King of the Dead

R.A. MacAvoy

© Copyright 1991 by R.A. MacAvoy
First e-reads publication 1999
www.e-reads.com
ISBN 1-58586-998-8

Other works by R.A. MacAvoy

also available in e-reads editions

Belly of the Wolf
Lens of the World
The Grey Horse
Tea with the Black Dragon

King of
the Dead

To a browser of dusty library shelves:

My name, in academic circles, is Powl Inpres. Otherwhere I am titled Earl of Daraln. I am enclosing with this letter a history of events of some importance to our nation: events which took place in the seventh year of reign of Rudof I. It was written by a man named Nazhuret, whose own history and surname are obscure (at least they have been while I could help it) and who was my first student. My most perfect student. In this I claim no credit, for anyone could have taught Nazhuret anything, as long as the knowledge rang true to him.

He was assisted, both in the experience and in the memoir, by Charlan Bannering, daughter of the late Baron Howdl of Sordaling. Of all swordsmen I have trained, she was the most elegant and the most deadly with a rapier, but she refuses to put pen to paper on her own account, and but for her lasting affection for Nazhuret, would not have cooperated even so far as to think back.

I have held this manuscript privately until now, because there is always a danger when officialdom becomes aware of a person, either

1

to disapprove or (worse) in approval, and I do not want my friends to suffer more entanglement than their own fates decree. But officialdom rarely follows the academic papers and never frequents libraries at all.

I have suspicions my health is failing, and lest death take me unprepared I leave this manuscript like an orphan baby. Like Nazhuret himself, may it linger in obscurity long enough to be safe from malice, and rise again in the hands of someone who cares.

Powl

My dear Powl,

I hope you will forgive my tone of bitterness; this year has been such a time of catastrophe: blood and confusion for all the northern world. Perhaps worst for Nazhuret is that I feel myself to have been part of the violence—a pawn of sorcery, and as a careful scientist I do not believe in sorcery. When because of sorcery men let themselves be butchered, it leaves me angry. When because of human arrogance, or twisted loyalty, or fear, they go out to be butchered, that makes me even more angry. I think war is a kind of black sorcery in itself.

In this, my twenty-eighth year, I have lost many things I grieve to do without: friends, peace, faith in the coming seasons. I, who was a happy beggar, have found my limits. All I have gamed in my turn is an understanding of my name, and it is a name I never wanted.

I wish you had asked for this history a year from now, or ten. Then I might have been able to show some understanding of all that happened to me in the country of my mother, or upon my way to it, or on my way home. As it is, I have nothing but images, locked in the eyes, and against them my understanding is useless.

But I know that what I have to give is what you want—my memories, whether sane or insane—for you will not let any other person do your understanding for you. You are the scientist in this, and I can be only your subject. Observe me well.

Watching through a window I saw five assassins assault my lady, who was carrying in her a four-months' child. They were armed with axes and daggers, with which they first attacked her horse: well-trained men. The white mare went down in a heap and I saw Arlin for a moment perched on the sinking back, and then she, in her black shirt, was hidden.

2

I went through the closed window, which was stupid of me, for the door was open to the summer air only ten feet away. I remember only the brilliance of scattered glass and the brilliance of my horror as I ran down the oratory walkway in my breeches and stockings, smashing against the ornamental maples that marked each curve of the path.

I was three hundred feet away; too far to be of any help. I came skidding along the gravel to a heap of bodies and gushing blood—red blood on white hide and blood staining dark woolens darker. Amid the pile of hands and teeth and staring eyes I sought for Arlin's, but in my shock I could not make out what belonged to what, not even horse from human, and then Arlin swung out from behind a tree, holding to the bole with both hands. Not standing straight. "Go," she said, and pointed to where the walk widened and met the wagon drive.

In leaving her alone and chasing the fleeing assassins I think I acted like someone else entirely, not Nazhuret of Sordaling. Not Zhurrie of the Forest Oratory, certainly. But Powl—who am I to say I know myself, and that self dipped in horror especially?

The river pebbles of the drive, so laboriously gathered and laid generations ago, slid and shifted and slowed me, but I did not feel their imprint against my stockinged feet, nor feel the heat of the effort.

Only a little way beyond, at the well with the stone benches, where even now local people did leave gifts of food and flowers, I found two men, leaning, gasping, one clenching one arm in the other and one holding his stomach. Holding his stomach as Arlin had. By this and by their dun hunters' jackets and breeches I knew them to be two of the assailants, and my mind reproduced the picture of slaughter and I could see now that there were three dead men around the dead horse, one of them pinned and obscured by the mare's bulk.

These two had no more than a few seconds' warning of my approach, but the man with the stomach injury already had a knife in his hand. The broken arm turned and ran.

The knife-fighter was experienced, and I hate encountering knife-fighters more than I do any armored knight, for their art is a deadly stroking, close in the belly and hard to predict. Arlin is a knife-fighter, however, and so I have had much practice. I let him think he was disemboweling me neatly, but tucked away and caught his hand at the end of its figure and disemboweled him instead. I did it of a purpose, for convenience's sake, because I wanted him out of the way. I wanted time to think about things.

Never before in my life had I killed a man for such a small reason. At times I wonder if that deed did not stain the events of the year to come.

3

(Perhaps that conceit is human arrogance—to think that events revolve around the condition of my own soul. Or perhaps it is a subtle awareness, and in reality my soul reflects the condition of events. Whatever, humans like myself will always think that way.)

Before the assassin could look down and see his own guts spilling, I broke his spine at the neck. That was not done for convenience, but rather because I thought he would want it so.

The last assassin did not try to resist, but stumbled away from me, face white, eyes black, his arm bone protruding from both skin and jacket. I caught him by the collar, and he watched as I dropped my breeches on the road. The poor brute of a man must have thought I was going to rape him—or even defecate on him—but I used the garment to wrap his ruined arm against his body and I led him back to the carnage.

Arlin was sitting beside her mare, regardless of the pooling blood, crouched over her own middle, and her face was not much better than my prisoner's. When she saw me she straightened and wiped the pain away.

"There were two," she said tentatively. I gestured behind me and made some sort of sound and Arlin understood. She rose as I came to her and, holding the man at arm's length, I let her lean against me.

She looked closely, not at him but at me, and she asked why my face and scalp were bleeding.

"I broke some glass," I told her and she made the traditional response: "God keep us from bad luck."

That was ugly writing, old friend, and I had to get up and weed the border for a while before I could go on. Above my desk is the very window I smashed—a window of fourteen panes—and it shows the signs of my own carpentry and glazing. (I am a better optician than I am glazier.) Now I must return to this story and write things much uglier.

Arlin had a red weal on her abdomen in the shape of an ax handle, and at the top was a patch of broken skin in the oblong of the back of an axhead. She sat on our cot, hands clenched, silent as ever and staring at the rotten old silk window screen. An hour passed and the mark darkened. Though I had explored medicine with you, Powl, in the last few years, I could do nothing to cure this and she would take nothing for the pain. I took the elixir of opium I had ready and went down the long hall to the closet where we had locked the broken assassin, and I forced a good amount down him. In a few minutes he was oblivious, and I set the arm as well as I could and wrapped it against him again.

The other beggars in the oratory warily watched me emerge with my lantern from the closet, and they said nothing. They were not used to seeing me take prisoners: no more than I was used to it. Nor did they attempt to enter Arlin's and my room, for her black silences and bright blades kept people at a distance. Some of them knew she was a woman and some did not. Some who had known had forgotten it again, as a thing too inexplicable. No one besides myself knew yet that she was carrying.

When I returned she told me she was beginning to miscarry. She said it as one would say, "I think I smell a dead mouse": with indifferent disgust, and she kept her gaze on the soft, discolored light of the screen.

We had raspberry leaf infusion, I told her. We had the stinking preparation you brought back from Felonka and left in the medicine chest, which was supposed to be effective to prevent such things.

Arlin said, "If it is dead, then it had better pass out," using the same dry tone of voice. I looked at the spreading weal and I tried to ask her if it was dead, if she had a way of knowing, but I could not speak at all. Then the blood started, and horrible cramping against the injury, and I could do nothing but hold her hand until from her grip the long bones of my own hand ground against one another.

When the worst of it had passed, I went down the hall to see to the other patient. Cown, the redhead with one eye, stopped me to ask about Arlin: was he well and would we want any dinner? I gave him a single "no" and brushed by.

The prisoner had awakened. He had hanged himself by his own belt from a roof beam and there he was, dangling, hours dead, his right arm still neatly bound to his side.

I cut him down. The next day I ripped out the silk screen (the last one left from when the oratory was rich and filled with religious). I could not bear to see the light shine through it.

This had been the third assassination attempt that summer, though the other two had been with fewer assassins, and both had been directed at myself. I had killed three men—four, if you counted the prisoner—and one had gotten away, first cutting the throat of his injured partner. This day Arlin had killed three.

And now our five years together, first with her as a student of my own teacher, and then two years wandering, seemed a paradise of innocence, not to be regained—certainly not by a man who killed as a matter of convenience.

I had been either arrogant or naive. I had thought I had the skills to control any man and keep him from injuring either me, my friends, or himself. That attitude was nothing I got from you, Powl. It had been nurtured by my years in Sordaling, where I was more experienced than any other student, and at the boundary of Norwess and Ekesh, where the worst enemy I encountered was a single renegade soldier. Now that I had met professed assassins, I knew I was not even a minor god.

The years of our honeymoon—I call it that though we could not be legally married—had been splendidly quiet. Even when Arlin pursued the blood-drinker (who turned out to be only simple and insane), that was more a matter of intellectual curiosity than of dread, and as I lay in bed in the late hours of this terrible night, I longed for the sunny triviality of worrying about the next meal, or keeping the resident beggars from one another's throats.

I had no real doubts where the assassins had come from. No one with money to hire such had any reason to want me dead except those who had inherited my father's dukedom, and who believed I would go to the king some day and demand it back.

I can understand their worry, for I know the love of countryside. I have learned to love the oratory King Rudof gave us, which is beautiful, and earlier in my life I learned to love a square block of brick and brass, which was not. I also understand the fear of being robbed, although all I possess is education, which can only be taken from me by rattling my brains hard.

And Arlin, of course. I can't say I possess her, but I might be robbed of her, and I have found that that possibility will cause me to kill.

It would have been simpler had there been only one gainer by my father's loss, but there were at least three—Towl Kuby: Viscount Endergen; Karl Bonn: Baron Fowett; and of course the Duke of Leoue, whose father Arlin had slain. The young duke was only seventeen, but his age was no impediment to employing a man for any purpose, and even if I did not find Leoue lovable, his son might have done so. If he did not, still there was the sting of humiliation and reduced holdings to spur him on.

Which of these men had sent the blight upon us, I could not know. I do not live the sort of life where I would be likely to meet any of them and judge. It could have been all of them, adding to a common fund. For this sort of problem I needed you, in your role as Earl Daraln, for politics are chess to you and you play chess very well.

But you were off alone somewhere, free of students for once, acting the eccentric philosopher and gatherer of exotic knowledge. The king, too, was off in Old North Velonya, acting the king, and there was no one here but Arlin, who is a social renegade, and myself, who have been called "simple" sufficient times for me to remember the word.

6

The next day Arlin continued to bleed from the miscarriage, and although she denied the loss of black blood to be dangerous, I feared her black mood.

Education changes nothing, nor does understanding. Before I endured your tutelage I was Zhurrie the Goblin, Zhurrie the Clown. Now I am ten times more the clown, and ten times happier to be one. Lady Charlan Bannering was a silent, saturnine girl and full of black secrets. Arlin the sword spinner took that persona further and darker, and his (her) secrets were deadly. As a graduate of our exclusive school (two students, one master, or perhaps three students altogether), Arlin was more brilliantly black than ever.

The next day a new beggar arrived, having heard of the shelter through a beggar's peculiar information services, and the original two beggars departed. One of these was short and rosy, and blond as a baby duck, and the other was wolfhound tall, with white skin and black hair. No one heard them leave and no one marked their absence, though according to the writ of the king, the oratory belonged to them and their heirs forever. Beggars have different writs.

The summers of high Velonya are as hot as the winters are cold, but the forests of maple and birch cut the heat into manageable slices, and even the short summer nights become cuddling-comfortable, soiled only by the presence of mosquitoes. For two years Arlin and I had floated from the North Cliffs down to Warvala City and back again, our only home being barns or byres taken for the evening in exchange for labor, or the occasional inn room which meant I had sold a pair of eyeglasses or Arlin had won a game of cards.

In the summer this style of life had been as comfortable as any other, and in spring it was paradise, but with the first snows it became deadly, and all our attention was necessary to keep us a step in front of starvation, or the loss of fingers, ears, or toes.

No man, however beggarly, sleeps in the woods of Velonya from November through March, and the gray downpours of April are not much easier. These past four months in the oratory had been an unexpected release from hell, teacher. We had refurbished the kitchen and cleaned every chimney. We had gone so far as to decide which room the baby would have. Like our own room, it had a private garden.

I didn't know who would take that room, or whether the others would use it to shit in now we were gone.

The first day we woke up in the woods, I felt a peace of spirit I hadn't known since before the morning in March when two men leaped out of the shrubbery at me with razors in their hands. Even had we been forced to flee into country strange to us, I doubt any Velonyan assassin could have discovered us, but these woods were our own park, by law as well as usage, and were like rooms of our house in their familiarity. Last year, passing north

7

from one market town to another, we had discovered a stand of vine maple on an acre's island in the stream that watered the oratory plantings, and I had braided a large stand of branches into a living pavilion three or four feet off the black soil. This spring, upon settling into the oratory, I rediscovered my architecture. All the braids had matured into elflocks, but that only added to the concealment. I had scraped the dry leaves out and scattered them into the stream, so that movement within made no sound, and corrected the roofing, twig and leaf, to minimize the effect of rain. No boy of ten years could have enjoyed the making of a hidden fort more than I had, though I was twenty-eight. When I was ten, there had been no opportunity for fort-making.

Now Arlin lay upon the faded carpet I had brought from our own room, and the sunlight through the red and green leaves of the maple ceiling gave the wool more exotic colors than it had ever known. Arlin's face, too, was a study of colored shadows, making it difficult for me to trace her expression.

"I had hoped to see your face in our baby," she said, having said nothing since our dry breakfast.

I was very pleased to hear her talk, though she sounded very weary. "Then you have a broad range of curiosity, or a broader sense of humor," I answered her. "But I expect you will have that chance yet. Why not?"

My question irritated her, and under the drifting lights of pink and green I saw an expression I recognized well. "Nazhuret, that question displays the essential difference between you and me. You wake up thinking your heart's desire may come today and I wake up wondering why a tidal wave has not washed us all away ere now."

She gave a great sigh and plucked a leaf out of the ceiling. "Why not? Because I do not conceive easily, even before having an ax blow to the belly. Because you or I or both may be murdered at any moment. Because there may come a plague. There are infinite 'why nots.' It's a wonder I ever got a child started."

I remained silent long enough so she would not think I dismissed her worries out of hand. "Yet I don't think murderers will find us here, Arlin. I don't think even hounds could track us over the running water. And as for plagues—well, what's the use of anticipating plagues?"

For perhaps a minute Arlin listened to the sounds: birdsong, the water, the hiss of leaf against leaf. "You're right about that, Nazhuret. About this concealment. Last year when we camped here, we were unobtrusive, but there was the horse. Now we are simply invisible."

I glanced out the hole in the shrubbery, small and at ground level, and thought no badger den was less obvious. By the sounds she made and the bitter smell of leaf juice in the air I knew she had destroyed the leaf in her hands.

"I miss her," said Arlin. "I miss Sabia very much. For a few days the loss of the baby overwhelmed that, but I had Sabia with me for fourteen years."

"She was a good horse," I said, though I did not have Arlin's educated appreciation for quality in the beasts.

"She was a valuable horse, when I had nothing else valuable. Three times I sold her, but I always got her back."

I almost asked Arlin whether "got her back" meant the same as "bought her back," but I decided if Arlin stole her own horse it was years ago and she was in no mood to be teased.

Still, I cannot hide my thoughts from her, even under a canopy of green and pink. "Once I stole her back, and once I bought her back—you remember that time, for I returned in time to find you stuck between the king's temper and Powl's obstinacy."

". . . In time to save the king, you mean."

She shrugged, her flat shoulder blades against the ground. "To save a king and kill a duke. Whatever. The other time I sold her I was honest about it, but she stole herself, and came to me bloody-nosed, dragging a chain cavesson. I heard later that she broke the buyer's head for him."

Arlin spoke with very little sympathy for the man, and she added, "I should have had her bred. Now there's nothing to remember."

I looked at my paramour, stretched out in all her length on the carpet, skin white against the dark wool shirt which was all she wore, and I thought of her father. "No matter, Arlin. Children are not much like their parents, anyway."

Arlin peered at me appraisingly with her cloudy gray eyes, but she let me have the last word.

There are three problems that dominate life for the homeless: staying warm, staying dry, and staying fed. The season took care of the first and the second, but it was up to me to supply the victuals.

First I raided the oratory garden—the garden I myself had planted and kept. It was an awkward time of year for vegetables, for the greenstuffs had already bolted in the heat and the filling crops of later summer—horsebeans, roots, and all the sundry grains—had not properly headed yet. I found that a large number of the parsnips and turnips I had planted were already taken out half-sized, and so I sneaked into the old pantry to dip into the grain stores.

Here had been further depredation, more than one would expect, considering that only five people besides ourselves had been staying in the oratory. I heard voices beyond the wooden door, and they were very merry. Peeking through the lock-hole, I found four of our five seated around the refectory table, with an assortment of jugs and bottles scattered about. I did not need to put my nose to the hole to scent raw wine and beer.

9

This gave me to think. We had lived in the oratory as beggars among beggars since the first one knocked on our door in April and found us scrubbing old mildew from the windows. At least we had announced the place to be a haven given by the king to the homeless (true enough as far as that went). We had lived soberly in all, since neither Arlin nor I have a great lust after food and we were usually cooking. And since there were always more mouths than anticipated, and we were conscious that the sacks of provision which followed us from court to the borders of Norwess were charity. One had better not become too used to living on charity.

The fact that our "fellows" had squandered their little capital within two days after our departure meant to me that we had acted more the part of the landlord than we had thought, and that these others felt no stake in the future of the place.

Well, why should they? Beggars were mobile by nature; their lives had taught them to take and go. For them this sour beer might be the equivalent of old wine in crystal.

I excused them, but still I was angry, and so I took bags of flour and of broken oats, and sneaked out again to snare a rabbit. Since I hate snaring rabbits, I was in a worse mood than ever when I splashed back to our shelter.

I found Arlin engaged in a short sword dance, and I watched as I skinned the animal. I cannot dance with Arlin's grace, though I have danced with Arlin often enough. After this exercise, she had a faint glaze of sweat over her face, which would not be the case with Arlin in good health. I made a small, almost invisible fire, grilled the meat, and made oatcakes while she sat in her open, empty silence: what I call the belly of the wolf. I was determined not to let her know I had been upset by my visit to our house, and so I hummed and mumbled in my work.

I do talk to myself.

The first thing Arlin said to me was "What's wrong, Zhurrie? Have they made trash of the place already?"

My expression made her laugh, which was an unexpected benefit, and she added, "Did they sell all the grain barrels already?"

"Just the grain out of them," I answered. "And the parsnips and turnips."

She widened one eye at that, and seemed to be my cynical old Arlin again. "You had to have expected it, my true knight. With the prior owners vanished without word, they would be waiting by the day for official dispossession. They have to make the most of the time they've got."

I thought about that while I cut up the rabbit, which was no fat baby and would have done better with steel than teeth to cut the bites. "I never told them the place was ours. Did you?"

Her smile was condescending. "No. But the usual beggar does not send letters to King Rudof two or three times a season."

10

"I handled that very inconspicuously," I began, but she cut me off with the words "Or get them from the king. By very conspicuous special courier."

She was looking at the rabbit with no more enthusiasm than I had shown. "One more wolfish feast. Until these two years, I never would have believed I would look fondly upon a diet of oatcakes and brown bread." We each took a bite and it was a while before we could speak again.

"I shall be constipated, on top of all my other problems," Arlin stated, and she lay back under the canopy (she was too tall to be comfortable sitting up) and dropped bits of food into her mouth.

Now the light was slanting to late afternoon, and the shadows of the big maple leaves were black as her hair against Arlin's pale face. I said, "You know, it's when you are disgusted about something that your upbringing comes out. You sounded then the true noblewoman. Very strange, in these circumstances."

She turned her eyes, not her face, to me. "Yes, My Lord Duke," she said.

This was the expected retaliation. "I was never brought up as a noble. You know that."

Arlin leaned up on one elbow and pointed at me. "You. . ." Whatever argument she had in mind she gave up, or something more important intervened among her thoughts.

"Norwess," she said instead. "You can't wait longer. You have to go there."

For a moment I was puzzled, for we were in the old dukedom of Norwess. "You mean the honor itself? God, woman, what business have I in that house? What could be gained?"

Arlin sat up again, crouching as dust and dry leaves fell onto her head. "You have three choices, Nazhuret, son of Eydl of Norwess. You can allow yourself to die, you can live as a beast for the rest of your life, or you can confront the people who want your death."

Arlin's phrasing revealed there had been a lot of thought before she spoke those words. Her tone hinted prophecy. I felt helpless as a rabbit myself, when Arlin turned prophet. "We don't know it's the young duke," I said. "Norwess is cut up like a big pie."

Arlin lay down again, chewing tough meat but still looking very like a prophet. "Where Leoue goes, the rest will follow," she said.

That night, as we huddled together against the wet, I dreamed of the Duke of Norwess's son, Timet. He rode by me on a tall black war-horse, which served to dwarf him and flush all the color from his pale skin. I ran along beside, hoping to catch his eye: hoping for recognition. Though I was too shy to shout it out, I was closely related to Tim o' Norwess. It was an unpleasant dream, for the man kept glowering ahead of him, black with the knowledge

11

that he had never had the opportunity to exist. His gear was blue and gold: Norwess's colors. I wore clothes of no particular color, of course. I ran barefoot and he never knew me.

This was not the first time I had had this particular dream, but as I dreamed it (knowing all the while it was a dream and to be endured) I realized I was destined to repeat it on many other nights. Through my life, perhaps.

I woke up to Arlin's sleepy protests; I was clutching her too hard. I asked her if she would prefer to call me a normal name such as Tim, and she replied that she would not.

It was my idea to leave Arlin in that island nest while I went on the errand alone. This was not her idea, and just as well, for I get into trouble explaining things. Though I like to talk (as you know well, Powl) and like to listen to others talking, I am never sure what they mean when they use the same words I use. Arlin, having no love for jabber, knows how to use the language as a pry-bar.

Norwess is mountainous; without too much exaggeration, one might say it is one enormous, jagged mountain. Our journey from the foothills to the palace itself took three days of hiking, and though Arlin had not recovered entirely from the miscarriage, she was not slowing us down.

We ate what we had packed, except the once when I was able to exchange chopping at a tree for a hot supper. That work humbled me, for I wasn't used to the air of the altitude—some nine thousand feet—and I felt my heart drum against my ribs. The local folk of Norwess think it the greatest hilarity to watch a visitor collapse, gaping like a fish. Perhaps if my life had not taken such an unexpected downward turn, my sense of humor would be the same. I like to think not.

The high waters of the duchy are more foreign than the air: black round lakes too deep to gauge, and rapacious streams floored in stone that fling down to the South, where they feed Vestinglon, or east, where exhaustion and level countryside turn them into the sweet waters of Ekesh. When I put my hand into one of the streams to fill our waterskin, the touch on skin was much like the sting of the dry-weather sparks that run from one's hand to a metal doorknob. This, however, may be sheer coincidence or the inexactitude of my human perception. I have heard you deny any connection between the nature of sparks and of cold water. If I had remained Timet of Norwess, these daunting lakes and streams would be normal waters to me.

Please believe that I keep returning to this "Timet" ghost not because I grieve for a life denied me, but because I fear it. At the time of my narration, it appeared that the very memory of Timet, son of Eydl of Norwess, was enough to doom Arlin and me both.

As Vestinglon is the heart of Velonya, so Norwess is its ancient bulwark and protection. From Norwess comes the tall, fair, lean-faced human stock we think of as true Velonyan, though Velonya possesses more folk as nondescript as I than it does heroes of the old stamp. In Norwess I felt more than ever that I was a dwarf who crawled out from under the stones of the earth—there were appropriate stones everywhere. But even in these high conifer forests, I noticed more people with Arlin's black hair than my own dandelion shade. (I have heard you say that blonds are an anomaly everywhere and inclined to be weak-eyed. But then, you are not a blond.)

When we were some five miles from the ducal honor, the road passed the highest point of our travels, and some man of wealth (perhaps Eydl, my father) had cleared a place and commissioned a stone table and benches, too heavy for thieves to carry away. Here we sat in a high, sunny wind, looking out over every quadrant of the compass.

I cut for my weary lady the last of our biscuits and cheese. I remember that the cheese had a coat of mold and an underjacket of shining grease. "There," I said, "behind you. That broad blue horizon is the North Sea." Arlin turned to look. Even from the mountain heights we could see a metallic sparkle of light from the water. The movement of the glitter implied that the sea was rough. "And over your right shoulder, that dark line like a cloud is the Great West Ocean. We can see both from here. And down the slope behind you amid the green is a flash of white limestone from one of the towers of Palace Norwess. Leoue, I mean."

Arlin has a special guarded expression (one of many) which I have learned means she is thinking about me. "So," she said, smearing the cheese onto the dry biscuits, fragmenting the biscuits in the process, "you did come here before. When I was with Powl."

"I wandered this far," I admitted. The white flashes of limestone disappeared as the wind died among the trees, and then reappeared.

"Wandered." She repeated the word without expression and ate the sticky mess she had created. Cold wind whipped her short black hair over her face. "Did you also wander as far as the palace, then?"

I admitted it. "I begged a meal. I cleaned stalls and slept in the home farm byre."

Arlin smiled her wolfish smile. "Don't apologize, Zhurrie. Anyone is interested in the place he is born. More so if he was ripped away early. It has to hurt."

I had to look away. I watched the white glow of limestone wink in and out. The bright glitter of water, winking. "It hurts," I said.

1 3

I saw my father and my mother once, Powl. Long after they were dead. I don't know if I ever told you about that. I was very sick at the time, and how can I prove the experience was real? Nevertheless, I saw them.

Arlin's beautiful, lean hero's face looked more wolfish, more dangerous. "At any time you can have it back. All of Norwess. I will get it for you, Nazhuret."

My wistfulness dissolved into laughter, but not because I didn't believe she could do it. "No," I said. "I don't want Norwess. You know I don't. It just hurts."

I don't think we said anything more until we came to the gates of the palace.

You, Powl Inpres, Earl of Daraln, must have seen Norwess many times, climbing the long slope in dry air with your ears popping. This was only my second sight of the place (second within adult recall, of course) and I had expected to find that memory had added grandeur. Memory had not.

The endless whiteness of it was the most impressive thing, for the only available stone was the native limestone, and though the structure had grown and rambled through many builders and many generations—turning from fortress to castle to manor to palace as civilization turned around it—it had maintained this unity of color. Against the backdrop of bare mountains, scarcely darker than its walls, it seemed a work of nature as much as a work of man.

It had hundreds of windows: tall ones, many-paned, slotted ones; without panes, arched ones rimmed in colored glass; and at the western face bottom, very ordinary ones with bad glazing and iron grilles. (These last I knew from the time I had begged breakfast in the scullery.) I could keep myself in steady work for years, maintaining the windows of my father's palace, if the owner would hire me.

The park of Leoue Palace is in two sections, the larger filling the valley that leads up to the gate and the smaller, scarcely two miles on a side, enclosed by a wall some eight feet high which shone with the same brightness as the house itself. Arlin and I approached the gate through the wood, which was largely conifer and riddled with large, protruding stones. The air seemed empty, lacking the incense I expected out of the evergreens, but that might have been only my unaccustomed nose.

The gate itself was of iron, higher than the level of the stones and very ornate. It was guarded by a soldier equally ornate, in the black of Leoue with Leoue's gold braid. He leaned against the round-arched cubby in the wall that was his only shelter, one hand on the length of a very archaic halberd.

I wondered if the man had any more reasonable weapon with which to face intruders. I did not think he could give us much trouble, even with Arlin weakened by travail and travel. But it seemed we could not win anything but ill feeling by overpowering the household defenses, so we decided to come in a good thirty yards from the gate, climbing over the wall.

14

Nowhere were there trees close enough to help in the endeavor, but I stood on Arlin's shoulders, lay myself along the top, and pulled her up after me.

I had not before seen this aspect of the garden. Someone, either Duke Leoue or my father or their wives perhaps, was of the school which likes to make plants look like animals. The juniper bushes that surrounded us were carved into hedgehogs, roe deer, standing rabbits, and other brutes less recognizable, and the winding paths were lined with pillars of ivy on wire, each of which was topped by a flock of vegetable birds. Through this fantasy slipped a bright small stream, which looked like nothing but itself, yet where it widened into a pond, I glimpsed a number of large goldfish with diaphanous fins, looking like orange flowers.

Arlin took me by the elbow and pulled me into the shrubbery, for I was becoming dazed by the place. "I prefer an honest rosebush myself," she said, and added, "You're sunburned. Things up here are different, even the sun. Be careful."

I rubbed my eyes to displace the oddities I had seen and reminded Arlin that I am always sunburned.

She got to see her rosebushes as we stole from garden to garden, and I got to see more ponds and fishes. The maze we avoided entirely, and we came to the main door over a terrace of white limestone and black slate, feeling dwarfed by all the magnificence and very dusty.

A footman in black and gold came out of the small, plain door hidden among the pillars. He took Arlin by the upper arm, or thought he had done so, and asked what we meant by our presence. He was left staring at his open hand, wondering why it clutched nothing.

Arlin looked blandly across at the man in the way she has when deciding which part of an opponent should be broken first. I announced myself to be Nazhuret of Sordaling, and I requested to be brought before the duke.

The footman, like most footmen, was very tall. He began to grin at my impudence, and he raised his hand to grab again. Before he could touch me, I used my last peaceful weapon, which is the name of the king.

From my purse I drew a red wax seal and envelope, one of which encloses every letter he has sent to us. The postal seal of the King of Velonya has no real meaning, legal or social, once the letter is delivered, but I have found that very few men will lay hands upon one who is carrying it.

I keep the king's letters with me. I value them highly.

Though it was the seal that brought us through the door, I believe it was my name that led us through to the duke. I remember counting steps and directions as we passed through that great, shapeless house as through the gut

15

of an animal. Servants in livery and in the clothes of gentlefolk passed by, their eyes flickering toward us and away.

If Leoue was our hidden enemy, then there was a chance we were about to be killed. We might be trapped in a room and shot from all directions. We might be trapped and simply left. Servants could be bribed or threatened to forget our existence. Perhaps these servants would not have to be bribed or threatened.

We passed down one very long hall, which was limed and gilded, into a large chamber of stuffed furniture, rather shabby by contrast. It looked comfortable. From there the footman led us into another hall, which was of generous proportion but quite bare, with red and white tiles on the floor and red stripes between the wall pilasters. There was a staircase, all in marble, winding up to the first floor, and the base of this staircase was flooded with light from a half-circle window. As the shine of the lit tiles caught my eye, I was hit by a memory and stood stunned.

I knew this place from before: the tiles, the russet uprights of the baluster, the quality of sunlight on a summer afternoon. My body had the knowledge of it, though nothing else in the house was familiar. I heard the footsteps of the servant recede and then scuff to a stop. I felt Arlin's hand tighten on my arm.

"Later," she said. "Feel it later."

Under the half-window was an open door, and outside that door stretched a small garden, divided from the park major by a wall of white-painted brick. This garden, like the room we had passed on our way, was comfortably shabby; there were uneven paths of brick, a patch of lawn, a small lion-headed fountain drooling into a pond with yet more goldfish.

First I knew the lion, and then the paths, and then I almost fell to my knees with the blow of memory, for this was the ducal nursery garden, and it was here I had had my first infant look at the natural world.

"He must have brought you here on purpose," whispered Arlin, and she dug her thumbnail into the sensitive point between the bones of my elbow until I was forced to shrug her off. And to stand upright.

The Duke of Leoue was sitting on a three-legged stool at the edge of the grass with a low table in front of him, and both the table and the grass were scattered with books. I looked at the man and I did not think he had met me here as a strategy.

I had expected to see in young Leoue his father, for I had never seen picture nor portrait of the new duke. No lifetime, however spent, could have turned this man into a great bear, like the Leoue I knew. He was almost as tall as old Leoue, but he had nowhere his father's breadth: not in shoulder, in chest, or in the fists like firewood that the duke had been known to fling at me. Maleph Markins, Duke of Leoue, was a graceful youth, and his black hair and sun-darkened skin were set off by large eyes of sky blue. Two bald furrows already running back above his temples, making inroads into the thick hair, served to give a greater intensity to what might have been a boy's face. He wore a white woolen shirt, side-buttoned, knee breeches of plain gabardine, and the knee stockings of a mountain shepherd.

He sat waiting for us to be brought to him, alert and quiet. By looks, by dress, and by the controlled way he held his body, this duke might have been another student of yours.

The footman brought us to within five feet of the duke and then he retreated, but only by a few yards. At an irritated flicker of his master's eye, the man backed further, but at the corner of my eye I saw him standing by the lion fountain.

"Nazhuret of Sordaling," said the duke, and by his hesitation I wondered if he even recognized the name. He unfolded long limbs, knocking the stool back onto the grass. His gaze was very cool and steady, but the muscles of his jaw stood out visibly, even under the soft skin of youth.

For a moment he seemed to withdraw from me without moving. His eyes went from a pointed sort of blue to haze-color, and had it been I looking at Arlin, I would have said he had taken his mind into the belly of the wolf. As his eyes cleared again I saw his lips move, and I think he pronounced the words "God help me."

". . . of Sordaling," he repeated, aloud. "Why 'of Sordaling'?"

I answered him that I grew up there, and had no other name.

With no greater expression than before the duke said, "No other name? Not Kavenen? Timet Kavenen? Of Norwess?"

This answered my question about being recognized. I phrased my reply carefully. "I will not use either of the first two, lest it be connected with the third."

I heard two sounds—a stir from the footman against the garden wall, and a quieter rustle as Arlin shifted to keep that man in sight. Leoue's intensity took on greater edge as he asked me, "Are you denying that as your parentage? It was my understanding you yourself claimed to be son of Eydl of Norwess."

I felt within me a bright spark of protest, for this was so opposite of the truth. Two men had claimed that descent for me, and one of them was this fellow's father. I waited until the spark blew out before I spoke. "It was claimed by others before I had any idea in the matter. I believe it to be true, but I have no desire to possess the things that were Eydl's."

17

We stood almost two yards apart, with Arlin behind my left shoulder, but I would never have turned my back to an enemy as Leoue turned his upon me. He crossed the grass in a few strides and took the branch of a bush in his hand: a woody peony, I think. He pulled it loose at the trunk, leaving a white streak of split bark on the plant. It looked painful as a hangnail. Without looking at the thing he began to pull the leaves off, one after another, methodically. "You killed my father," he said at last, as though that one sentence explained everything in the world.

As a matter of truth, Arlin, not I, had killed his father, but only because I was not in position to do so. That would make no good answer to the man, nor would it help to state in turn that his father had worked the death of mine. I saw a swallow dip over the garden wall, shimmering in the queer high air, and everything seemed to shimmer. I wondered if I had made a mistake in coming, for I could scarcely gather my wits.

"Your father was trying to kill the king," I answered, because it was true as far as it went.

Now Leoue's garment of calm left him. He took two strides toward me, swishing the naked branch over the grass where undoubtedly both he and I had toddled as babies. "So *you* said!"

"So the king said." I hoped I did not sound as heated as he did.

Hearing this, the duke broke the stick. "The king can be mistaken. He was mistaken. I know what happened clearly. I see it in my mind's eye. My father wanted the head of Daraln—to protect the king from the old illusionist—but the earl made a game of all of you and you slew the wrong man!"

"If that's what you think. . ." It was Arlin, trying without success to be heard.

Leoue pointed one jagged fragment of his stick at my head. "Only, seeing that it was Eydl's son who struck the blow, it may be your role was not merely that of tool. I have never been certain. . ."

Now Arlin shouted, "If that is what you see in your mind's eye, fellow, then your mind's eye needs spectacles! When your father struck, Daraln was nowhere within reach, and he stood in the opposite direction from the blow. And further, it was not Nazhuret who killed your father."

She had his attention for the first time. I could see him taking this lean shape into account. Dark and dressed in dark, speaking in the gravelled voice of a pipe smoker, my lady had never looked less like a lady. Or like any woman. "It was I," she said.

The swallows stitched over the sky and the footman's jacket glowed like red flame against the gray of the wall. Beyond garden and wall I saw the tips of mountains, white even in summer against the sky. They appeared unsubstantial. I thought the peaks might float away, light as the purple swallows.

18

The duke's response came slowly, and he had himself well in hand before he spoke. "Your man?" he asked, speaking again to me, as he might have said "your horse" or "your knife."

Arlin and I answered together. "No." I said more. "Not my man, but my friend. Arlin, also of Sordaling."

Arlin interpreted the tight grimace on the duke's face. "Of Sordaling, yes, but not another hidden son of a duke. Nor of any noble." (My lady takes endless delight in using the truth to mislead people. She is not the son, but the daughter of a noble. At times of moment, such as this was, I hesitate to speak at all, whereas Arlin likes to speak at no other occasion.)

Another footman came through the doorway, and behind him, more steps. I measured the height of the garden wall, and the anger in the duke's clenched hands. I thought I had better get my business over quickly. "Is vengeance for your father the reason you have sent assassins out against us, Duke? Or is it simply worry that I will petition the king to re-create my father's honors?"

Once again I had turned his attention from Arlin to myself. The duke's young forehead roughened at my words.

"Assassins?" Again he fixed that sharp blue gaze upon me. "Do you come here to accuse me of assassins?"

I did not shrug, because shrugging puts the body at a disadvantage. "Who else? Endergen? Fowett?"

By the time he answered, the duke had his composure over him as perfectly as when we had first seen him. "I'm sure a man like you has many personal enemies, without having to search for those of a previous generation."

Until he said those words, I had been convinced that the young duke had nothing to do with the attacks against us. The coldness of that verbal thrust made me less certain. "Just answer me that you are not the employer of these killers, my lord. Only that and I will bother you no more."

His large eyes searched my face. "You call me 'my lord'? You do?"

In irritation I replied, "I will call you 'my God' if you will only answer my question. Of course I call you by honorific; you are a duke of Velonya!"

Leoue looked away. "You insult me, Nazhuret of Sordaling. Do I seem like a man who pays for murder?"

Once again I said, "Just answer me," and the duke scowled at his heap of books. "I have sent no assassins to murder you or anyone else." As though forced out of his throat, the words followed "Though I don't wish you well. . . though I have a certain sympathy with the man whom you have made your enemy."

I wanted no more of Maleph Markins. The assurance I had come for I had gotten, and whether I believed it or not was my problem. I backed away from

19

him a good ten paces before I turned; let him think it was out of respect. Arlin came behind me.

In the doorway under the half-moon window stood a woman dressed in white like the white of Norwess stones, with a footman in red at either side of her. She was elegant, with silver and amethyst around her neck, and by her face, she was kin to the duke. She did not move aside, but stared down at me in the manner people use when they want a short man to realize his height. I am very familiar with that stare.

Leoue called to her to move aside, calling her "Mother," speaking very respectfully. His voice, though controlled, had a lot of feeling behind it. Without a word the woman slipped to one side, and the bright-garbed footmen adjusted themselves next to her. I stepped into the house and noticed that Arlin was not with me. She was a few yards behind, and her eyes were locked with those of the duchess: no difference of inches there.

Again the duke spoke to me. "Servants talk, Nazhuret. There is no help for it. My men are loyal, and it would be better if you left the province with reasonable speed."

"The province," he had said. The ancient name of these high mountains is Norwess, not Leoue. The duke did not feel comfortable using the name in front of me.

I left grinning. Norwess—the honor to which I was born, and to which so many expect me to aspire again—seems as foreign as the moon to me, and leaves me dizzy as a kite.

"My men are loyal," he had said. Did he mean his men were too attached to his honor to be obedient, or did he mean they would do murder at his command? Either manner, the threat did not weigh upon me; even in strange territory, Arlin and I are not so easy to find. That evening we spread ourselves out in a dry pine wood, ate drier bread, and discussed the results of our visit.

Arlin was convinced that Leoue was the heart of our problem. She had enough reason on her side, for surely we had found anger in our reception, and the man convinced that we were responsible for the griefs of his life. My only argument against this was no argument at all: that I thought the duke looked too much and dressed too much and acted too much like a student of Powl's to be so devious.

She raised her head and dusted the needles from her black hair. "I am a student of Powl's. I am devious," she said.

I had to admit that, and so was forced to contradict myself. "But he is not Powl's student, so how could he be so good an actor? He seemed so outraged that we should be there. Not wary, not smug—not like a man who had planned and paid for our deaths. Could he be such a consummate actor at the age of seventeen?"

"Consummate actors are born," Arlin answered. "Or made in early youth. My father honed my instincts in that direction. Wouldn't you say the son of the Black Duke had opportunity to learn at least as much as I?" Arlin was taking apart a pine cone as she spoke, and her hair still wore a halo of dead twigs and needles. I remember that she looked like a stern sort of angel as she compared her own duplicity to that of Leoue. I remember that this was the first evening we were too occupied to think of the assault, and the death of the baby. And the death of the horse.

I poached rabbits in my father's preserves for the next few days while we tried to decide our next action. It began to rain, and though we should have been glad for the sake of the dry countryside, we had not prepared for it. Arlin began to sneeze and I thought it best, threats or no, to seek out human habitation. The nearest village was a handsome place of steep-roofed wooden buildings with their eaves painted in bright colors. When I saw them the thought was forced upon me that such sights would have been a joy and a solace to me in my childhood, and I was aware that the ghost of Timet of Norwess was encroaching further into my mind. I would have to exorcise him somehow.

The first tavern we came to was glad to trade supper and space in the stable for my wife and me, for work in these high altitudes is more plentiful than people. Arlin retired to the warmth of horses to let her clothes steam dry, while I warmed up more quickly chopping the ever-needed firewood.

(I call Arlin my wife, but the truth is that we are not married by any law or order besides the natural one that marries geese and wolves. I have never yet dared to engender a legitimate child, lest its very ancestry doom it to murder. Until the assassins came, this lack had been my only grief. Now, I had others. Now, I knew bastardy was not enough protection.)

I am not bad at reading human expression, and there was nothing in the face of the innkeeper or the potboy that led me to believe they knew my identity and felt obliged to inform the soldiery or take matters into their own hands. The villagers were more polite and reserved than I was accustomed to in my travels, even though my mongrel face must have surprised the folk of Norwess more than those to the south.

It was a small pleasure to be able to speak to strangers without adopting the Zaquash dialect I had learned so laboriously from you. The burghers of Norwess speak a very pure Velonyie.

I brought our supper to the stable, because Arlin was very tired. We washed in water borrowed from the animals and then cleaned our clothes as best we could. Letting the wool dry over two crossties snapped together, we wrapped ourselves in a blanket on a heap of good straw and let night fall.

It was Arlin's belief that whoever had set the killers upon us now knew we were seeking his identity, and to visit Fowett or Endergen would only be asking for a knife in the ribs. I was dissatisfied, however. I felt we had learned very little in all our climbing.

We discussed the matter very softly in the dark, so quietly we were aware when the grunts and snores of the horses stopped, and I could sense one beast raise his head and sniff the air. Our conversation died at that moment and Arlin and I rolled back to back, letting the blanket fall away. In another moment we were crouched in the darkness, and there was not a sound from inside the stable. Slowly I reached for my dowhee and some beast kicked his stall partition once. My skin felt a very strong sense that someone was moving in the dark before me. Black against darkness, Arlin shifted beside me. No sound.

How many assassins could we handle, naked and trapped in a three-sided oaken box two feet deep in straw? How many assassins, well trained or no, could move together so silently?

"I wish I could have been of some assistance," said your voice out of the blackness. You were far enough away from us that neither was likely to strike you in pure startlement. I took a deep breath and laid my dowhee against the loose-box wall. "But until two days ago, when I reached the oratory, I had no idea you were pursued."

(I will repeat your words as I remember, and later we can argue whether I was correct.)

"Good evening, Daraln," answered Arlin in her drawling gambler's voice. (She only called you Daraln because she was irritated by the surprise.) "Don't think of it twice. You can't be forever nursemaiding us."

I remember you replied with a little sound in your throat, more polite than a grunt. In it I felt that you communicated you understood many things, including the loss of the baby.

"Who it is that designs your death I can't say, offhand. I am inclined to believe that the source of your problem lies up here, however: Leoue or Endergen. Perhaps together. Perhaps even Fowett, although the man is old and without male heir." You sighed, rose, dusted yourself off, and stepped into the loose-box with us, whereupon you took a tiny flint and set spark to a charming small lantern of a sort I had never seen before. Your own design, or I miss my guess.

We found our teacher dressed neatly in indigo broadcloth, with gold lacing around the double row of buttonholes in his jacket. Had I asked you why you dressed in so different an apparel from that which you recommend to your students, you would have said once again that you were in disguise. If so, Powl, you live most of your days in that disguise.

"Once more, it is my influence which has led you both into danger. Had Nazhuret merely agreed to be the son of his father, the king would have placed him in such of his father's honors as was possible—Leoue's spoils, at least—and all would have grumbled but moved over for him. That would have been understandable to the heads of cork we call our aristocracy. This denial of your 'place,' my boy. . ."—you pronounced the word place with poisonous irony—"is something they will not and cannot understand. Especially while you maintain ties with King Rudof."

"I have never even been tempted to ask. . . ," I began but as I spoke, suddenly the ghost of Timet of Norwess sat beside me, bitter as the high frozen wind, and I did not know whether I was telling the truth.

What you saw in the lamplight, or what you heard in my voice I don't know, but you have always been very good at reading people. "Even though you are not tempted, Nazhuret, I might have used my influence to press you into such a role. . ."

In astonishment I said, "But you always have said the most perfect life is. . ."

"Yes. Running about the landscape with the clothes on your back and infinite possibility in your future. As you are, in fact." You made a small gesture to include Arlin and myself. "But I might have been willing to sacrifice your happiness, my son, for the sake of political simplicity."

My amazement was total, both because you spoke of sacrificing me and because you called me your son. You only said such a thing once before, and that in a letter.

"But the truth is, you would make a very bad duke, Nazhuret."

Here at last was a statement that was no surprise. Yet Arlin contradicted him.

"As for that," she said, in the pipe smoker's voice that meant she was concealing feeling, "it is my opinion that Zhurrie would make a fine duke. His dependents would love him."

You turned your face a bit and smiled at the straw. "Some would love him, certainly. Those in need of mercy. But you cannot love forever what you cannot understand, and how many understand either of you, even now?"

Arlin's gray eyes widened and lost focus and I knew that she, like I, was remembering the oratory and how quickly the other beggars had forgotten the life we had established there.

"Zhurrie, I can see you as the headmaster of a school. I can see you as an archbishop. Our nobility in Velonya more resemble wolves—no, feral dogs—and among them you would cause only greater carnage."

"Then isn't it a good thing I don't desire a position among them," I answered, and Timet of Norwess sat silently beside me.

You were quiet for some time, your eyes flashing with the light of the lamp. "I wish I had come to help you with this, instead of pulling you out with the matter unfinished," you said at last, and both Arlin and I frowned in puzzlement. "What do you mean?" she asked. "Why else did you chase us from the oratory here, if not to help?"

Your shrug, my teacher, is very elaborate, very foreign. Perhaps I think of it that way because you shrugged so frequently when teaching me the Allec language.

Another thought rose. "Where did you come from, Powl? You've lost a lot of weight. Have you been traveling?" I think there was some envy in my words. I would like to go to foreign countries, as the Earl of Daraln does. It is harder for a beggar.

You answered, "I've been in the capital. Largely with the king. And the parliament, damn it."

Arlin lifted her head. "What's up?"

"War is up," you said, and with those words Timet of Norwess faded, like smoke from a quenched candle.

We three leaned against the rough oak boards, and I remember that you smelled faintly of sandalwood and of roses. Arlin and I smelled not-so-faintly of horse manure and sweat. The little lantern threw the shadows of your small gestures against the straw, and I felt taken out of reality altogether.

"Sanaur Mynauzet is seventy-eight years old," said Powl. "His sister's son—his heir—is dead this past winter, perhaps naturally. *His* oldest son is in his middle twenties, and is Minsanaur of Bologhini as well as heir to all Rezhmian territory. It is with the Minsanaur we shall have to deal."

"Reingish? This is the same man who wears the dagger around his neck, day and night?" It was Arlin who spoke. I knew the famous dagger of the Bologhini minsanaur was only three inches long and made of gold, but still it was a dagger.

Powl nodded, causing a flood of black shadows before the lantern. "Yes. Possibly it is merely a symbolic gesture. Possibly the minsanaur's well-known hostility toward his northern neighbors is equally symbolic, or will fade as his responsibilities increase.

"Or possibly we will suffer an attack that will break our nation." As you spoke these words, you let your lantern go out and we were left in cold darkness.

I reached for it, hefted it, and finally shook the thing. I heard oil sloshing. Then you began to tell us about the lantern's experimental nature and the difficulties you had had increasing light at the expense of heat and soot—as though nothing of greater moment than the malfunction of the lantern had been discussed so far.

For me the darkness was filled with a hundred thoughts, a thousand images. I had never been to Bologhini, though I had spent one winter close to the border, and lived and worked with the trading guilds that moved between Warvala and the South. I knew the flavor of the speech of Bologhini, and I knew the flavor of the mind.

I could taste the cherry liquor that was a Bologhinese specialty. I could hear them in argument (another specialty).

War. I was raised in a military school. I had seen horses and men exploded by a petard. I had been blown into the air myself and only by mercy could I hear at all.

My father had been commander of a Velonyan invasion of Rezhmia.

My mother was Sanaur Mynauzet's niece.

"You are sitting very quietly, Nazhuret," you told me. "Have you heard any of what I said?"

"You want me to go to Rezhmia," I replied, "don't you?"

You inhaled in careful manner, as you do when you do not want me seeing your feelings. "So you are paying attention."

I shook my head, then realized that would do no good in the darkness. "No," I said aloud. "I haven't heard a word. I only knew it."

I hid myself in the belly of the wolf—in what others call "meditation," though I do not understand that word—for long black moments, and when I looked around again the two of you were still sitting beside me and the lantern was still malfunctioning. "Am I supposed to presume upon my relationship with the sanaur?" I asked you, and I thought your answer slid a little—was too diffident. Too diffident for you. "You are to do what seems advantageous to you."

Arlin cleared her throat then, and spoke as though she had been rehearsing words for a long time. "Which sister was eldest?"

She had never asked that question before. Nor had I—aloud. I waited for your answer in a sweat of fear.

If you sweated I did not know it; you were fiddling with the damned lantern; I could smell lamp oil in the air. You put on a lecturing voice. "It may seem unlikely to you that the eldest daughter of the royal house of Rezhmia would be given to the general-in-chief of a foreign invasion, and a defeated foreign invasion at that. But at that time the sanaur had a healthy, ten-year-old son and a wife not past bearing age. And Eydl of Norwess was gallant, the sanaur himself whimsical, and the girl. . . determined. It was not a bad bit of politics."

25

It was hard to remember that this bit of history we were receiving was out of your own memory, and not a crabbed footnote in the Sordaling archives. "And was it politics: the marriage?" I asked him. Though I knew the answer in my heart.

"No. It was madness," he answered, and in those words the pain in your voice broke free.

"So she was the eldest, and Nazhuret, as well as heir to the Duchy of Norwess, is. . ."

". . . a penniless lens grinder with a hedge trimmer on his back," I finished for her, because I could not endure the rest of the sentence.

Arlin let the silence sit for a while, and then added, "But a gallant one. Like your father."

The next morning I took a step up in social class; after washing under the stable pump, I tucked in my shirt and put on one of your burgher jackets, which was too large for me. I wonder, Powl: is your neat burgher dress the earl's equivalent of my peasant woolies? Is burgher gabardine, which was my proudest tailoring, a greater humiliation for you than homespun? Answer me later.

With this change I altered my accent to court standard. Arlin did nothing, but she never looked or sounded like a beggar, anyway. We were both grateful for the good breakfast you bought us at the same inn where I had cut wood the night before, but I had not slept and so was too weary for appetite.

"You are not to be a spy, Nazhuret. The king would not ask you out so against your mother's people."

"No. I am to do—what? Prevent a war?" You regarded me blandly from behind a loaf of sweet bread, from which you were peeling a charred bottom with your penknife. No one but you can do this without getting fingers greasy. Wonder of wonders.

"Preventing wars is generally a good idea," he answered.

I was unaccountably angry, with you, with Arlin, who sat across from me and kept such a wary eye on my responses, with the morning, bright and bland as my teacher. "But Velonya is strong, and Lowcanton would come in if she needed it. Rudof says so."

With no change of expression you said, "Rezhmia is strong, too, and Lowcanton will not 'come in' for us. Whatever the king says. War will be catastrophic. We will lose the largest part of a generation."

"A generation of whom? Velonyans?"

"Humans," you said, and you watched me not eat my breakfast for a few minutes. "Nazhuret, are you afraid?"

"I am terrified," I said, and I looked over your head—over the shining bald spot that never seemed to grow larger—at a Norwess sky of blue and white.

"Good. I am glad you understand the situation."

Weren't we walking from the table to the outhouse when you tripped me? After my first shock, this was a greater relief than the rich breakfast. I managed to come to earth on top of you, at least for the moment (or were you letting me do it?), and we had five minutes of contest, which proved a more reasoned and meaningful argument than all our night's talk, while Arlin leaned against a tree and supervised, one hand resting on her sword pommel. I seem to remember that the bout ended with me in a headlock with the breath choked out of me, but that may be a confusion of all the other, similar times you choked me. Whatever, the interlude cured me of my sullens, and my creeping dread. It also ripped that seam out of your spare jacket.

I was disappointed that you would not come with us, though I understand why the king would not release you from court. But it is my guess you would not have come at any rate; not while you had influence in Velonya. Not while he had the ear of the king.

You certainly extended your couriership long enough, considering all this. I think we must have looked odd: two ragpickers walking beside a small burgher on horseback (with sunburn on his balding head) plodding down the long southeast slope of Norwess. It was a gentle progress in beautiful summer weather. It was good of you to try to give the horse to Arlin. You failed to move her, possibly because riding would have been more difficult for her. Equally possibly it was merely as she said—she didn't like your horse.

I hope our teacher was as happy to have our company again as we were to have his. Rarely did the three of us travel together.

(Like most men, I have taken the years of my schooling and converted them in memory into paradise. They were not paradise, old teacher, but they were equally strange and unworldly.)

A week's westward progress had us solidly into Ekesh Territory, just north of the Satt boundary, and as soon as you started to hear the whine of the Zaquash dialect on the roads, we began looking around for suitable mounts for our southeast journey.

Your idea of suitable was not Arlin's idea. She would certainly have purchased a close approximation of her assassinated Sabia, if a horse so splendid could have been found in this land of shallow green waters, deep soggy fields, and large mosquitoes. None of these were to be found, however, and at last she consented to ride your choice: a smallish, short-coupled mare with flat

27

sides and a dull, black coat. Her rolling eyes and flattened ears spelled trouble, but I wondered whether equine temperament would be a useful distraction for Arlin. I was very happy with my gelding, short, lean, and colored as yellow as a summer squash. Since I have neither Arlin's background with nor abiding interest in horses, I was relieved to find the fellow was not full of himself, but inclined to abide by majority decision.

I recognized these beasts as cousins of blood with the animals of the traders of Warvala, who come north from Bologhini and even Rezhmia Capital with the most exotic (and expensive) of goods laid across their dusty backs. Cobs, we might call them, but about them is nothing bunchy or round. Nor are they heavily boned, and yet I have seen one of these creatures all but buried under the mass of a large carpet that it had carried hundreds of miles: eating and drinking under that burden also, as though it had all the ease in the world.

Also in that equine family are the ponies of the Naiish nomads, I believe, which are their workbenches and easy chairs as well as transportation. Some of the animals I have seen have spent such a large portion of their lives under saddle that their very spines and ribs have taken the shape of the underside of the little leather-and-tendon saddles, and yet they often remain in service until their thirtieth birthday.

None of these attributes endear the beasts to Arlin, however. They are not beautiful, not inclined to affection, and riding them is not riding the wind.

Once we were mounted, our speed of travel increased, and increased further when we purchased two other ponies (as such became available), and packed them with travelers' food and with Rezhmian-style garments and weapons. It was possible to purchase bows: the little, lip-shaped, cherry-colored bow of the South, which I knew by experience and Arlin knew to her regret, carrying still as she did a large, puckered scar from five years ago, when she had been sure an arrow could not travel three hundred feet.

For a man neither landowner nor landowner's hireling to carry a bow in Velonya is a crime. South Territory operates under Velonyan law, except when it doesn't. The bows were easy enough to find in the markets, along with the short, lacquered arrows that go with them.

Ekesh passed behind us, and we were in South Territory, which is really more east than south. Warvala was a day away, and Warvala is the balance point of our subcontinent, where the culture of my mother's people begins to overwhelm the imposed manners of Velonya.

That morning, after washing, I folded my decent homespun and put on the tunic, trousers, and high boots. My hair was not long enough to tie back,

28

as is strict Rezhmian custom, but with the triangular scarf tied back of the head, the lack was not apparent.

Arlin stared at me for half a minute unbroken, with no expression upon her face that I could read. At last she shuddered. You, already in your reputable burgher clothes, said, "The last time I saw you dressed like that, Nazhuret, you were not so dark."

I found I was very self-conscious. "I have been outdoors almost constantly this year," I said, as though in apology.

You said my name again, with your impeccable Rayzhia court accent. "Nazhuret. For once the name needs no explanation."

Through the floorboards, I felt Arlin shudder again, as a frightened horse will. She kept to her garb of gentlemanly, travel-stained black.

It had been a few years since I had traveled that hard, rolling country, all sky and stone. The presence of my companions did much toward alleviating that feeling of being both impossibly big and completely invisible which South Territory imbued in me. I was experimenting controlling my yellow horse with my feet, for that is how such Rezhmian mounts are trained. My fellow, for all his homeliness, had a great sensitivity in him; I felt we were well matched. I tried riding with hands clasped behind my head, swinging Daffodil from one side of the road to the other, singing the "Hymn of Sordaling School" to the rhythm of his hooves. The horse obeyed, but he sighed frequently, the sound rolling under me like wind in a tunnel. It could be he found the language of my heels too prolix. It could have been my singing.

At this time, I recall that Arlin and you rode together, considerably in front of me. That also could have been my singing.

I was singing when you noticed something and shushed me. You were also riding without reins, but making no large thing about it. "You *could* have a company of horsemen for protection, you know," you said.

"Now you tell us," said Arlin.

"It's not too late. There is a small military station south of Warvala. I have the letter of authorization here."

I met eyes with Arlin and then said, "I don't think we would have much use for a company of horsemen. I wouldn't know what to do with them."

You nodded and resettled yourself in the saddle. "That's why I didn't mention it until now."

I thought the matter was over, but Arlin kept staring from myself to you. At last she said, her voice very compressed, "Do you think that Zhurrie can't command loyalty?"

When you turned back to her, you seemed very guarded. "I don't think that at all," you said, and a moment later I could see you were laughing.

Your horses spontaneously widened the distance between you by two feet. Arlin's mare flung up her head, white-eyed.

This was not the first time I witnessed a display of sparks between you and Arlin, always with myself as object of contention. I'm not blind.

I don't believe there is a lack of affection between you. It's not that. But your quarreling never fails to upset my equilibrium, and I fear I gave too strong a signal to Daffodil, who turned on his haunches until I was facing the road we had just traveled.

A row of dots crested a rise not a mile behind us. "Horsemen," I called, glad of the distraction. "A company of them. Coming south. Riding like military."

I have very good vision, both close and far (ironic, in a spectacles maker), and both of you squinted to verify what I had seen.

"I have been gone for weeks," you said. "Could it be things came to blows already?"

Arlin now turned her squint from the horizon to you. "Did the king know what road you would be taking? If you found us. And if *we* went?"

I had not taken my eyes from the apparitions, which were increasing, four abreast. "This is not blue and white," I announced, and my voice cracked like an adolescent's.

"Then what?" It was Arlin who asked, "Is it a livery at all? Who else would ride in formation but soldiers?"

"Black and yellow, like a bee," I answered her.

You cleared the dust from your throat. "I understand you, Nazhuret. But I find it hard to believe, with your connection to the king, that Leoue alone has been responsible for these attempts against you both. That he would move so openly. . ."

Now there were six rows of horsemen visible on this side of the last hill. Six rows at four abreast. I didn't know if more would follow. "Black and yellow," I said again, and I pressed Daffodil between the others' horses. "Ride," I called in what I hoped was a commanding voice and I snagged the reins of your horse under its chin and took it with me. Forgive me that arrogance. I took only your horse, because in respect to these attacks that had come upon us, Arlin and I were of one mind.

Our three horses were running, and my innards were sloshing with fear. Half of the fear was for the company that pursued us, and half for the liberty I had taken with my teacher's horse. I expected to be launched from the saddle in some subtle manner and dragged unsubtly behind. Instead you leaned along the horse's neck and shouted into my ear.

"Enough, Nazhuret! Release me. I believe you."

I let go and let my horse run between the others on loose rein, while I looked again. There were eight lines of four horsemen, all in Leoue's colors, with one lieutenant before them. Their horses averaged two hands taller than ours and they were coming at a controlled gallop. Our ponies could not out-run them. Your face was unreadable behind the kerchief and dust scarf, but you did not look Velonyan and you did not look afraid. "We have never fought together: the three of us. Have we?"

"Yes, we have," I answered, and Arlin added, "What about the cutthroats in Morquenie, my first year? And the Apek police cordon, that I'm not sup-posed to talk about?"

Then, to my surprise, I saw you smile. It was not a Velonyan smile. "Those don't count. Here the odds are ten to one. This will count. As you spoke, you were pulling at your saddlebag, and you had in your hands the gaudy Rezhmian bow, which you bent in the hole of the saddle pommel that is for that very purpose. "Let me relive the battle of Bologhini. This time on the winning side."

You prodded me with the end of the weapon. "Go on, you ugly little Red Whip. You go out on that side."

In another moment Arlin was pressing her black horse left and off the road, onto a sandy soil not designed for speed. I swung out right, and found that Daffodil's round hooves and short legs were scarcely inconvenienced by the terrain. I saw that Arlin's bow was already strung and I locked my own reins around the horn and did the same.

Now we were drawing back toward the pursuit, back but wider, and through the cloud of dust they were raising, I saw the lieutenant raise his hand in a signal to slow them. The elegant, long-legged animals almost hit the earth in a pile; one did roll on his rider.

The officer must have thought we had split off the road for escape, and were heading backward merely to confuse them. The officer had never done battle against the Naiish nomads. Along with half his men, he swarmed and floundered off the hard-packed road toward me.

Was I within three hundred feet of them? I guessed the distance to the lieutenant as two hundred and fifty. A crankbow bolt split the sky toward me and fell skidding on the dirt some sixty feet away. This was a surprise, for the crankbow is not a usual weapon among the horse-soldiery of Velonya. It is used by siege artillery. Or by assassins. It has a range more than comparable to the Rezhmian reflexed bow, but having no feathering, it is not as accurate.

I had only eight arrows, and did not dare waste them. Drawing to my chest in southern manner, I took aim for the lieutenant as though at a target and let fly. In the instant the string slipped my fingers, I realized I ought to have shot at his horse instead. I saw the man go down with red feathers stick-ing out the base of his throat, and I heard a roar, either from the men or in my ears.

31

The next shot was more difficult, and while I rode and sweated, with the closest rider locked in the parallax of my eyes and arrow tip, a metal bolt slid over the earth before Daffodil's hooves, close enough to make that stolid horse shy out. I finally shot the man's horse in the throat, and felt worse about that than I had about the lieutenant.

Through all this my pursuers had come closer and now I could see the worker of the crankbow, who had a metal dally on his heavy saddle, and who was presently cranking for another shot. His horse was being led by the rider at his left, and I had a moment's opening, which I took.

I hit the man imperfectly, driving the arrow through his bladder and into the saddle, pinning him grotesquely. This so sickened me I turned my horse and ran straight away from the pursuit, vomiting hugely over the side. I am sure the old animal had never been so scandalized by his rider, nor ever run so fast.

When I could I turned again and shot twice. My first arrow hit a man, though he did not fall, but my second only scraped along a horse and made it rear.

The pursuit had spread itself out behind me, with less than a dozen men mounted and three of these so bogged in soft sand that their horses were floundering. I could not see what had happened in the other wing of the battle, nor catch a glimpse of Arlin, nor of you.

I could do harm with these tactics—massive harm—but I could not win, so I turned Daffodil to the middle of the line, where there was most empty air, and as I galloped in I shot at the man directly in front of me. My accuracy was going steadily down, for I hit him a glancing blow on the skull, but he dropped both his short pike and his reins to lift his hands to his blood-soaked face.

From the left and right, men pressed their horses toward me. I saw blades catch the light and, without dropping my bow, I took my dowhee in my right hand. I made 'eights with it at either side of my horse's neck, remembering every story I had ever heard about a swordsman cutting off his own horse's head. Daffodil seemed to have heard the stories, too. He lowered his neck and kept his face immovably forward.

The soldier at my left had a simple saber, but there was something unconventional about his appearance; I couldn't say what. He tried to reach me, but the bloody-faced man was in the way. His uncontrolled horse was in my way also, and as Daffodil feinted left and right on his own to find our way through, from the right came a horse white with lather, and a mace descending upon my head.

My dowhee is not made to take that sort of impact, but neither is my head. I raised my blade obliquely while my horse plunged forward, and the spiked iron weight scraped down the steel of the blade and the bone of the arm. I felt a great shock, not seeming to belong to my arm at all, and then I was through the line and galloping.

Before me was a clutter of cavalry, disorganized, encircled by a white ghost and by a black shadow. At least eight men lay on bloody earth, only a few yards from the road. Someone was screaming in a horrifying manner. By the raucousness, I expect it was you. A sliver of red flew as I watched, and another soldier fell off his horse.

I realized that I was only leading fresh opponents toward my people, and I swung right and south along the road again, hoping to take my pursuers with me. As I fled, I tried to draw the bow again, but my right arm had no strength in it. Glancing down, I saw a red stain of such size it astonished me, and it was growing momently. I would have to finish this left-handed, and with the dowhee only.

Daffodil once again took the signal to turn with such alacrity I was almost thrown, and what I saw behind me came close to unseating my mind. The ten soldiers who had marked me for their own were far behind me and heading in the other direction. Toward Arlin and Powl, I thought, and I named various kinds of dung, animal and human, as I set back after them.

There were my friends on their ponies, running as wild a circle as before, but there was no dark hub to their wheel. Their pursuers—their prey—had broken out and away, and by the force of their panic they were taking my own personal enemies away with them. Back up the empty road they went, this time without the military organization.

But the road was not empty. Coming down from the hill was a donkey cart filled with baskets, led by a small human figure. The person was not a woman, for it wore no skirts, but that was all I could tell at this distance. I saw, through rising dust clouds, the mob of horsemen approach the donkey cart and converge upon it, and then I saw winks and flashes of steel. Though I was a thousand feet away, I began to shout against this. Futile noise, for as the horsemen rode away there was no human figure, but a blot upon the dry road and a donkey plunging, dragging a cart behind it onto the dry sand.

This is all I remember of the battle. I am told I rode up to Arlin and asked her how she did. I am told I handed the reins of Daffodil into your hands. That I said the words "I did everything wrong," and that I rode another few minutes until we could find a hidden place before I fainted.

I am told all these things but they are not my memories.

My next recall is of a crude strip of linen, onion-dyed, being dangled under my nose. I remember that you dropped it beside me, along with a jacket

33

of dark fustian. "Here is your black and yellow, Nazhuret. I think the duke clothes his soldiers better than this."

With these words came a shock of burning pain down the outside of my right arm. It took me some while to separate the two stimuli. I looked down to find my arm wrapped in what had been a white undershirt, now torn into bandages and seeping brown and brown-red. It smelled of blood and mint and one of the more disgusting herbs. Powl, your medicine is always as much experiment as altruism. It worried me.

"How badly—" I began, as you forestalled me. "The spines of the mace sliced along the muscles of your arm, from just above the wrist to halfway up your upper arm. If you are not careful of yourself for the next month, you will lose some use of that arm."

"I will see that he is careful," said Arlin with some heat, but I had heard correctly.

"You think the muscles will scar and shorten?"

"Almost certainly," you answered, and you kept your eyes on your hands, which you were rubbing clean with the rest of your fine linen shirt. "You must stretch it daily. Though. . . that may not help."

The pain was enormous, distracting, and I glanced from yourself to Arlin only to see fear and loss in her large eyes. Arlin always had an exalted idea of the value of my physical prowess; I hoped my own face did not reflect a similar anxiety.

I tried to stand up, and sat down again, hard. I needed water, to build up the volume of my blood. I asked for it, and, to turn the subject of conversation, added, "So how do you explain the masquerade of our assailants? And, have we surely left them behind?"

Your bland face grew more bland: a sign you had taken some offense. "Both Arlin and I are satisfied we hid our tracks sufficiently."

You taught us that art, and so I had to accept the reassurance.

"And, as for the masquerade, I can think of a number of explanations." When you sat down beside me I found I was looking at your rough shoes. A myriad of times I have been nose-to-laces with your footwear, usually because you knocked me down. It was astonishing to see those feet without good leather and gold-plated buckles.

"They might have been mere brigands using a noble's colors to confuse and intimidate their victims. . ."

Arlin made a sound not quite contemptuous but dubious.

". . . or they might have been Leoue's men, ordered to travel incognito, but attaching the duke's colors so we might know who killed us."

"The duke his father would do that," said Arlin, coming to rest at my other shoulder.

"That would be illegal and dishonorable," I said to her. I have a tendency to state the obvious. My excuse was exhaustion and loss of blood.

34

"Or it might be that they represented the interests of a different party alto-gether, hoping—if we escaped—that the blame would rest at the obvious door. It could be that Leoue is not your enemy at all."

Arlin scratched her shiny black head. "What do you think, My Lord Earl?" she asked. Every once in a while she had to remind you of your bothersome worldly position. She never called me son-of-a-duke, however, or nephew of Rezhmia. Arlin does not tease me often.

You pursed your lips and stared at the pale sky. "From that boy I would have expected a different show of resentment. Cruel but not covert. He seems really to be as bluff and honest as his father seemed to be."

Arlin sighed, took my injured hand in hers, and sighted down my arm as though it were a doubtful arrow. "It took us many years to discover the other face of the old duke. Some people still cannot believe."

Feeling in that arm was growing: not a pleasant thing. "What shall we do about it?" I asked, looking neither at Arlin nor at you, but you answered first. "Do nothing about it," you said to us. "Stop thinking about it. Go to Rezhmia."

Arlin put my arm down on my lap. "Like this? The way he is?"

I told her I could ride, not knowing whether it was true or not, and you replied heatedly "Yes, like he is, and yes, like you are, My Lady Charlan Bannering, who have had a miscarriage some seven days ago and traveled hard since then."

We were both quiet then, as was your intention. "We are breeding insan-ity in this land: a huge insanity. Neither of you has survived a war, and I can-not expect you to understand, but such as you are, in your present unready state I must send you south."

"To what purpose?" asked Arlin. She did not speak insolently.

In reply you only asked another question. "Do either of you remember what inoculation is?"

Arlin answered for both of us. "Yes. You described it as the process of exposing a body lightly to a disease so that it does not succumb to that dis-ease more heavily. I have never understood it, though I know that fewer nurses die of the diseases they treat than one would expect. But how we—"

"You and Nazhuret," you interrupted her (and I think I have your words right). "I have made you both a little mad, over our years together. With this little madness I have inoculated the nation of Velonya, and I must also inoc-ulate Rezhmia itself, in an attempt to avert the insanity worse than pestilence which man breeds up in himself."

These were no new expressions from our teacher: either to call your stu-dents madmen, or war insane. But I felt obliged to add, "Powl, if we're a little mad, Arlin and I, it's you yourself which are the source of all our madness. I don't understand why you don't go in our place."

35

Your smooth oval face went empty. You wove your neat fingers together and blinked several times at the dry turf. "You still don't understand me, my old friend. How to say it. . . ? I am myself a jackdaw of wisdom. I have been many places and carried away with me whatever tools the people used to add to their science, to their understanding. I have used these tools at my whim and inspiration, and what I created was you two. As different as a monkey and a cat, you are, and that must be some proof of the integrity of my work."

Arlin and I exchanged glances, with no doubt in our minds which of us was which animal.

"But I myself remain Powl Inpres, Earl of Daraln, irritable and opinionated, forty-one years old with a career of many highs and lows and gifts primarily for politics and pedagogy. I am not very mad, myself. My own strength lies in argument. And in my sometimes odd acquaintanceship. Old alliances. Now, for Rudof's sake, I must gather in outstanding debts.

"And besides. . ." You slicked your hair back, smooth upon your smooth head, and concluded, "I have taken vows of loyalty in my time. To Velonya. That in itself invalidates me for this act."

We left you that midnight, under no moon, and we headed south. In the next large bit of this history you are not present, save in our minds.

You always encouraged me in the use of Sordaling's Royal Library, and I took that bit between my teeth, my teacher. I have wasted many hours reading memoirs when I should have been grinding lenses for food money. I know what characterizes a good history: it is a sense that the author had understanding of what passed under his eyes, and honesty in relaying it.

My own understanding has always been odd-angled to the usual. I have lived through the heart of a cavalry encounter and gone away remembering only that the horses appeared angry and their riders did not. Last year, when a brilliant, idiot crow designed to steal the eyepiece out of my big telescope and left mess and irritation behind, I put out a dozen painted glass buttons around the instrument instead of a crow trap. It worked.

So much for my understanding. Whether I am honest in my perceptions, you will have to judge. If I were to continue this memoir with the facts that Arlin and I rode through South Territory toward the border, under a dry wind and with no one accosting us, that would sound like the report of a businesslike scouting team. It offends my sense of truth; it is a lie made up of facts.

My ride through South was an awkward exercise, with an arm swollen as soft as a calf's-foot jelly, smarting each time my yellow horse broke into a trot. Arlin was gray-weary and concerned for my sake. (Her concern tends to exhibit itself as irritability.) We were not two troopers on extended foray, we were old lovers, each wounded in heart and in body, and we did not know where we were going.

We had money—rare commodity for either of us—but this far south there was no store in which to spend it. Most of the natives here spoke Rayzhia and lived by driving small flocks of goats or smaller herds of cattle over large stretches of poor grass. I had lived among people like these more than once; they trusted neither Velonya nor Rezhmia, and especially would not trust the yellow Velonyan stubble of beard on my otherwise Rezhmian face. We camped alone, burning dried cattle manure when we dared have a fire at all.

I have never learned the standard mannerisms of being a husband in fact. I had no way to reassure Arlin, to make her accept the loss of the baby and forget the present risk. I have not the gift of lying bold-faced. I could not speak confidently about our absurd pilgrimage, nor say that I believed war would recede again, like clouds when the wind changes. She would not have believed me, anyway.

What I could do was to keep us under one blanket, Arlin and me, to pretend to sleep (by way of example), and when that became unendurable, to spend the black hours wrapped in a horse blanket, sitting in the belly of the wolf.

I am sure she pretended to sleep at least as many hours as I did: tiny, difficult gift to each other.

There is an official boundary between South Territory and the nation of Rezhmia, and there are numerous markers of the obelisk variety, placed at intervals of a few miles, so in these treeless plains they ought to be visible one from another. They are not visible because though they were once stood up, none of them are still standing. The Naiish tribes rope them, knock them over, and drag them by a dozen saddle horns apiece. It is the largest communal effort in which they commonly engage.

These nomad tribes mark the real boundary between Velonya and Rezhmia: a boundary as wide as the sea of dry grass that fosters the pony riders. They live off each other, off the less martial herders northeast and southwest of them, and off their own herds of cattle. They are as poor as any starveling in Velonya and prouder than our most impossible nobles.

It was our intent, insofar as we had an intent, to travel the width of this territory without encountering the herders. Though my arm improved daily, and Arlin gathered her strength—from where I don't know, from the black night as likely as anything—we were in no shape to survive an encounter with them.

On a very windy morning we were dived over by a pair of plains eagles, and I recalled what an old woman had told me in the inn called the Yellow

Coach, five years before: that the huge birds were the scouts of Naiish magicians, or perhaps their other shapes.

Eagles, these creatures are called, though by shape and by their naked necks they are certainly more closely related to vultures. They eat aged meat when they can get it, and living meat when that is more convenient. Their wings are oblong and the feathers spread like the fingers of a hand, and the span of them is twice that of my own arms. These creatures glided from behind us; I heard a whisper in the air, and at the same moment I saw an angelic shape descend over Arlin, who was leading. The bird was white and silver and tipped with that elusive blue that is found only on birds' feathers and fish scales. The red, ropelike head and neck were not visible.

The shadow of its body darkened over her black mare, and the mare flung herself out of that darkness, plunging three or four steps before Arlin brought her head in. As I was watching, a breath of coolness came over my own head and I reacted without thought, to block and grip the descending claw.

I heard a ruffle of feathers and my fingers closed upon what seemed a warm bar of metal, sharp-tipped. My yellow horse reacted in his own manner, which was to come to a sudden stop, and I felt myself rising out of the saddle.

Though I am not a large man, I am not especially light either, I gaped up in astonishment at the bird large enough to carry a man away and saw among the angelic feathers, that red, grotesque, flabby snake-head, seemingly unconnected to the beautiful body and the iron claw, strike down at me. I had grabbed the thumb-claw of the bird with my right hand, which is my hand of instinct, but was not now my strongest. It was my left hand that came up to fend off that beak the size and shape of a cow's horn, and next I had the thing around its neck. I felt my horse disappear from me and I was rising, first five, then ten feet above the grass, the huge wings beating the dust up on each side of my head.

Arlin was calling to me to drop the thing, but I could not see how to drop it without being dropped by it, and I trusted that with its head trapped among its toes, it would hesitate to rise far.

This was clearly one more peculiarity within my peculiar destiny, Powl, or at least my destiny to *find* peculiarities. Grabbing the attacking arm is what I have been trained to do all my life. In most situations, it is the safest path. I was very fortunate the thing was too flustered at being trapped this way to think about its other claw, which could have taken either of my arms off at the elbow.

The ground unrolled beneath us. We were rising up a hill, keeping a fairly constant elevation, and at the top of the prominence the creature sank slowly until I was on my feet and supporting its great fanning body. On the other side of the hill at least one hundred and thirty mounted nomads were pulling their ponies to a stop and staring at the sight. In another moment Arlin had ridden up beside me. She regarded the nomads without expression, pulled the bird's head from my grip, and stuck a tiny dagger into the base of its skull. With Arlin on her black mare and myself holding the dead bird by one foot, we waited.

Their forms and faces looked alike to my eyes—and my eyes are half Rezhmian. They were all short, gaunt, black-headed, with faces like squares stood on one corner. They do not indulge in marks of office, these wild men, though each band has its magician and each has its chief. The chief bides until he is supplanted, but the magician remains through his life.

It is common knowledge that each of these men wears silk against his skin, a silk finely enough woven to cloak an arrow as it penetrates the skin, so that the arrow might be removed intact and the man survive. The image of silken-clad warriors thus engendered is very misleading, for I have seen the silk undergarments of the Naiish, my king, and they are crusted, malodorous, and largely rotted out at the armpits. What one sees upon the Naiish is homespun, sometimes the hair of goats, woven on portable looms by the men in winter shelter. There is very much hardship and very little color about the Naiish, though I have seen the little girls gather meadow flowers in the spring.

I was not thinking these things while I waited for the nomads to sort themselves out. I was thinking that the Naiish do not take captives because they consider no one but their own small tribe to be human. I was thinking that our horses were far from fresh, even could I reach mine. I was trying for some argument by which I could convince Arlin to leave me, since she could at least have the satisfaction of trying to escape, and I was finding none worth uttering. I was trying as best I could to face my old colleague, death.

Out of the milling mob of ponies, brown or dun, came one rider on a dun pony, dressed in brown. His face was dusty, his eyes opaque. He seemed oddly familiar—he reminded me of an old gentleman who had frequented the Yellow Coach when I was peacekeeper, five years ago. That one would visit us on the coldest days of winter, drink himself unconscious, and be dragged before the embers for the night. In the morning he would pay his shot most peacefully, and if the weather had turned, walk away. I had to remind myself forcibly that this was no old dog I was facing, but a red wolf, and a man-eater.

His horse climbed until he faced me evenly, he on horseback and I on my short legs, and then he stopped. He unfolded his left hand to me, and upon it was a glove, every finger of which was tipped in one of the wing feathers of the eagle, and the base of which was sparkling with bird-feather blue.

39

I had killed their tribe totem.

The magician leaned forward from his pony and examined the beautiful body. "You have conquered the male," he said, and had we not been traveling through South Territory for these few weeks, I would not have understood his accent. "The female is larger and more fierce."

Arlin had not descended from her horse. She was much more at home in the saddle than I. She rose three feet above the Naiish magician, only two of those feet being due to the hill, and she pointed to the sky. "Then bring her back to us, magician," she said, her gravelly public voice speaking perfect, courtly Rezhmian, "and I will allow her to join her mate."

I looked up and the magician joined me. Above us, in wide circles and high up, rode the plains eagle that had played with Arlin. It was crying out in its improbable, honking voice.

The magician snapped his feather glove shut with a sound like the birds' wings. "I like her where she is," he said, and his eyes shone with dry intelligence. He put his glance back on me.

"What can you do, snowman, besides this?" He pointed with his naked hand to the corpse.

To the Naiish, the term "snowman" is a filthy insult. I cannot take it so, having made many satisfying snowmen in the practice fields of my youth. In actuality it only means yellow-head. I answered that I could do whatever was needed. I did not think humility would endear me to him.

He rocked back and forth on his pony, which was trained to weight in the Rezhmian fashion and so rocked with him. "Can you die, if that is necessary?" he asked.

I noticed that the mob of horsemen had edged halfway up the hill and that many of them were missing. I judged that the hill was surrounded by now. The riders beneath me did not have their bows drawn, or even strung. Their swords, axes, or lances were in their hands. They had a catholic armory. I felt the pressure of Arlin's leg against my shoulder, and that of her mare behind it.

"All men die," I answered. "And all things."

The magician smiled widely, as a nasty instructor will when a student misses a question. "Ah no, snowman. Most of them are only killed. To die takes strength."

I thought the riders were advancing. I made the obvious challenge, the only that held any hope. "I will fight your chief," I shouted, and since Arlin had ruined our chances of being taken for local—not that it mattered—I also used courtly Rezhmian, which contains some very insulting intonations.

"I will challenge him for our lives."

The nasty instructor smiled more broadly. "Our chief has neither desire nor necessity to fight you. Nor does he want you to live."

40

I thought further. "I will fight any one of you or any number, for *his* life." I pointed at my companion. It would do Arlin no good at all for these creatures to discover she is female. No good at all.

Arlin shouted above me, "I will fight all of you together for *his* life." They laughed at that, for all together was how they intended to take us, but she added, "And I prophesy that you will be a very thin band of riders, afterward. There will be too many cows for the number of you. Too many women."

At this the laughter stopped, for to wish a tribe "too many women" is a great curse, a great insult. Yet Arlin had not spoken it as insult, but as prophecy, and there was a halo of darkness around her that I could feel through the skin of my face.

The riders themselves carried another kind of darkness, and with no weapons in my hands, I approached the line of them, and put myself before the pony of the man I guessed to be the hidden chief. "Chief of the Eagles, let me dance over the knives," I said. "If you want me dead, and think me a snowman, let me do it for you. No snowman can survive the rope."

I said this because they believed it; I had heard it out of the mouths of southerners in my bartending days. No Velonyan can dance the slack rope which is tied to two horses. The knives I mentioned are set into the dirt below the dancer's feet.

No Velonyan has ever tried to dance the slack rope, just as no Rezhmian has any feeling for the bonfire dance. In this instance I was entirely the snowman they had named me, for even you never made me dance on a rope tied to horses. Only the Naiish have made that ordeal part of their rites, and most of the Naiish who choose to attempt the ordeal die also.

I had guessed this man to be the chief by the way his eyes roved over his troop, like those of a herder upon his cattle. I was correct. "What would we get out of that, but wear upon our ropes and bent knives?" he said.

"Amusement," I answered him. "Plus knowing, if I fall, you will save the lives of a number of your troop, who otherwise will die trying to kill me."

This arrogance raised a chuckle among the riders, and the chief could not entirely ignore that. "And you, tentpole," he called, turning his attention to Arlin. "What do you say about our dance?"

I don't know whether Arlin had any notion what the Naiish chief meant, but she has an unerring grasp of theater. "I am night, I am darkness," she said, gravel-voiced, sitting black upon her black mare. "I am a plague upon you. But he. . ."—her long arm pointed down at me—"is King of the Dead."

The laughter died, leaving a moment's utter silence, though my companion had merely named me aloud. The horses, following the instincts rather than the signals of their riders, began to back away from me. I saw in many faces a form of dread: that feeling which hits the bowels instead of the brain.

I think it was the very triviality of my appearance that did it, with my hair like raw linen, only partially hidden under the three-cornered kerchief, my face, which was neither foreign nor familiar, and the litter of white feathers that stuck to my face and my hands. I tried to turn this moment to profit. "Let me dance above the knives," I said again, this time loudly and publicly. "I am the only man living or in legend who has ever flown. I deserve it."

The old magician had led his pony behind me and I was pressed between hairy noses. I was ready to leap left or right, depending how the blade sang in the air.

"But you did not fly far," said the magician.

"And we don't want you to live," said the chief.

I was beginning to feel dizzy with desperation, which was undoubtedly what they wanted me to feel. I called to my aid both my training in calmness, and my own sense that this game was ridiculous.

"Well, I don't know why you don't like us," I answered, with obvious hurt in my voice. Again I spoke not to the chief but the whole troop, using the broadest Zaquash accent to my Rayzhia. Everyone knows a Zaquash accent is humorous, even those who speak it. I heard a few more giggles by way of reward.

"Here are we, two travelers as like out of a puppet show or the spirit world as on a highway, belonging to nowhere and desirous of making you a story to tell your babies, and what else do you have to do but watch us and hear us?" As I spoke, I was looking around as sharply as I knew how, to find out more about these "eagle tribe" people. I peered between the flanks of the ponies.

Down below the hill were wagons, and around the wagons were spread the cattle that are the wealth of these people. My distance vision is a great gift to me.

"Nothing but to push the cows from yellow grass to yellow grass, and watch the calves getting thinner."

"You have young eyes," said the chief grudgingly. Unsure of my own wisdom, I answered him, "I am older than you, Chief of the Eagles."

He looked at me doubtfully, though I was now more sure I had the right of it. The constant weather of the plains loosens the face around its bones, and I guessed the battle chief to be in his mid-twenties. They usually were. But no Naiish will tell his age out loud. "Who are you, snowman, to claim so much and look like so little?" he asked, speaking publicly as I had done, and I took a grateful breath. Insulting or no, he had showed interest.

42

I could not tell him I was the son of a Velonyan earl and a Rezhmian princess. Those attributes would only qualify me as a pincushion among these people who hate the governments of North and South equally. I also feel every inch a liar when I say it.

"I was born on the edge of a knife," I said instead, which was more true to my own perceptions.

"I grew up confined in stone and under stone, but I burst out under the sky and am free forever, past my own comfort, past the judgment of kings.

"I was dead and live again.

"I myself am king: King of the Dead.

"I am Nazhuret."

This time the silence lasted longer, and once again the chief tried to break my effect by turning to Arlin, but Arlin never fails.

"What is your name?" he asked her, and without expression she answered, "My own."

I was glad the chief was as young as he was. He was still trying to find the words that would destroy our impression when the magician spoke. "Let the rope be unwound," he said, and then I knew who was the real power in the tribe.

We were not allowed to use our own horses, which the magician did not know was a blessing, as I had no idea whether either animal had ever been saddle-tied before. Neither, however, did he pull crazy young stock or half-broken pack animals out of the line, but instead called for two riding horses from the remount stock, little dun animals with each rib showing (much like the men who rode them).

The rope itself was neither flax nor hemp, for the Naiish have no agriculture and all their produce is animal. It was a strip of braided cowhide some ten yards long, and even as they unwound it I could see it stretch and bounce in its loops.

I could feel Arlin's leg press against my shoulder, giving what support she could without destroying the job of acting that was keeping us alive. She still sat upon her mare; unlike me, Arlin would rather fight on horseback than afoot.

My memory becomes sporadic, here. I recall the voices of the men urging the horses apart (one may not hold them by the headstall). I remember the sound of holes being pounded, to be wedged with steel blades. I saw the poles being slid across the ground at both sides and lifted at each end, to prevent the horses stepping back and hamstringing themselves. I must have taken my boots off, for there I was with my bare feet splayed out on the back of another horse, ready to step onto a bridge one half inch wide, strung over the points of knives.

43

The nomads were shouting, some the traditional blessing on the dance, and some merely shouting. The blessing may have been ironical, but I took it for its worth. Arlin made no sound, which was perhaps the greatest blessing.

I touched my right foot to the rope as close to the middle as the horse's position would allow. I was surprised it was not more slick, and grateful, but as my mount swayed, I swayed and the game was almost finished as it started. The riders gave one single, rapacious shout, but both my feet were on the rope and I was standing. I was wobbling, but I stood.

Such was the slack of the rope that my feet were only inches above the tallest of the blades, which were old sword blades, broken and kept particularly for this use. With all my attention on my balance, I did not at first notice that I was steadily sinking toward the earth as the rope stretched and the horses' tackle shifted on their backs. I gave the breathy little whistle that the nomads use where we kiss our horses along, and although one of the animals chose not to hear me, the other pulled forward with a will and I was bounced clear off the suddenly taut leather line.

The public roar with which I rose and then came down again on my feet and on the rope was almost lost to me under the roar of my heart. Usually in moments of emergency one's emotions lag behind, making it possible for good habits to outstrip panic. This time, I was so terrified that my body's sweat-chill started to shake my teeth.

This was not what you taught me, and your teaching has been directed toward moments such as this. I stood quiet on the rope for the next few moments, recalling my times in the belly of the wolf, staring at nothing over the heads of the men and ponies, and then it was time to whistle the horses apart again. The lazy horse refused to move as the responsive horse stepped forward. The lazy horse's hindquarters touched the pole and he twitched his back. The lazy horse was going to kill me.

I was facing the responsive horse, and unsure how I could turn on the rope, but I backed, foot behind foot, until I began to climb upward toward his croup. I turned my head over my shoulder and almost lost myself, causing a cry of great excitement, and issued what I hoped was a very personal whistle to this single beast. I tried to make it threatening.

The horse put its ears back and stepped stolidly forward three paces, where it stood at attention.

The riders wanted more of me. They began to clap in time, chanting, "Dance, snowman, dance." I was not sure what dance they expected; most I have learned are strongly three-dimensional and would not last long on a rope. There is, however, the walking dance "Minselye," which closes every Yule celebration, and which every human who can walk can dance: forward three, back two, forward three, and stop. I gave them forward three, back two,

44

forward one, and stop; and in my trembling concentration I might have missed the beat a few times, but I did not miss the rope.

The horse by which I had mounted was no longer there, but the magician was. "Not so easy as it looks, snowman. Is it?"

I did not look at him. "As I have never seen it done, I cannot be the judge of it. Tell me, elder, have I done the thing?"

"*You* have," he answered me, and once again my balance was precarious. Would Arlin now have to repeat all this, with me watching? He told me to back up, and I saw, amazed, that Arlin had been pressed into standing on the back of her horse, and her shoes were off, and it was to be both of us together.

My fear turned to ice, and the roar that accompanied the sight of Arlin stepping onto the leather line had, for the first time, its own share of doubt in it. I heard one voice shout, "It will not hold them," and another say, most remarkably, "It has never been done. It isn't fair!"

That a Red Whip should protest so, when they consider none but their own small troop to be human, and kindness to animals is unknown. . .

The rope did stretch alarmingly, and as we sank toward the field of sharpened steel I met Arlin's eyes. Although they are light eyes, like my own, they give a darker impression, and now they were forbidding and black. There was no fear in her face, nor yet warmth. She was taller than I, which was no advantage in this game, and she swayed disturbingly. My own body was hard pressed to make up for it.

The total of our weights was enough to make the lazy horse start to give backward, shuffling his feet as though he hoped no one would notice the defalcation. As Arlin was still finding her balance on the line, I felt the sole of my boot give against a spearhead. I did not dare whistle the horses apart, for fear of dislodging my companion, but Arlin is observant, and Arlin can master a horse. The whistle she gave, while not loud, caused both horses to strain forward until the line snapped taut and popped us both in the air.

I landed slightly overbalanced to my right, but Arlin landed slightly overbalanced to *her* right, and we were holding hands at the time, so our excess balanced out. We were standing as though at a formal dance, and if our steps forward and back were an attempt to maintain equilibrium, they might do for dance steps. The Naiish cheered for us, even the women in their wagons at the base of the hill. The rope, however, was doing its own cheering. It was squeaking like a mouse and I knew it would give soon under this treatment.

Arlin's face was calm and blank as the face of the statue of justice at the Sordaling School entry hall, and she said to me, "Back up to the horse behind you, Zhurrie. Stride him and point him down the hill." With no other word she released my hand and slid backward along the trembling rope: left foot back, right, and then left again.

45

I followed, though I kept my arm raised as though preparing for a couple's return at dance, and when I felt the croup of the horse behind my heels, I leaped up, spun around, and came down sitting on the saddle. I broke my descent with both hands but it still hurt.

Arlin had an edge upon me, so I grabbed the bit end of the reins, man-handled the little beast's head around, and beat him forward with my heels. The Naiish who had the ends of the reins dragged a few steps and lost me, and I was plunging down the dry, turfy hill, attached to a leather line that took every horse and every man on foot at windpipe level.

The first row of nomads were hit solid and went down. The second had time to turn broadside and it went even worse with them. The third row had not understood what was happening and we mowed them, and then the leather line broke, whipped, and spooked both our horses.

Mine floundered, skidding into the herd of calves, where it did some dam-age and caused more panic. Arlin's animal was bound for the assembled women, and she plowed them down regardless; Arlin is not sentimental regarding women. In another moment we were free of the band and running up the side of the next low hill of grass.

Three little arrows raised clouds of dust between us, and later there was the sound of hooves pounding. The beats were regular and even familiar, but there were not many of them. Arlin's horse was larger and better fed than my barrel-ribbed pony, but he had little difficulty keeping up.

Both horses were wheezing when my ears reassured me that there were only a few riders following us. Arlin and I slowed enough to lean back and try to release the rope from our saddle-cantles, but our long trawl through the ponies of the nomads had jammed the leather into knots as solid as wood. I had out a little knife to cut myself free of the line when I heard a bel-low of protest.

"Cut the rope, snowman, and it is ruined. It's already broken once. And it is my rope." I saw it was the old magician trotting up to us, and the sweat-soaked horse he rode was my own daffodil-yellow gelding.

I marveled, not so much at the sight of the Naiish rider, but at the empti-ness of the plain that surrounded him. He had no companion at all, unless the yellow horse counted as one, or the black horse that he led, or the dead eagle strapped behind the withers of the black, shedding blood and feathers with each step the beast took. Ten yards from me he brought his mount to a stop—the four-square, attentive stop the nomads elicit from their mounts by body weight alone. The horse stood there, steaming, golden in the shine of its sweat: a much more impressive creature than usually it was.

The magician extended his left hand slowly—the ritual hand with its fan of eagle feathers. He seemed to have no weapon except his own strong presence. "The horses you ride are also mine, but in that matter I think a simple trade will please all parties."

Arlin had been off to my right as the magician approached, but her horse had milled uneasily over the grass until by chance—seemingly by chance—it had come to stand between our visitor and me.

The Naiish magician might have sensed that a rider of Arlin's ability does not ride a horse that wanders by chance, or it might have been some expression in her usually guarded face which informed him, but he was not fooled by her maneuver. His seamy face split in a grin that showed excellent teeth, and at that moment he looked remarkably like the old drunken Zaquash who frequented the Yellow Coach.

"I have seen stallions protecting mares," the man said. "And I have even seen stallions protecting geldings. This is the first time I have seen a gelding standing in protection of a stallion."

Arlin did not move, and though I was behind her, I could see her response reflected in his, and I am sure she showed only the watchful inexpressiveness of the cardplayer she was. It was left to me to ask, "What do you mean by this talk of geldings and stallions?"

"I recognize a gelding when I see one," he answered in good humor, but out of Arlin's sword range. This time the word he used was a variant of that used for castrated horses: a word particular to the Rayzhia language. "What other sort of man is so tall, so light-boned, so fine-faced. . . and so bleak of mood? I mean no insult by this; many men of consequence are geldings—servants of the mysteries rather than of lust."

How on earth to answer the man I had no idea. It was a shame he had perceived anything unusual about Arlin, but given the choice, it would be better for him to think her a eunuch than a woman. I pressed my horse up beside hers and looked at him squarely for a moment. "At the Yellow Coach Inn there is a man—or was—who comes in only on the worst of winter days, drinks himself sleepy, and falls asleep by the ashes with no thought of a blanket. I know, because I have often draped him in a blanket only to find it kicked off in the morning."

The magician extended his finger-feathers meditatively, while his eyes, silvered over with age, looked somewhere into the middle of my head. "You would do yourself a great damage to equate that man with myself. Just as I would do a great damage"—and his face split into a grin of brown but serviceable teeth—"to look at you and see a half-breed tavern functionary whose purpose in life is to translate for the fat merchants."

I felt we had made a great deal of progress in this one exchange, and I felt myself settle more relaxedly onto my horse. Arlin had been listening to us with one ear, most of her attention concentrated on the horizon behind the nomad. Arlin is not distractible.

He noticed. "I came alone," he said. "I forbade them to chase you." The grin spread afresh. "They did not want to, truth to tell. One gains power and respect, forbidding people to do what they do not want to do."

"Why did *you* follow us, then? Not to be sure we got our property back?" Once again Arlin's pony was shuffling between the magician's pony and me. This was beginning to irritate me, so I moved my own mount up solidly against her. I hoped the man would miss this byplay. His face told me that he did not.

"No, nor to get my own horses back, though mine are the better beasts. You are a story happening. You have called yourselves so. I am a keeper of stories and I want to know the rest of yours."

We were still staring at him, trying to understand his intent, when he slipped off my horse (just as though he were a natural man with legs and not a Naiish nomad at all), left both animals ground-tied, unbound the limp eagle carcass, and sat on the naked earth, cutting the skin from the bones of his sacred animal.

Arlin and I sat beside our demure little fire, while on a round bump of a hill, some fifty yards off, our magician burned most of the carcass of the eagle on a fire of cow pats and brush. His fire stank up the night, and the bits of mineral powder and compounds that he sprinkled over the flames made a great show of color but did not ameliorate the odor.

We, in our manner, were aiding in the disposal of the corpse. The breast-steaks and thigh-meat had been donated to our dinner. The magician insisted; it was not our sacred animal, after all, and no nomad appreciates waste. The bird tasted better than I had expected, but it had the texture of damp leather.

"There is some phosphorus in that fire," Arlin said in my ear. "Phosphorus and perhaps sulfur. I wonder where he gets it? Do they have mining, out here on the plains?"

I shrugged. "He probably buys it in Warvala. From a 'pothecary, like anyone else."

Her glance at me was guarded, looking for something in my face that would tell her I was joking. Arlin had not been with me during that winter five years before. "You really recognize him? And he recognizes you? That being the case, I am surprised we were able to put over our poetic drama back there."

At this moment I felt more akin to the bird-burner on the hill than to Arlin. "Why be surprised? We were not offering lies to him. The man who sleeps the blizzard away on warm tiles with warm wine in his gut is the magician: a real leader of the most really deadly people on this earth. That I know of.

"And I am Zhurrie the tavern bouncer, translator, mercantile mediator of Warvala. (I miss the place, do you know? Perhaps it is merely the effect of seeing a familiar face.) And I am also Nazhuret. . ."

I shut my mouth on all the possible ways I could continue that sentence. I had said it once that day, and once was too much. So I continued. "Think of Powl, who at court is the Earl of Daraln, adviser to the king and to the king's father.

"And was also to my own father. But who as P. Inpres has written more articles for our own Royal Academy of Sciences or that of Lowcanton. And as simply Powl—"

Arlin put her finger in front of my mouth, which was one step more polite than plugging it altogether. "Enough, you. . . you snowman. I have the message that truth is not what it seems, or rather, that it is that and more besides. But I tell you that at no time, blizzard or sunshine, withindoors or without, am I any kind of gelding."

I looked past the fire at her gleaming eyes and realized three things: Arlin had recovered from her pain and her tragedy, I had recovered from my arm wound, and the magician had finished his oblation and was proceeding down the hill toward us, making as much noise as a mortal man.

I took the opportunity to kiss the fingertip within my reach and steal one private glance. "What a shame that would be," I whispered over the fire.

"Two days from now these plains will become ridges, and then these ridges will become mountains, and it is a good thing we do not pass through them any later in the year," said the magician, riding between us. "The winds are terrible in the autumn, and in the winter, the snow is worse. And after the mountains we will descend into warmer country, where the sweat sits on your forehead even in winter. And then we will rise again toward the fortress.

"That is, if no one has killed you by then."

"What if we run into another of your. . . of the Naiish tribes?" asked Arlin. "You would be in every bit as much danger as we."

The magician laughed. "More, fellow. But we will not. There are no horsepeople within a hundred miles of us."

As we stared at him uncertainly, he continued. "Believe me. I would know if there were. My ear can read the ground as well as anyone's."

You neglected to tell us such an ability exists, my dear Powl, but I believed the man. Considering the hatred the Red Whips feel for one another's tribes, they must have some means of mutual avoidance, or they would all be dead. I decided to watch him do it.

"Magician," I asked, "when you describe the wine country—the lowland beyond the mountains, am I to understand you dislike the place and the climate?"

The magician chuckled. "Ah no, Nazhuret. I find it very sweet. You can fall asleep in the middle of a field and wake up rested. You can pop fruit right into your mouth." His eye, as he met my gaze, was cloudy, but his sincerity was clear. "But I do not own any of that land, do I? And as Naiish, I own the entire grassland. Still, I'd rather have a vineyard." The old magician laughed like a little boy.

He played with the kite he had built of twigs and eagle skin. The salty skin, though dry and translucent now, still gave off an odor. Through the next few days he worked on the balance of the thing, and weighted the tail with pebbles, until it was flight-worthy and sailed out over us in the steady wind of the plains. I didn't think the horses would ever become used to it.

It was sometime that day or the next that the magician ceased calling me by the epithet "snowman" entirely. Arlin took up the practice instead.

Travel across the plains in summer took on some of the aspects of contemplative discipline. More specifically, it was like staring at the empty wall when one was ill; all things were bright, confused, and far away. There was no rest to be had, either under the hard stars or the vengeful sun. Arlin's skin turned a color somewhere between brick and leather. My bothersome complexion merely burned, until the smell of my own cooking skin drowned out all other odors for me. The magician gave me a jar of some sort of mud with which I covered my face and forearms. It didn't stink, at least not after it had dried, but I must have looked like something dug unwisely out of the ground. The claypack made me very conscious of my moods, as it yanked against the expressions of my face, and it did nothing to keep the broiled skin from splitting over my knuckles and wrists, but it did make it possible for me to cross the width of the grasslands.

During the last Rezhmian incursion, I am told we lost many blonds to the infections of sunburn, and that was in mid-spring, right after the thaw. Skinburn would be a nasty way to die.

The image that stays in my mind of that first trip across the empty spaces is that of a white line of horizon topped by silver-blue and founded on pale tan, broken in the middle by the shape of a single auroch, that ancestor to the broad-horned cattle of the Naiish, and perhaps of our lesser northwestern breeds as well. As the beast sensed us, we had a full view of its spread of horn, eight feet from tip to tip, over a body as tall and lean as that of a racehorse. Its beauty overwhelmed me, and though I am as fond of the soft eyes of a cow as is the next man, I felt man had done a huge disservice to nature in diminishing the creature.

As we watched, it gave out a cry something like a bell and something like a goose. It spun on its haunches and began to flee, swishing its horns alternately over the dry grass. Its manner did not encourage us to chase it, had we been so inclined, and though the beast did not run as gracefully as a horse, it ran very fast.

I cannot recall there was anything visible on the landscape to which the creature's bellow might have been directed. The land between the auroch and the horizon was as shimmering flat as a tailor's press. Was it merely giving voice to release its own emotion, or perhaps to dissuade us from pursuit? (This is the sort of question I should have asked our Naiish magician, but I cannot remember that I did.)

It was after this appearance, or perhaps another like it, that the magician said, "It's in the history of our people that those animals created the grassland."

Arlin, with her eyebrows, asked for elaboration.

"The plain was once forest, they say. Black, forbidding forest, like those where you live in caves, huddled over your fires against the snow."

Neither Arlin nor I bothered to correct him. This man did not for a minute believe the Velonyans lived in caves, and one can only suffer one's tail to be pulled so many times.

"The aurochs lived in the forest, along with every other sort of animal that now lives on the plain. But their horns were too wide; they banged them into the trees everywhere they went. So strong were the fathers of the aurochs that every time they hit a tree, it came down, and at last there were no more trees, and it has been grassland ever since."

I savored the image of great bulls and cows, scything through the fir-woods of my home. I liked it. "And are your people grateful to the aurochs?" I asked him.

When the magician smiled, his dry face creased into fan-folds. "No, they are not. If the aurochs hadn't been so thorough, wagons would be cheaper to build."

Arlin must have had her fill of whimsy, for she asked, "Do you believe this, magician of the Plains Eagle People? Did the cattle really knock down all the trees of the forest?"

He laughed. "It is complete superstition. It is for children!" His glance at her was wary, half offended. "What you must think of me!" he said. Then he cleared his throat and pushed his horse to a more energetic trot. "Still, the aurochs did create the grassland. . ."

Both Arlin and I had to work to catch up in order to hear his next words. The old performer planned it that way. "Or so I think."

He forced me to ask him how.

"It is simple, Nazhuret. The cattle eat without discrimination, grass, bushes, and young trees. The grass comes back, but the bushes and trees do not. Tell me, what is going to happen to the ground?"

51

As the magician's words resolved themselves in my mind, I was struck by a realization, heavy as a blow. It was not merely that his observation was acute and correct, but that this character, who had acted the role of persecutor, pursuer, aide, and comedian to us, and whom I remembered as a drunken geriatric in the tavern and as the manipulator of a mob, had shifted image again, and now was our teacher.

No different from you, Powl; he was dirty, small, and stinking and yet no different at all from the immaculate Earl of Daraln.

And in another moment my perception had focused differently, and I saw in the man something that was not Powl nor Naiish magician, but was of identical nature, shining through both names and faces. I think I made a sound.

My memories rose like birds, and I saw this same identity in the eyes of a wolf I had known (or dog. I never knew which). This thing, which was teacher and not exactly teacher, suddenly seemed to be everywhere in my past: in the slant of a sheeting rain outside the barn where once I slept, in the face of my mother (which may be not memory but an invention from the needs of my heart), and at last in no image and in no disguise at all.

I came awake again and my arms and back were cold with sweat and I had let my horse drift. Arlin was staring at me. She edged the black mare over and took me by the arm. I met her eyes and again I saw this thing—this teacher—before me, bright and real under the light of the sun. I cried out without words.

"What?" Arlin shook my arm, and in her face was a taut, martial concern for me.

I don't know how much time had passed while my perceptions had knocked one another along in my head. The magician was speaking again, or still. He was pointing his finger at me.

"As a legend, King of the Dead, you should know these things already."

I did not know then and I do not know now whether he was speaking of the aurochs' eating habits or of what I had experienced a moment before. The moment was still ringing around me like a struck crystal, and the sweat had stuck my shirt to my back. I felt very calm and light, as though I hadn't eaten for days. "I don't have any desire to be a legend, magician," I said, and I meant it wholeheartedly.

He laughed wholeheartedly in reply. "Of course you don't," he said to me. "It works that way."

By the evening of that day (I think it was that day) the horizon was smudgy. Arlin noted it first and guessed there was weather coming. The magician denied it; though his eyes were cloudy his nose was keen. I stopped my horse, examined the distance, and found the smudge to be mountains.

52

That night we celebrated. Arlin and I each spared an hour to stalk game, which is not easily done in the open land. The magician did not hunt, for though the Naiish are the best archers in the world they waste little time on game, living instead on the herds they follow and saving their arrows for human beings. He stayed at the fire instead, boiling a huge mess of cracked barley and roots to which we were able to add a large desert hare and a little wild chicken. I remember that feast, because it set to rest in my mind all the horror stories one hears about Naiish cooking.

While I sanded the pot and Arlin sharpened our swords—for Arlin gets more satisfaction out of that task than I do—the magician lay his head upon his saddle and instructed us.

"No man over the age of forty likes to see other people's blood spilled. Not if he has had children, he does not."

"So that was why. . . ," I began, at the same moment in which Arlin said, "Even among the Naiish?"

He glanced at each of us and chose to answer Arlin. Firelight gleamed upon his cataracts. "Even among the riders. Yet you must remember that traders and wealthy parties travel between Rezhmia and Velonya along the strip of wet land south of Morquenie, by the sea. We rarely see strangers cross our property, and when we do, we take it as an insult. You would also, if strangers rode their horse trains over your property."

This simile was amusing, but I asked, "Can a hundred people call a thousand square empty miles their property?"

The old magician cast me a chiding look. "Of course we can. We *do*. All the world knows we do. That was not a clever question." Before I could interrupt further, he continued. "And then you killed our eagle right before our eyes. It is not that we like the old vulture, you understand. But it is our totem.

"Still, I would have been happy to see you fleeing back the way you came, but the young men made that impossible. Our young men are like no other men on earth. They are mad wolves.

"You will say we make them that way," he accused me, and indeed I had been thinking exactly that. "But it isn't so. Our children are brought up like any other children, but they grow up to carry the red whip!"

His voice rose with emotion and in his face shone a mixture of pride and disgust: very odd. I took the chance of offending him to say a thing I had grown to think over the years of roaming the Zaquash territories. "And yet, magician, by appearance the people of northern Zaquashlon are of the same stock as the Naiish nomads. Certainly you can pass back and forth at will and be unrecognized."

53

By the silence I thought I had done it; the man would say nothing more of interest between here and the mountains. But after a minute he replied, "It is a dangerous thing you know, Nazhuret. We avoid letting snowmen know so much about us. But you have taken the information wrongly.

"It is true we are born looking no different than any small child of Warvala. And it is true a rider can get off his horse and labor in a tinware shop for years without anyone suspecting what he is by birth. In fact, many young riders do this.

"I will go further and say that any rider who has it in himself to behave reasonably and mind his own business *will* get off his horse and do this. And always has done so. The tribe is poor and pleasures are few."

The magician gazed blandly into the fire and spread his brilliant feather glove in its light. "Old age is an agony among us. It is enough to drive a man into taverns.

"As a result of this winnowing, the young men who are left to us are the ones who cannot moderate themselves. Like certain cattle, certain horses. . . The plains, however, have the power to do what the rules of man cannot, and under the sky our men learn discipline or they die. Sometimes both.

"If you were stock-raisers, my comrades, you would know that you cannot breed the wildest to the wildest for generations without getting some effect."

I asked him about the women; were they also the wildest of the wild? He chuckled, snapped his hand closed, and said, "About the women you will have to ask a woman."

That night I considered all the man had said. I had plenty of time for reflection, because I could not sleep well apart from Arlin, and our blankets are not really warm enough unless shared. The next day, as we fixed our eyes on the smudgy horizon and willed the mountains to grow, I asked the magician if he had been a mad wolf as a boy.

His answer was cheerful. "Oh no, I was clever instead. I ran away to Sekret when I was ten. I was every inch a snowman! Later I went as far west as Grobebh, and I lived in Bologhini until my children were grown."

My expression of surprise at this revelation won another bout of laughter. "I have no secrets!" he cried loudly, and I gaped again at the inaccuracy of his statement. After another minute he added, "Men like me are necessary among my people, too. Otherwise the poor brutes would die of their own fury."

The next day was windy and bright, and through our morning's ride the flattened expanse of earth rose into ridges, just as waves of the ocean rise higher as dawn leads to midday. The peaks along the horizon were clear now to Arlin as well as to myself, and though the old magician could not see them, he knew they were there. What had been grass all of one color, topped with the dried spikes of its husky grain, was becoming a carpet stained with various pigments: gray-green bushes of sage, blue-green plantain, ribs of rock not green at all.

It occurred to me that we were out of the grassland and into the foothills of the mountains. I recalled to mind that I was going to visit the Sanaur of Rezhmia, that most consistent enemy of Velonya, devil incarnate to all Velonyan schoolboys—my granduncle.

Who did not know I lived. Who would not be made happy by the news. I reflected upon this.

I felt a cold wash of fear over me, so strong it seemed to originate outside myself. I heard a beast growling, huge as the earth.

This fear and this growling were not particular to me, for my daffodil-yellow horse reacted to them also, and his heart beat between my knees like a drum. Arlin's horse, too, had started, and so had Arlin.

In another moment I was flung off the horse and rolling over the stony soil, heels over head. I thought I had been bucked off, but no horse has such power as this had shown, and then I heard the poor creature's shoulder hit the ground.

I had spun three times around and came out of the roll standing upright, thanks to long and stringent teaching, but it seemed I was still rolling anyway, or at least the earth was. The horrifying growl had grown into a roar, and the ground disappeared from under my feet. This time I came down on my chin.

This was enough, I told myself. It was time for this to be over, but the earth went on bucking and heaving. I raised my eyes, tasting the blood from my own lip, and the air just above the ground was white, nearly opaque. I could see the black shape that was Arlin, flat out like myself with only the position of her head to tell me she was still alive. Beside her the larger black shape of her mare threw her neck about in a vain attempt to ride the bucking earth.

The two Naiish ponies had kept their feet in some miraculous fashion, but they stood with their stubby legs braced out at angle, like furry, fat spiders, and the magician himself lay flat and motionless. I feared the beasts would step on his face, and twice I got to my feet and made a few steps toward him before being knocked down again.

The third time I stood, it was over. The mad beast went quiet and the earth was as still as it had been a few minutes before. I knelt beside the magician, and in a moment Arlin joined me there. We met each other's staring eyes and neither of us pronounced the word "earthquake" lest we call it back upon us again. I could hear horses floundering, and horses running.

The old magician opened his eyes to the sky and took a deep, laboring breath. Holding his ribs in both hands, he inhaled again, shuddering. He bent his knees and arched his back from the ground in an attempt to pull air into lungs that had been violently emptied. It took him over sixty seconds to reprime the well of his breathing, and just as he sat up, the predatory growl began again, followed by a sensation of something huge stalking the earth all around us.

We held him up by each elbow and did nothing but witness this invisible calamity around us. This time when I heard the "beast" I knew what it was, and I recognized (or perhaps merely trusted) that it was of smaller magnitude than the tremor that had preceded it. I felt calm enough, and indeed felt my consciousness descend into the belly of the wolf, but nonetheless, two long seconds after the growl, when the earth was well into its trembling, I was aware that my heart leaped and started racing. An instant sweat was chilling the skin of my arms.

It seemed the earthquake had pulled these changes out of my body, with my mind having no part in the process.

When this tremor was over, the magician got to his feet. "To think," he said in a very casual tone of voice, "that an earthquake could throw me and wind me like that. At my age." In his cloudy eyes I read contempt: for himself, for the event, for us who were holding him when he could stand perfectly well.

Arlin released him first, for his pride called to hers. "Tell me, what animal causes the earthquake? According to your people, of course?"

He didn't answer her.

Around us I found my own baggage, Arlin's saddle, and the magician's eagle-skin kite. Only the last of these seemed to have escaped harm. The old man picked it up, arranged its flight feathers, and proceeded toward the mountains. "The horses will come back to us," he said portentously. I didn't ask him how he knew.

For Arlin and me, it was more difficult. I would have liked to carry the saddle for her, since it was more awkward than my own burden, but I did not know how rules of gallantry applied to eunuchs, and I did not want to share her secret with the old man.

Twice in the next hour the beast growled around us again, once so strongly that although it did not knock me to my knees, I found myself sinking down for security's sake. I had always thought of a large earthquake as something like the hammer of God, which would strike and be done with, but I learned that it works more the way a burnt house caves in, piece by miserable piece. Each time I heard the tremor announced, my body reacted in the same manner: two seconds of shocked calm followed by a storm of pulse and sweating like a kettle gone from simmer to boil. I resented the calamity's intimacy with my physical person. I wished to snub the earthquakes, and my body answered their every growl.

The dust in the air made it difficult to know exactly where we were going; the mountains were invisible behind white curtains. I followed Arlin, who followed the magician, who couldn't see well anyway, and though the journey seemed hopeless and pointless, the tremors were like whips to keep us moving.

Indeed, before that first hour was up, the horses had started to come back to us. First was my bright yellow gelding, still wearing my saddle on his back, and I might preen myself on my ability to attach affection, but I suspect he was always the laziest of the herd. On the other hand, perhaps he was just the most intelligent, and knew what a handicap the saddle would be in the feral life. Arlin's black mare came over the horizon shortly afterward, leading the Naiish ponies, but while the mare returned to her life of duty, the others shied away and kept clear of us until nightfall.

The magician didn't care, or pretended not to. He was not carrying anything but a kite.

The summer had been dry, and there was a good deal of dead brush to make a campfire, with which we attempted to keep the earthquakes at bay. Arlin had taken a heavier fall than I, and her neck was stiffening. I massaged it as I could, while in Allec I suggested to her that as times were difficult even without masquerades, we might be better off informing the magician she was female. She responded that such would be a very bad idea, and when I pressed her for a reason, she said, "Tell him nothing. He has not told us his name."

There was sense in what she said, albeit oblique sense. I glanced up at the old man in time to find he had been watching us. Without asking what we had been saying or in what language, he began to lecture us.

"The legends of the riders don't say much about the earthquake, because the earthquake does not belong to the grassland. It is a monster of the mountains." He pointed into the darkness. "You are headed now toward the home of all the world's earthquakes."

Arlin chuckled at this bit of drama. "Well, so are you," she said. "Heading toward. . ." In the middle of her words the growl came, and the ground shook again. All the horses started and one pulled wildly, but unsuccessfully upon its tether line.

Two seconds' pause and then my heart raced, my skin sweated cold. I was very irritated at the earth and at myself.

The magician laughed. I think it was a laugh of real amusement; I cannot be sure. "You have had quite a trip down to Rezhmia! First two eagles come against you, then a full troop of riders, and now the earth itself. It would seem you are not meant to go to the City."

I felt Arlin stiffen under my hands. I straightened, walked around the fire, and sat down beside the magician. "If we are not meant to go to Rezhmia, we will not get to Rezhmia. But nothing has shown that."

I made sure I had his attention and added, "Fate can stop a man's heart with a hiccup, properly timed. There is no need to disarrange the earth."

Arlin coughed, groaned, and said, "The earth and sky herald great events, rider. We are only receiving our due."

The magician's eyes grew brighter as he stared over the fire at her. "Earth and sky, you say? I can't wait to see what the sky will produce!"

The next day it produced rain, but I do not have such a sense of my own importance to believe it was a gesture directed at me or my fellows. As though for balance, we enjoyed the end of the dry east wind that blows all summer across the grassland. We were now in the Bologhini foothills—no mistake. The ridges ran almost due north and south, and passage through them above Morquenie's trade road was only by horse or by foot, through the occasional crack in the walls of the peaks. These mountains, however, crack frequently.

Between insufficient blankets and steady rain, Arlin came down with a head cold. To me it seemed her sneezes were too unmistakably feminine, but I had never paid much attention to the few eunuchs inhabiting Zaquashlon, or at least not to their sneezes. Perhaps it was all my own anxiety; Arlin's male impersonation is harder on me than upon her.

The magician claimed to know where we were going, though he did not pass on enough information for us to understand the route. I remember going south along a well-trodden path, between two rows of rock teeth only fifty yards apart. Along either side, the herds of the mountaineers had cropped the herbage to a fine lawn (as the aurochs did the grasslands, according to our magician), but above a certain height, different for each individual stone tooth, the grass gave way to stunted cedar and pine. Sometimes the lower surface of the lowest branches would be shaved to the bark, which was scarred by the teeth of sheep and goats. The manure of sheep and goats dotted the road.

As we rode down this improbable landscape, I began to catalog in my head the stumbles that fate had thrown in our path since receiving the king's commission. First we had been attacked by ambiguous cavalry at the borders of Norwess, and then in close sequence by eagles and by the Naiish, from whose hands and hooves very few escape. Building upon this experience we had an explosion of the earth, and now (to finish in whimsy) a leakage of the sky. What was the purpose of all these obstacles? Not having killed us, what had they accomplished?

The answer came to me like a prompting voice in my ear. They had, each of them, served to keep us from thinking about the job at hand.

I was going to the Fortress City in order to prevent a war.

I was not certain the war could be prevented. Or ought to be.

Arlin and I had been sent because of our training, an education which the king trusted would help us produce alternatives to war that other men might not discover. But alternatives are not always an improvement over things as they are. They do not always (I hate to admit it) exist.

I personally had been sent because I was the sanaur's grandnephew. His cross-bred grandnephew, and child of a "snowman."

I did not imagine the old man knew of my existence.

I did not for a moment consider he would be glad to know of it.

I pondered my mission while the rain soaked my headcloth and liquefied the claypack on my face, and at last I decided that the soldiers, the eagles, the Red Whips, the earth, and the sky had had no reason to bother. I was utterly unable to think about the job at hand.

The first people we saw since leaving the Naiish were a family of perhaps ten individuals, who had pitched woolen tents on the small width of flat land and were waiting out the rain. The fabric of their tents collected water in droplets all over the surface, each drop serving as a lens for a ray of light. The traditional brass witch-chimes of the Rezhmian peasant echoed that light into sound, that was punctuated by the bleating of their animals from within the ring of hurdles the people had set up.

I remember most of all the seagulls, that wheeled gray and white like rain-clouds above the tents, obviously expecting something of the residents. Their own cries echoed among the stone teeth above us.

I was riding beside the magician when we first heard the sounds of the camp, and my eagerness to see human dwellings again put me in the lead. I paused long enough to hear a voice from within one of the tents; it was that of a woman speaking Rezhmian, and not the Rezhmian of the Naiish either. I would have ridden in among them, had the old magician not kicked forward and snagged my yellow horse's bridle in one hand.

We had a short, whispered argument in the rain: I, feeling justified in greeting these herders or at least riding past them, and the Naiish utterly set against it. Arlin broke the tie against me. She said she was feeling too incompetent to meet anyone, dangerous or not. We were forced to draw back an hour's ride before we could find a break among the teeth to the east that looked like it might be gotten over.

59

It was not a path in any sense, but a channel choked with rocks, and the recent earth movements had sent any number of fresh rocks, pebbles, and boulders to wobble atop the earlier ones. A fall might have been the end of a horse's leg, and so of a horse. It might have been the end of a rider.

I gave my Daffodil his head, tying the ends of the reins together over his gnarly blond mane. I considered getting down to spare him my weight, but the magician advised against it. The lurching sensation we felt as the horses hauled themselves from one level to another is not something I can well describe. At the end of another hour, we were scrabbling down the east end of our rock channel, a journey Daffodil completed on two forefeet and his broad behind.

We were not in another clean-cut valley, but along an uneven, stony ledge that might or might not keep parallel to the way we had been going. It was so narrow that I had to press forward to enable Arlin's black to skid her way down from the rocks.

I think it was within five minutes of reaching solid ground that I heard the sound of hooves ahead: a horse trotting. The rock tooth over which I rode opened out into a cuspy molar, and a man came riding toward me from the west.

I looked at the trail behind him and surmised that the other end of it hit the herders' valley right past their camp. It looked clear and inviting. I sighed.

I looked at the horse, a gray, shining like marble in its rain-slick but undoubtedly white when dry. It was beautiful as Arlin's Sabia had been beautiful. Its trappings were also rain-darkened to a deep purple. They were beautiful, in the Rezhmian manner. The rider's clothes, too, were black-purple and beautiful in the Rezhmian manner.

I looked at the rider's face and he was me.

His eyebrows were dark, as I remember, and under his broad-brimmed rain hat perhaps his hair was also dark, but the face itself, and the hands—one of them around the reins and drawn back over the pommel of the saddle and one pointed at me in astonishment or accusation—were my own.

Was my own hand pointing at him? Was this encounter only with some mirror of distortion, perhaps in my own head? As best I remember, my right hand remained at rest and my left loosely on the reins, for Daffodil did not demand strenuous discipline. I think we looked at him quietly enough, while his horse danced.

Then the immense growl began again, though which of us the earthquake had as quarry I do not know. My horse skipped sideways, while his horse screamed and plunged ahead along the path he had taken. He was gone before the earth had stopped shaking.

Arlin's mare bolted toward us. She halted at my side. "What is it, Zhurrie?" she whispered, as though the old magician were near enough to overhear.

60

"You look dazed by that one. Did a rock fall? Your horse slam you into something?" She put her hand over mine, only for a second.

My heart was racing, of course, and cold sweat mixed with the rain.

On the stones, streaming with water, I saw no signs of a horse's passage. Arlin, who is as much a tracker as I, got up from her soaked knees with no better results. The old magician came up even as she was rising, having lost and found again his pack pony. Without getting down from his saddle he contradicted us both, saying the "silk" of the rain on the rocks proclaimed a horse had passed that way only minutes before, scrabbling wildly over the trail.

Neither your teaching, Powl, nor my own experience had taught me to read the glint of wet rocks. I could not say the magician was misleading us. I could do nothing but ride on, following out between the teeth of the ridges.

By evening the ground was rough around us, but easier going than the first ridges of the hills. We passed another herders' encampment, but this time the surrounding was not so much a trap, and our guide allowed us to ride through. So did the herders.

Our own camp we pitched upon a height that overlooked the east, and the rain ended in time enough for the rocks to be dry beneath our blankets, though there was nothing for a fire. Arlin was sneezing regularly and her eyes were swollen. She allowed the magician to brew her a tea of herbs that allowed her to sleep. It seemed to my eyes, fingers, and nose, to be made of bark, bones, and opium. When I said as much to him, he denied the bones.

The sun went down as it does every night. It left a red glow in the western sky, but also a yellow glow in the east. The red glow faded, but not the other, and I was driven to stumble over stones in the dark, to find the cause of the light. Behind me I heard the halting steps of the old magician, and I remember wondering whether a man half-blind was more handicapped in the dark or less so.

What I had thought to be a murky sky was actually the next rise of the mountains, and little yellow stars and stains decorated the slope. The display was very broad, taking in one hundred degrees of horizon from where I stood, and in two spots the demure glows were clearly dancing in flame. It seemed to be I could smell burning wood, but that might have been suggestion.

"It is Bologhini," said the magician, sitting down heavily close to me. "In the times of earthquakes, Bologhini is always on fire."

I sat down next to him, astonished. "Bologhini, the city? We're nowhere near a city, out here. We haven't seen a permanent building since before we met you."

61

I could barely see him shrug. "Yet that's Bologhini: the 'Crescent.' It runs north and south between the layers of the mountains, that are like onion scales. Travel comes down from Sekret and up from Rezhmia. It comes from every way but the plains. Our way."

He stared out over the black decline. I could see yellow lights winking over the milky skin of his cataracts. "It is a grain house burning. That's a shame, for prices will be high and I'm almost out of barley."

He got up again, and reluctantly I followed him. "You will permit us to enter Bologhini?" I asked him, meaning to be flippant and still resenting our clamber over the rocks that day.

He took the question as earnest. "Bologhini should be safe. All large cities are safe, for who is to call you an enemy among so many strangers?" The magician let me pass before him, so that I might discover our path by hitting my toes against rocks.

"I really like large cities," he said, and gave a happy chuckle.

In the morning the city was before us, and I wondered why I had heard so little about so odd a place. We of Velonya think of Bologhini, when we think of it at all, as second city to Rezhmia itself, lesser in history and culture.

Whether it is lesser in history I cannot tell, for Bologhini is built out of wood-weavings and wooden boards. Such a building may last a thousand years, except that every piece of it will have been replaced by another. As to its culture, a man without introductions is not likely to discover the culture of a city. He is lucky to discover its taverns.

No one, not even you, my teacher, thought to tell me that Bologhini was flat as moss on a rock, and largely composed of domes. Nor that the stucco upon the wooden frameworks was dyed delirious colors. Nor that the city spread out over the valley and up the face of Mount Hawtel Azh, covering much more ground than does Vestinglon itself.

We breakfasted on jerky provided by the magician; I never asked of what animal it was made. Arlin was too fatigued to rip at the stuff, and I remember thinking it a pity I had too much culture and education to chew it for her.

I had not realized how high we had climbed, not only in these last few days, but over the long rise of the grasslands, until I heard in my ears and tasted in my mouth the same buzzing I had felt in Norwess. The air was thin and odorless.

I remembered that Rezhmia's fortress was even higher in altitude than Bologhini, and it struck me that both of my parents had been raised in an environment I find strenuous. Arlin leaned over to ask me why I was laughing, and all that I could reply was "It seems I cannot live up to my ancestry." She asked no further explanation. She was not feeling well.

Ten minutes' sliding ride left us at the lowest level of the city, close to its south border. The stone below us was rain-scoured and even, but at the flood mark on the other side the camps and houses began, nudging close against the water-made "road."

The first, farthest out, and poorest building of Bologhini took me by such surprise that I reined up and stared. It was a suspension building, like certain suspension bridges. It was a tent of boards, stucco, and rope. Outside the square perimeter of its walls stood a rank of timber pegs, and wall and pegs were connected by heavy, tarred ropes that entered holes like dovecot doors at the level of the rafters and, I assumed, held the walls upright. I wondered what damage a good plague of rats could do to such a house.

The next thing I noted along our way was a cluster of domes all connected, rather like the ice lodges of the Sekret hunters, but of plaster, and in various shades of pink. The cluster was surrounded by a border of colored gravel, in the same way that a house of Sordaling would be surrounded by a border of annual flowers. The very next thing was a troop of Rezhmian soldiery.

One moment the way was clear save for a few children and a lop-eared black kid. The next we were swirled among dozens of horse militia, each man wearing his little cap with big sun visor, each visor stamped with the sigil of the sanaur. Reduced to this size and replicated in such number, the sign of the book, the sun, and the mountain becomes no more than a froth of gold threads: what we at the Sordaling School were wont to call "yellow birdshit."

I felt no desire at that moment to insult the sanaur's sigil. My Daffodil, gold himself, attempted to meet the random charge broadside, and for a moment it seemed we would go down, bringing a few of the unorganized soldiers with us. As I hauled his head keel-on into the flow, Arlin's mare came breasting this current to reach my side.

"Zhurrie. These are not soldiers," Arlin shouted in Allec. "Not real soldiers. They're raw recruits. From a press-gang, perhaps." At this point we were separated by a small horse ridden badly by a large young man who called polite excuses in very good Rezhmian before he was pushed through by the mass behind him.

In another few minutes it was over, leaving us clattering over an empty roadway, almost back to the place where we had come out of the hills. It took another while to find the magician, who had lost his pack pony in the melee and had to charge into it again to regain his animal. We caught up in time to see him accomplish this; he was Naiish and cut the pony out of the horse troop as he might have cut one cow from his own herd. When he retired with his prize he still held in one hand the eagle kite, taut and undamaged.

"The city is preparing for war," he said and he pointed the eagle at me. "Explain."

I had to smile. "Me, explain? It's you who explain everything: the grass-land, the earthquake, the rain. . ."

He didn't move and I couldn't pass. "You summoned the earthquake. And the rain. Did you summon this?"

Arlin stretched and cracked her back with the show of feline laziness that I know means she is roused about something. "This," she said (meaning the soldiers, the city, or something else known only to her), "summoned Nazhuret."

Under these gray skies I could not continue to wear clay over my face, and I felt that my shining pink cheeks were conspicuous. We withdrew from the flood-road and became one more of the poor camps that filled the yards of South Bologhini. It was necessary, this time, to buy dried dung for a fire. The magician separated from Arlin's medicinal tea certain of the bark, mashing it in his pestle and brewing a concoction that was vilely black but smelled light and spicy. I asked Arlin to show me her tongue and was thus assured that the Naiish skin dye was permanent. She held my dowhee before me while I painted my face with a fine brush the magician was carrying. I remember it was stamped with the seal of the city of Grobebh. I remember the reflective blade gave back to me a most peculiar image: a doll with a wood-brown face and pale linen hair, with blue eyes as unnatural as diamonds on a cow. When I replaced the concealing headscarf, however, the effect was unreal in a more ominous way. I was glad I did not have to look at myself. I did my left hand and the Naiish did my right.

We pressed through the crowds of Bologhini all that morning, and by noon we were in a section of the city that possessed such amenities as inns and stables. The inns did us no good as far as accommodations went—being filled three to a bed with soldiers and their attendants—and the stables scarcely more. We were at last able to find one establishment that allowed us to turn out our beasts in a paddock filled with goats, and the horses stood there in the gusts of rain with their companions nibbling their manes and tails.

Though the beds of Bologhini were full, there were plenty of glasses to go around. We squeezed into a tavern surrounded by small trees in buckets (all that grows on this mountain of stone must grow in a bucket), and steamed our wool against the tiles of the stove.

I chose this establishment, for while I am no great drinker I have a certain appreciation of taverns, that have been my occupation from time to time. It was a dome building, which in Bologhini was to say that it was more than respectable. Its inner bowl also pleased me, being whitewashed and trimmed in colors of salmon and seal brown. Seven feet from the ground hung a circle of small brass bells, too high to be hung for the musical delight of the patrons,

64

but even as I lowered myself to the hearthstones the bells rang all together and the great stove itself made a noise of discomfort and my heart raced and I sweated.

The tremor left the crowd silent for a moment, and then they broke out into laughter as one man. There was even a scattering of claps and foot-stomping.

Arlin and the magician had frozen in tableau, with legs bent and arms out for balance, and only after the clapping subsided did they seat themselves. "I suppose," said Arlin evenly, "that if earthquakes are the specialty of your town, you must take notice of them."

"I take the most conscientious notice," I answered, and the Naiish only grunted.

About that meal in the tavern filled with soldiers I can remember most clearly the poppy-seed pastries. I have an addiction to pastries, especially poppy-seed pastries, and these had a clear casing of honey and egg whites that raised them above the level of the ordinary. The crumbs scattered in the air as the little bells jangled, responding to every shift of the earth and to the passage of heavy vehicles.

(I am returned from ten minutes' journey of the spirit, my old friend. The pastries proved more potent than many another memory of real importance. After reflection, I come to think that my worship of these sweet cakes springs from the fact that they are of ordinary material, like myself, that has had a lot of time invested in it. Pastries presume a kitchen somewhere, with a heavy stove, and a table ghostly with white flour and a woman with a roller leaning over it, rolling the dough still thinner. Perhaps she is singing.

There is no real reason she ought to be singing. There is nothing in the little, crisp, folded shape of a pastry to imply that it was a woman at all that made it. Inn cooks are as often male as female. But I—who have so often in my life been where there is no roof, no stove, no woman, and certainly no song—I hold the pastry in my hand and fall half asleep in the warmth and the sound of her voice.)

There must have been people in Bologhini before the military call-up, but one got the feeling that everyone in that tavern and everyone on the street outside was on military business. We sat against the stove like three stones along a riverbed, listening to discussion of troop sizes, bad food, uniform allotments, competition among the career colonels and the land colonels, pay, press-gangs, bad food, the shortage and poor quality of horses, the shame of unqualified officers rising from the ranks, the shame of unqualified officers coming in from outside the ranks, the bribery of noncoms, the shortage of decent blades, the unreliability of any harquebus, and bad food.

The two things never mentioned in all this tintinnabulation were the purpose of the call-up and the name of the enemy.

It was this more than the swelling masses of young men and the prevalence of Rezhmian salmon and gold that convinced me this military phenomenon was real, and not merely an artifact of the mountain's bottleneck and of the season. I spent fifteen years at the school in Sordaling, weathering four separate war scares, and I remember most poignantly that the closer we came to fighting, the stronger became the unwritten prohibition against discussing the enemy, even to the mention of his name. Had any cadet cursed, insulted, or even joked about the Rezhmians, we would have stared at him. He would thereby have declared himself an outsider, a civilian, not a boy in the know at all.

We wandered from this pleasant tavern to another less appealing, and from there to an open yard with stone benches that was aflutter with brilliant ancestor-flags and pools of water: the Bologhini equivalent of a garden. There Arlin chose a sun-dried bench, glared right and left, and sank down upon it with doglike territoriality. Her sneezes had become coughs according to the normal pattern of a catarrh. After a minute of sitting slumped and weary, she drew her feet out of her black boots and folded them under her, pulled the woolen shawl over her head, and retired from us.

I saw the magician glancing covertly at her face under the shawl. "What is he doing?" the man whispered to me. This was not (I think) the first time he had observed Arlin or myself in this activity, or this lack of activity. He seemed neither disquieted nor impressed, but merely interested to know.

I had to reply that I could not tell him. "Not to say I don't want to tell you, magician, but that I don't have any way to. He is sitting still, with discipline, and letting the rest go. . . empty."

The magician smiled, tightened his mouth, and then smiled again. "My riders don't need this. They are empty often enough already."

That evening the sky was clear, brilliant, and very cold. As it would be very difficult and expensive to keep a fire going, we delayed making our night camp as long as we could keep awake, and spent hours tavern-hopping, drinking hot ale, and listening to the news. The most interesting piece of information or misinformation was that Minsanaur Reingish himself was going to make a surprise inspection of the Bologhini call-up. He of the dedicated knife, of dangerous repute. My own cousin. I wondered if I should see him.

66

Other stories running through the city that night were that "they," which I presume meant the Velonyans, had filled Morquenie Harbor with Felonkan mercenary boats, and that these "devil's darning needles" (as they are called) were about to move south along the Old Sea and attack Rezhmia's capital through the mountain channel.

I knew this was so much horseshit, because the king could not have made a productive alliance with the natives of Felonka since I left Norwess. No one had ever succeeded in making a productive alliance with the Felonka tribes, in any amount of time. Furthermore, sending these consummate sailors over a mountain pass to assail the most populous city in the northern world was a threat equivalent to that of sending a school of whales to besiege the city.

The rumor was idiocy, but it had the power to chill me, for it was the sort of rumor that accompanies imminent war, or the early days of war itself, and we huddled on a bench provided outside the poorest tavern we had struck yet, and I wondered how all this had come to pass without my knowing of it.

I felt cheated; I should have had months or years of ascending worry and decision before being confronted with such a thing as a major war. Though I have fought often and in deadly earnest all my life, though I have been in two battles and been blown up once, I am of the generation that has never known war with Rezhmia.

For Velonyans, almost no other war is war. No other enemy has such a power to terrify us, and I, of course, am my own battleground of just this war.

The night was cold, and I listened to Arlin's increasing cough, which sounded as dry as ripping paper and seemed to cause her pain. We had spread our blankets under a grainery wall that by the quality of its salmon-pink paint seemed to indicate it was not used too heavily as a urinal. I had strongly considered attempting to buy out some patron's hotel room, having still almost every penny that you, my teacher, left with us, but it was more likely that space was going by shares of a bed, and it was too risky to subject Arlin to that. Besides: wasn't this tumult in the city a military call-up? I knew what happened to friendless poor men during a military call-up. It would be too ironic to be flung back against my home country as a member of an impressed company of Rezhmian infantry.

What I could do I did; I wrapped my arms and my blankets around Arlin, regardless of the presence of the Naiish magician a few yards away. She was cold in hand and foot, and sweaty-hot in the face. She shivered occasionally, and I could feel the stiffness in arms and thighs that means the body cannot keep its heat.

After I moved my blanket, I heard the magician laugh: at me, I knew. The impression I received then was not that he laughed at my action, but at the fact it had taken me so long to decide upon it. Arlin also heard the laugh, and I could feel a wave of hostility sweep over her, as though she had turned to stone.

After some hours of sleep, the discomfort of our situation outweighed my fatigue and I sat up. I heard the magician scrabbling through his baggage, and got up to sit with him. Arlin did not move, and I left her both blankets. There was no moon.

"I have not seen you shave," the magician said, much to my surprise.

What did he think, that we were a pair of assorted castrati, Arlin and I, marching back to the land where our kind were common? Somewhat defensively I told him that it was my usual practice to begin the day (or at least every few days) with a shave. When not pelting across enemy grasslands, enduring flood, earthquake, or altitude, I shaved regularly.

"But what I am saying is that you do not show it, Nazhuret. Most snowmen are as hairy as ponies, in a very dirty fashion, around the mouth. You have little hair, like a Naiish rider, and that is very valuable, right now. It will make things easier for us."

I had thought dyeing my face had been enough to create me a worthy Rezhmian. It was my belief I looked much closer to a native than did Arlin, at any rate, with her height and high-bridged nose. I suggested to the man that if he did not want to endanger himself with us he could return to his grass, his cattle, and his riders.

I heard the magician shake his head, and I heard a rustling. "No," he said, "I'm not about to do that. Autumn is coming on. It will be winter soon, and I would rather be somewhere else. Anywhere else."

I could not think of anything to say to this statement, coming from a recognized spiritual leader as it did, but the magician heard my silence. "You think that I am abandoning them. Abandoning them in what, I ask you?"

I shrugged, for dawn was almost upon us and he might be able to see that much. "In the winter. In disease. In the hardest time of the year."

He laughed and rustled again. "In the winter the grasslands are death for old people. No one is forced to stay among the tribe all the time. We are not a military, like these poor brutes up here. And as for disease, there are six women who know as much of the medicine as I do. I tell you, Nazhuret, that there are twice the number of Naiish on the grass in summer as in winter, and even more during our beautiful springtime."

Now it was my turn to laugh. "So you live your lives of raid and plunder at your comfort and at your convenience?"

He leaned away from the wall toward me and replied, "Of course we do. Why not? It is not ourselves we desire to destroy."

There was something odd in the shape of the black outline against the salmon-colored wall. The magician's head was too large. There was also something odd about his voice. For a moment the dissonance between what I saw and heard and what I expected to see and hear was so intense as to cause nausea, and then I was able to make sense of both. I said, "You are wearing a winged headdress. And a skirt. You are masquerading as a woman!"

"It took you long enough to notice." The old magician scooted forward into better light. For five seconds I stared, able only to see his male face framed by the stiff cloth folds of the Naiish woman's coif, and then my mind let go of its habits and let my eyes see what was there: a perfectly acceptable old woman of the nomads. She was not beautiful, but neither was she a travesty.

"What I have done, you must also do, for our protection," said the magician, and if his face was the same, his voice was that of a stranger. "That is why I was glad you are not hairy."

I had no idea how the man thought he could disguise me as female, for my shoulders are wide for my size and my arms not spindling at all. I would not have thought he could do it for himself, though. I asked him if he had carried an entire female equipage over the plains on the chance he might have to escape a military draft, and he answered, "Of course not, Nazhuret. I carry it always, for the times a spirit is in me to be a woman." I was still trying to encompass that statement when the magician added, "Now you can ask me what it is like, to be a woman of the Naiish, and now I can tell you."

But I couldn't. I couldn't speak at all.

When Arlin woke, she fixed her gaze on the magician for a good five seconds, closed her eyes again, and seemed to be trying to return to sleep by act of will. I was weeping at that moment, because the magician had me pulling out the straw-colored stubble of my face with steel tweezers. Before this day, I had had no idea how full of feeling was the upper lip.

Perhaps to give myself a respite, I said to her, "Press-gangs are sweeping the city. Our friend had the idea we are to dress as women and escape their notice."

The Naiish magician shook his finger in the air. "No, no, my chicks, I did not say to dress like a woman. That would never fool them. You must *be* women."

Arlin looked from him to me and saw what it was I was doing. My face must have looked as raw as meat. I saw her color rise and her jaw come forward. She began to shake her head. "No. No, I won't. Forget it. Not me." Her

69

head still went from side to side, like a beleaguered bull showing his horns to one dog after another.

"He has strong feelings on the matter," I said to the magician. He put one finger over his lips and looked regretful. "Then what are we to do? Hang on his coat when they nab him, wailing that he is our sole support and we will starve without him? With those bruisers, it will only cheer them up!"

I have to admit I had difficulty understanding Arlin's attitude, too. She could scarcely still be afraid the magician would assault us at the discovery of her sex, especially now he was in a skirt himself. As for the disadvantage women suffer from predacious strangers—well, womanhood had suddenly become the greatest protection available against the present danger.

Arlin's "manhood," however, or to be more accurate, her "rascal-hood," was a lifetime's work of art, and she was no more apt to drop this persona in the middle of the business than is a good actor.

In fact, there are only two human beings before which Arlin moves easily from male to female, and these exceptions were won with labor. She had no intention of showing her female nature in the Fortress City of Rezhmia, and she was not going to dilute her act now.

My own garb was bought by the Naiish, using our Velonyan money. It was the bright but luckily shapeless dress of the women of the Sekret wasteland, made of strips of pressed animal hair, in more colors than has a good sunrise. I knew an uneducated form of that language, in case my authenticity was challenged. It is a tongue closely allied to old Vesting; a fact unpalatable to those proud Velonyans who call the Sekret people "den-diggers" and "the bear-folk."

Another observation I made was that the old Naiish, of a people known as the world's best murderers and thieves, returned me a penny-by-penny account of the expense. It was less than I had expected, for the old man was a bargainer far beyond my own powers.

I sought my reflection once more in my dowhee. My felt cap was sky blue. (As the magician said: to match my eyes. If I were a Sekret woman, he assured me, I would care about such things.) The earflaps of the cap had tin dangles with bells at the ends of them, for the women of the Far North wear earrings on their headgear, instead of in their flesh. My dress was enormous; perhaps I was supposed to be increasing. I did not look pretty, but I did look like a young woman. A young woman who was clearly Nazhuret.

I felt a cold helplessness, as when I had met my own image, in the rain, on the mountain. It was the sort of feeling one has when some incident recalls a dream that had previously been forgotten, or when a word disappears from the mind as one opens the mouth to say it. This feeling is bad. It contains dread, and also panic, as though the strange face, the missing word, the half-remembered dream were the beginning of one's final forgetting.

There we were, two men dressed as women and one woman dressed as a man. We sat on deplorable horses, or at least horses Arlin would once have called deplorable, two of us with our skirts hitched up and our unappealing calves and ankles bare to the world. To the world and his wife, I might have better said, for we did receive a good bit of public attention from the natives of Bologhini, in addition to from the soldiers who swarmed all over the town. Considering the habits of soldiers, it is as well I was an ugly woman, and that the Naiish magician was an old one. Considering the habits of "recruiting parties," it was much the better we were women.

Leaving Bologhini was different from entering it; it took longer and was without drama of any kind. The road south and east drew the city out as a string will draw honey from solution, and we spent the best part of the day milling slowly among other travelers on the road, both military and civilian, and pressed between houses. It was time for supper before we could say certainly that Bologhini was behind us, but that observation was followed within a few minutes by the disappearance of the rock walls to our left.

It was Rezhmia we were looking at: a country half green and half gold. Below the road began orchards, vineyards, grainfields in their end-of-summer stubble, pasture for the large speckled cows of which the Rezhmians are as proud as the Naiish are of their horses, and houses, barns, and enclosures at every crossroad. Nowhere was there any waste, nowhere any wildness.

I had seen drawings of the southeast countryside, and even a few paintings, but I had assumed that each artist had chosen all the notable features of the area and concentrated them as maple sap is concentrated over a fire back home. Thus my cynicism was my own naivete, for now I found Rezhmia really did look like that. At least from the mountain pass east of Morquenie, it did.

That night we were able to withdraw from the stony road into a dell where the mountains' bones were well padded, and there was enough summer-baked brushwood for any size of fire. Even above the level of the countryside, the old magician swore he could smell fallen grapes. I myself thought I detected an odor of the sea. Arlin used a kerchief and ostentatiously did not talk about smelling.

That evening I sprawled on the grass and watched the shadows of the mountains close eastward like the jaw of a trap. Though I remember this dire image, I cannot say I was in dread of the land before me; it appeared so pretty, so prodigal, so very feminine in its lineaments that I could only wonder that

71

a part of me had its origin in such a place. My own youth was so bleak and empty of beauty, I do not know how I lived through it, if I were born of this.

It had been only two days since I had met myself in the mountains, in the rain, during an earthquake, riding a horse that left no hoofprints I could see. Was that apparition the shape of what I would have been had my father stayed with his wife's people, or if I had had some other father entirely? In my brief, impossible meeting of the eyes, I saw nothing but the shock my own face must have shown.

I was almost asleep when the memory returned to me of that vicious springtime just passed, ending in our trudge to Norwess, and the ghost child that had haunted me there. Again a home I could not remember but that perhaps remembered me.

Even through the night, we heard troops moving above on the road, massing for war. Both my ghosts were awake in me, the big blond one and the slight dark one, along with the forms of brutes and angels: all me. I sat up in the shelter of two rocks and spent all the moonlight in the belly of the wolf.

I did not relate these internal visions to either of my traveling companions. I inflict them only on you, Powl. They are your sort of conversation.

The lonely rockiness was gone; plantings and settlements slanted down at either hand, and the military atmosphere we encountered in Bologhini was cut by the even more disciplined actions of harvest.

Arlin, the magician, and I rode toward Rezhmia Fortress with the year's grapes. These overflowed wagons and wains and spilled from the huge panniers of small donkeys, and over each caravan hung a cloud of flies, hornets, drunken bees (yellow, not black like our northern bees), and sharp odors. By the side of the road sat men in small booths or under umbrellas, selling fresh grape juice or that pulpy, beerlike stuff they make from broken grapes and age all of five days.

I liked the fresh juice better, but Arlin said she could not taste the fresh juice, whereas the fermented stuff at least gave a tingle to her tongue. The magician made no claims for the taste, but he drank the fermented stuff for what it did.

We slept in an inn, either that first night or one soon after. It was no different from the Yellow Coach, where I had worked, except that here the Rezhmian accent was purer. I cannot even say that there were fewer blond heads along the bar that evening than there would have been in the territories. My own coloring, which had become rarer the farther we traveled from Norwess, and disappeared utterly amid the heights of Bologhini, had retrenched in Rezhmia itself.

It was not just a matter of dandelion-fluff hair on Rezhmian faces, but an entire set of men might have passed at Sordaling (of course, I had passed at Sordaling) and women who might have passed anywhere. These last were crowded at the bar with cups in their hands, shouting good Rayzhia into each other's ears like so many Rezhmian princesses.

In the middle of the afternoon I had taken the temperature of my sur-roundings and, having seen no press-gangs nor recruiters for many miles, changed from my lady's draperies back to men's ordinaries. I had done so because the stark reversal of our small procession seemed too much a chal-lenge upon fate, and because you failed to teach me how to maneuver a skirt. Now, wanting drinks for my companions and myself, I felt I had erred. In woman's clothes it would have been permissible to shove and shoulder my way through to the bartender. I, at least, would have permitted myself to shove. As it was, I could only quarter territory three feet from the bar and wait for someone to offer me an opening. I pressed through as soon as I could, almost losing my headkerchief, which is a social error in Rezhmian eating places. (Perhaps they have an outsized abhorrence of hair in their food, or perhaps this is only more of the human tendency to fence about pleasure with rules.)

When I got my belly to the bar, I was in a very bad mood, and my call to the bartender sounded sharper than I had intended. The reason I addressed him in the familiar, however, was merely that I had worked a bar so often and I simply forgot I didn't know the man. Putting aside all excuse, I admit I sounded autocratic and that I made no attempt to adjust my accent to the local patois, but spoke as you taught me, six years before.

There was not immediate silence after my order; that took two or three seconds to rise tidally along the chatterers at the bar and another five seconds to spread throughout the room.

The bartender, who was a man of fair complexion and some size, turned from another customer to me and stared and stared. So did the drinkers with their elbows on the tin of the counter. The room full of people began to rise, with a scraping of benches.

I heard a roaring in my ears, my heart raced and I felt sweat cooling on the skin of my face, but whether there had been another tremor or whether I merely recognized a bad situation I do not know. With an attempt at non-chalance I asked the bartender if I had said something out of the ordinary.

His almost-Velonyan face darkened. "No, lord," he said, standing before me with hands folded over his belly. "What can I do to please you, old lord?"

All around me were eyes. Never had I been so much the public cynosure, and I did not like it a bit. I had not removed my pack in shoving up to the bar, and I had room to draw out the dowhee, but how could I hack my way clear in a room as full of flesh as a well is full of water? I glanced from the bar to the rafters to see if I could swing clear back to Arlin's table, but that would be a flight worthy of one of the magician's own plains eagles.

I pointed to my stained and ragged tunic. "Do you see an old lord here, good bartender? An old lord in rags?" I asked, and looked at him as comically askance as I knew how. There was a sprinkling of laughter in the room, but it was all nervous laughter.

He clenched his hands together more fiercely and blinked at me. "Oh no!" he said.

"My old lord," he added.

The man was not doubly blind; he did not see in me both a noble and an ancient. The common people of Rezhmia have a habit of referring to the house in the person of the man, and therefore even an infant of a house of ancient power might be an "old lord."

The sanaur was my granduncle, but that did not mean I looked like him. I had seen enough likenesses of the man to know we only resembled each other in the way of common humanity. The minsanaur I had also seen in etchings, and though horseback portrayal confuses an image, he certainly seemed a head taller than I. Of the rest of the swarming nobility of Rezhmia I had never concerned myself. I did not know who the barman had mistaken me for, and could not judge whether the greater danger lay in ignoring the mistake or confuting it.

I slapped money down upon the bar. It was Velonyan money, but my years on the border had taught me that no one cares too much what portrait stamps the silver, if it is silver. I asked for hot wine for three, as politely as I knew how, and directed it be brought to me at the table end where Arlin, the magician, and I were sitting.

Perhaps I was wrong about the Velonyan coinage, for the barman was very reluctant to touch it. "Oh no, old. . . You must not pay, my. . . ," he said, and the ellipses in his phrases were wide enough to lose a horse in. Meanwhile, the staring circle around us had withdrawn to a respectful distance, but by the same token it now contained more eyes. I was more than daunted, I was defeated, and I went back to my bench without another word, my eyes on the floor.

My Naiish magician had cataracts, but he was not blind. By the expression on his old woman's face, he found the situation very enjoyable. "They know you for someone," he said, prodding me in the ribs jovially.

"Then they know more than Nazhuret himself," Arlin answered for me. She put her handkerchief to her swollen nose for emphasis. "He is determined to be no one at all.

74

"But then. . ."—her gaze upon the man went from vague to pointed—". . . we don't know who you are either."

The magician shook his head until his starched headdress rattled, and his belly also shook with laughter inside his skirts. "That is true, rider. Names, for us, would lead to misunderstanding."

He had called Arlin "rider." To a Naiish, no outsider merits that title. What exchange of names could have been more important than that? For a good five seconds I forgot my own confusions, until a pitcher of hot wine arrived, smelling of spices and brandy, and surrounded by three tumblers of chased silver.

I had ordered wine, yes. Rezhmian beer is not as good as that of home. I had not thought it necessary to stipulate that the vintage of the wine be ordinary or the presentation simple.

Arlin was the first to dare the offering, perhaps because she had been raised as daughter of a baron, or because her cold made her want the drink more. She took a long sip, sniffled, and announced what my nose had told me before.

"This stuff is half brandy. And very good."

The dinner that followed the wine was of a quality Arlin and I had not enjoyed since our last visit to the capital: the capital of Velonya, that is. I remember five different sorts of meats, each wrapped in tissue dough and drizzled with honey, and a sort of fish stew flavored lightly with lime. Neither Arlin nor I did it justice, being more wary than hungry, but the magician maintained honor for us all.

After dining not leisurely but long, we rose from the table and left the inn, looking neither left nor right. At least I didn't look. Among my various regrets was this: that overwhelming service requires payment, and it was necessary for me to leave a large portion of our travel silver on the table behind us. I suppose I could have stiffed the house and dared them to ask us for payment, but things were already very tenuous for me as well as for the man dressed as a woman, and for the woman dressed as a man.

And also, I have worked taverns.

We slept outdoors that night, when my body had been primed for a mattress. (In such manner does one pay for notoriety.) I believe that night was the most lively for Arlin and me since we started traveling with the Naiish magician, for we were rested, well fed, and travel-hardened, and she had recovered largely from her cold. The sweetness of the Rezhmian countryside inflamed us both, and I don't know what the old magician made of it all.

I remember there was a bird singing all that night, a series of liquid trills interspersed with bell sounds. His song was too complex for me to memorize, and besides I was distracted.

How can one discover a night-singing bird? He is only heard from windows, or under blankets on the cold ground: a gift to us out of the unknown. As was that night.

The morning was clear and very fine. We started late, giving the horses a chance to feed on the good grass that now lined the road. In the midst of the greenery and the smells of harvest, I could not keep my mind upon my task—my shapeless task. At midday, however, we passed a group of cavalry, led by a grizzled and scarred lieutenant, and though there were no faces I remembered from our tavern mystery, these troops reacted to the sight of us—of me, rather—in the same manner. To a man, they bowed over their horses' heads. Unfortunately, they were traveling in the same direction as we were, so there was no quick way to leave them behind. We trotted on and they trotted on, becoming a sort of terrifying honor guard for our ponies. I considered stopping to replenish my face stain, but I feared that if we were to stop, so would the entire troop of them, and I feared that as one fears challenging a dream that may turn real.

In the middle of the afternoon we passed through what seemed a reasonably sized city, not after the Bologhinian pattern but much like any city in Velonya. We were forced to rest and water our mounts here, and took some dinner ourselves. To my delight the Rezhmian troops did not stop at our heels, but rode on past us, only pausing to steal glances as they went by. We found an inn and things began well, but halfway through our meal I started to hear whispers, and Arlin's wine cup was filled three times before she noticed it had begun to empty. Looking around the place, I noticed a man in cavalry boots and tunic, seated at a table alone at the other side of the room. This alarmed me, for soldiers on maneuvers do not eat or drink alone. As a rule, soldiers do not do anything alone. I ate my bread and drank my beer with the best composure possible, but I let the Naiish, with his unmistakable accent, do all the talking. That afternoon, as we took to the road again, we found our honor guard waiting in two files at the grassy berm. They let us proceed then.

The town we had encountered did not fade away as it had begun, but continued in a series of interlocked neighborhoods that paralleled the road. Soon the smell of the sea was clear, though no view was to be seen, and I wondered aloud whether we were actually in the outskirts of Rezhmia's capital.

Arlin, feeling much better today, took a breath of the saline air and looked around her. "The difficulty is," she answered, "that the capital is called Fortress of Rezhmia, and we have seen no sign of such a thing. Besides, I have seen paintings."

The old magician squeezed his pony up to us. He was still demure in his skirts and headdress. "This is the Fortress City. It is not the City Fortress yet, but it is the City. We are there. Didn't you know?"

We rode through the city outskirts all that afternoon, and there was nothing in the architecture to inform us we were in a foreign country. The inhabitants were dressed in lighter, looser garb, certainly, but that could be explained by the sweetness of the climate. They appeared in no way more exotic than the territories people, unless one called the men's headscarves exotic. Late that afternoon we found ourselves in a neighborhood where even those differences failed.

I remember rounding a corner occupied by a shop selling small leather goods and hearing the voice of a boy calling to another boy in Velonyan. It was not perfect Velonyan, but the imperfections were those of any young boy. Another child answered, and then both ran across the road in front of our horses, in the careless manner of boys. One was fair-haired, one was brown. They were dressed like any boy of Sordaling City.

Because I was tired, and because I was far from home, this anomaly hit me very hard. I thought for a moment I would slip over my horse's neck and lie on the road with my hands over my eyes. Arlin's gasp of disbelief did more to strengthen me than would any words of comfort. The boys were Velonyan, and in the heart of Rezhmian territory.

The old magician trotted up. "Well, what do you want? We have entered the City along the snowmen's quarter. Would you expect to hear Felonk?" As he spoke, a girl somewhat older than either boy chased the two across the road, explaining to her brother all the ways in which he was erring, and what Mother was going to do about it. Our horses started forward again, and around this corner we came upon a commercial street with many gallows signs, each written in Velonyan, Rezhmian, and picture-language.

The magician gained a great deal of amusement watching our astonished faces. I tried to explain. "To come so far," I began, ". . . and to find things becoming more different every day, and to reach the heart of difference and find it just like home. . ." As I spoke, I realized that what I was now saying was all I had learned of life. And of death. I could only shake my head, which amused him further.

"You are not the usual idea of a great spirit," he said. The word he used for spirit was the one that among the Naiish is used to describe ghosts, great storms and messengers of the gods. I made a crude noise. "I never said I was such a thing!"

His grin grew naughtier. "You didn't say you were, and I don't say you are not!" He squeezed his pony between ours and led us through the Velonyan quarter.

"This is not the first time I have been in the City, of course," said the magician. By now we had left the Velonyan quarter, but we had not left all the blond people behind. In this heart of the East, I found heads on almost every street wearing as bright a yellow as my own. Of course we could only see the women's hair, and Arlin whispered to me that much of it looked as though it had been bleached in the wash with the linen.

We had taken the chance of stopping indoors for the night. There was nowhere to camp anyway, and in Rezhmia City we had seen very few press-gangs. "Stopping indoors" seems a wicked insult for the hostel in which we were abiding, however. So fine was the service that we were able to toss all our desert-abused clothing out into the hall, and it was returned to us after a few hours, sweet-smelling and with the wrinkles pressed out. It was now obvious that every stitch of clothing the Naiish had worn—each malodorous rag—was made of fine silk.

Myself, I had reclined so long in the scented water of the bath (a clever device with a fauceted tap and a charcoal furnace below the copper, keeping the water constantly warm) that I felt I had slipped out of a skin of dirt and callus as a snake might, and when I rose up I expected to see a hollow shell of myself hanging limp in the water.

The Naiish magician had bathed first, and I was slightly surprised, not knowing that the plague of the plains engaged in watery amusements like bathing. Perhaps the magician indulged for the novelty of soaking in a shining copper tub, or perhaps his traveling life had made him cosmopolitan, but he emerged looking a much younger person and less like a Red Whip rider.

The cost of this establishment worried me, but we had a good amount of your silver left, and tomorrow we would reach our goal. If the sanaur killed us or threw us into a dungeon, we would have no more use for the coins.

Now my bath had been drained through a pluggable hole as clever as the rest of its design, the tub had been scrubbed by a hostel servant, and it was refilled for Arlin, who was spending even more time than I at shedding her skin. When she was done we would order a dinner, and I had great hopes of that, but for now I was spread out on a mess of cushions, limp as a weed on the beach, listening to the magician.

"It is not even the first time I have been in the City in the company of a snowman," he added. "Though it has been many years.

"That fellow. . ."—the magician showed a reminiscent smile—". . . had a great deal of balls." (And here I must interject that in many Rezhmian dialects, the word for testicles and the word for courage have been confused. They will even speak of a mother cat having balls when she throws herself at a mastiff in defense of her kits.)

"Because it was not long after the crazy war you made, when the old sanaur turned you back and left the Naiish to butcher you in the plains at our convenience. . ." The magician's smile grew even sweeter. "So you know what kind of risk the man was running. He picked up Rayzhia with a baby's ease and had better profanity than I, who have studied all my life. We were thieves together."

He raised one of his half-moon eyebrows and his eyes glinted at me. "You must tell no one this—that I was a thief. Among my people it would never be forgiven."

I was silenced in astonishment by this: one more evidence that I did not yet understand this man or his culture. Before I could think of a proper response, Arlin emerged, clean and glossy, from the bath, and supper took all our serious concentration.

The next morning was magnificent, clear and breezy, with the birds twittering on every branch as though it were spring and the horses as high as kites, whinnying and skittering over the road in a manner that makes only Arlin happy.

After worrying the matter from Norwess to here, I had determined to use no subterfuge in my attempt to speak to the sanaur, or in the interview I hoped to gain. I might have equally well made this decision in the beginning, since I am hopeless at subterfuge, but worrying must have been necessary to me.

Now I was through with worry. This morning we would reach the fortress itself, Rezhmia's famed citadel of red stone.

Perhaps the sanaur would not be at home. Perhaps he would not be receiving beggars. Perhaps the world would fall down, but the autumn morning was very bright.

Here the streets were narrower and the buildings taller. Our misbehaving horses stood and sweated as the way was blocked by a misbehaving donkey. The magician led us down a still-narrower street where no sunlight reached, except for a splash that squeezed between rooftops and landed on one of the usual hanging signs, giving it unusual brilliance.

I remember it. The picture was of a man on a horse, holding (with difficulty, I imagine) a viol in one hand and a sword in the other. The sign was old, and what must have been royal purple in the man's garb had faded beyond color, and the rich brown of both his moustache and his horse had gone entirely yellow. The name, in huge black letters, quite unfaded, read

NAZHURET, and, under it for the sake of foreign visitors, in smaller letters, KING OF THE DEAD.

I sat under that sign for a very long time with no feeling and very little sense, save for a small buzzing in my ears. It was only through the coldness of the wind against my face that I perceived that I was weeping. I was cold all over, despite the balmy weather, and at last the sounds of hooves scuffling at some distance distracted me from my trance, and I twisted on my horse to find Arlin's mare lodged sideways in the street and her, with dowhee glittering in her hand, holding back by threat the progress of six Rezhmian cavalry.

The picture is still fresh in my mind: Arlin in black on a black horse in the shadows, the whole cut only by the white of her face and the nickel of the bridlework and the light of her blade. Even the worn patches of her sleeves and elbows shone with more an effect of dread than of comedy. It is the peculiar, original gallantry of my lady that she would risk her life to allow me room to cry in public. You taught her much about life and death, Powl, but you never succeeded in giving her common sense.

I swung my yellow horse around with all speed and let her know she might release the flood, and Arlin pressed her horse sideways out of the center of the street, weapons still at ready. When she reached the brick wall of the nearest shop, she bowed to the men she had just defied, with a great flourish and an expression set in stone. I echoed her gesture with less theater, and the cavalrymen passed, their eyes and those of their horses rolling at us. In a small alcove across the street, the Naiish magician and his pack horses waited, observing all.

"You got away with that because they had no corporal or sergeant to unite them," I felt it necessary to mention.

"I got away with it," she echoed, and put her dowhee back into her pack.

The magician joined us again, in a street that remained bare of traffic as long as we loitered. He glanced at the sign, at me, at Arlin, and at nothing. "Today," he announced to us and to every head poking through the windows above, "something very large is going to happen." Having said this, he trotted down the street, leaving us to trot behind.

Arlin caught up to him, thereby blocking the street again. "A little bird told you that?"

He was wearing his eagle glove, which he spread and closed again before answering. "Yes. And my pony told me." He gave a large sigh that jangled the little bells on his lady's headdress. "Also, today I am going to leave your company."

Arlin was silent a few moments and then said, "I am sorry to hear that," although from her tone it was impossible for me to tell whether she really was sorry or not.

"When I came this road with the snowman, it was early springtime, after the Velonyan War. I met him in a tavern in the City. He said he had become the fifth wheel of a carriage and didn't want to go home with the crowd he'd come with."

We were climbing again, and the golden fields dropped away through the houses at our left. Here the buildings had triangular basements, giving a flat base to the living quarters above, and I had to wonder if the trunks and boxes stored in the basements were triangular to fit. The basements might have been dug out, of course, but if the road we traveled was any sign of the firmness of the earth, it would not be worth the effort.

Travelers approached behind us, and I recognized in the sound of hooves those same cavalry that had accompanied us—driven us, to be precise—the day before. The old magician seemed to ignore their dust and bustle, but he had to raise his voice to continue.

"I remember he was cleaning copper off the table, taking bets: odd bets. Unheard-of bets, such as being able to hold an orange and a knife in the same hand and skin the thing. Another was to dance a shofaghee with an ale mug on his head. Not the sort of thing one would expect of a snowman, since you people are known for having neither grace nor humor."

"Thank you," said Arlin tartly. I did not reply to the magician (if there is any appropriate reply to such an accusation) for I had gotten a scent of something salty and cold, and in the context of this city I could not place it.

I turned my head to the right and I felt my yellow horse pulling upon his bit with the same idea. At that moment we crested the long, long hill we had been climbing and found ourselves riding past a public garden, where all planted things were low and the view was vast.

I caught my breath.

"Look! Nazhuret!" called Arlin, and I answered that I saw it, and the blue glimmer and white sparkle of the sea in the harbor overwhelmed me.

"No, no. Look this way," she insisted, and I let my glance slide back from the cliffs and the harbor to where she sat pointing at the City.

Here was the circular wall of the pictures: a city buried within a city, and it was as beautiful and rose-colored, with the four towers of direction rising up.

It looked small, but then it was ancient, so what need had it had to be big, those centuries ago? Around the walls were vines, and the pink of the walls showed through only occasionally, dotting the surface as though with blossoms. After a good minute's stare, I began to think the pink dots were blossoms and nothing of the walls was visible after all. Surely the towers were a different color of rose.

"Ah yes." The old magician nodded as though he had ordered the decoration himself. "We have arrived at the good hour, when the roses have their autumn bloom. Of course in the spring the flower is so thick one cannot see the leaves at all, but still it is better than midsummer. Or midwinter, for that matter." He spanked his ponies forward.

As a city it was tiny, the sort of place that could stand as a symbol from generation to generation. It was a place one could love; I loved it, though I came as a stranger and most certainly as an enemy, and my eyes wove back and forth from the bright ocean to the walls that lay like a wreath of roses over the land.

Our horses, immune to the effects of art, had plodded steadily on while we wondered, and now began the last, slight ascent toward the city gates.

The cavalry now began to intrude around us, and there was no chance Arlin could threaten this many away. To the right and to the left they came, and their tall bay horses, so different from our plains ponies, enclosed us in a fog of dust. Their tackle and the garb of their riders were trimmed in purple. Arlin pressed her horse close against mine, while before us the magician continued as though he had heard nothing happen.

"Another thing the man did was to challenge anyone in the bar to come at him, hand to hand, for a wager of three 'naurs. He put them all down, this snowman, and there was not a chair broken at the end."

By now we were on a causeway that led nowhere except to those black gates in the pink and green wall, gates that rose impossibly high as we drew in, gates that were certainly closed. We could turn neither left nor right, for the crowd of riders around us and the much larger crowd coming up behind.

Suddenly from ahead came an astonishing shout of brass, as six cornets at the head of the troop announced themselves to the City. Arlin's black mare reared and one of the magician's two pack ponies tried to turn donkey for him, but even the horses could not resist the inexorable procession.

I tried to catch the attention of any of the men riding beside us, but they had no more than to meet my glance before shying like horses themselves and darting away. I feared we would be dragged around the walls or through them, ending lost in some enormous cavalry stable where we had no right to be at all.

The black gates of wood and iron opened with no more noise than a sighing of wind. They stood thirty feet high, I believe, and yet what I most clearly remember is a twig of rose not far above my head that had grown into the crack of stone and iron and then changed its mind and grown outward along its own length again. It had a broken rose blossom at the nether end and a perfect bloom at the hither end. Both blossoms bobbed in the wind that escaped from the City, through the open doors.

Under the gateway, my yellow horse walked heavily into the hind end of the magician's horse, for he had stopped still and I was forced to precede him

into the fortress. Arlin had to push through on his far side, around all his
ponies. She reached out her hand to me, as though to keep me from being
swept away by events, and then her hand found mine and we were inside the
City of Rezhmia.

I saw that the buildings were as pink as the walls, and I noted that the
streets were surprisingly wide. The roads were all paved, and not in cobble-
stone but in brick, like parts of old Vestinglon where the winters are impossible. Certain of these roads had been worn for so long that the centers of them
were hollowed out and contained water.

All visible dirt, too, was in containers and doing valuable labor with fruit
trees and assorted flowers. The buildings themselves, albeit pink, were not so
different from buildings in the West.

These things I saw in snatches among the legs of the cavalry horses, and
glimpses stolen above. What impressed me more immediately were the
glimpses of people, for these were few and mostly in uniform. Regardless
of manners, I pushed my horse forward and left, toward the lieutenant of
the column.

He watched me come with the same rolling eye a horse will show when
nervous, but then cavalry often begin to look like their horses. "Sir," I shouted
over the noise of the hooves, "you must tell me: is there any objection to our
being here within the walls? You have brought us with you by your very numbers and through no desire of our own!"

He hit the heel of his hand against his forehead in the most respectful of
Rezhmian military salutes, and I knew then that we were in deep trouble.
"Most gracious lord, the fault is mine," he said.

Which explained nothing.

The street along which we were herded opened into the sunlight of a
neat square, and the front file pulled their mounts in abruptly, while the riders behind had less warning and served only to spill the three of us out
before them.

I saw the base of a tower of pink sandstone heavily inlaid and more heavily still grown over with roses: these not only pink but in colors of white and
red. I remember that the white roses were almost all past their bloom while
the red were just opening, and that the clothing of the people who lounged
before that wall of roses put the blossoms to shame.

There were ladies in sky blue and ladies in silver and there were gentlemen in all shades of purple and gold, making a clash of color as flowers will,
if the gardener has not been thoughtful. There were pillows and hassocks
strewn everywhere and one white goat, engorged with milk, which was being
restrained with difficulty from eating the roses.

In the middle of this, surrounded by the emptiness of awe, stood a very short, bent old man in faded purple, holding a wooden basket and a little pair of shears. He was deadheading the roses.

He looked over his shoulder at the milling horses as a householder will notice boys scrimmaging in the yard. "This is the season for pruning, not manuring, lad. I prefer it delivered in barrows, anyway."

I looked at his face. He looked like someone I ought to know, and had no business not knowing. He did not look like his portrait. He glanced past all the tall horses and grand riders directly at me. "This is a new trick, Reingish," he said, with great familiarity and not much warmth. "Whom did you hope to catch in misbehavior? These cavalry?"

"Sanaur Mynauzet, I am not who you think I am," I said to him, and as he still stared, I tore off my kerchief and revealed my yellow hair.

The old man stood up at this. He dropped his basket of spent flowers. "Then who are you?" he asked me.

There was a sudden silence. By this I don't mean that the men all waited for my answer. I mean the doves on the flagstones stopped pecking, the horses froze with their heads up and even the wind seemed to stop itself. The only sound was of the hooves of a squat pony as the magician forced his horse to the front. He spread his eagle hand as a herald unfurls a banner.

"This is he who was born on the edge of a knife, who is free past comfort, past judgment. Who was dead and lives again. This is Nazhuret: King of the Dead."

I was torn between astonishment that the old Naiish had remembered our "bit of theater" from our first encounter with him, and that he would have the poor taste to try it out in the sophistication of a court. I expected to hear hoots but instead heard more silence. Terrible silence.

The Sanaur of Rezhmia took a step toward us, his pruning nippers in his hand. My horse, I noticed, was shiny with sweat.

The earth then exploded.

Every image I think to write, describing how this happened, only insults the horror. But I must say something.

The flagstones bucked, throwing my horse into the air with me on his back, in one piece like the statue in a town square. I saw the pavement shatter crazily and raise a cloud of pink, as though the sandstone were only talc.

All of us, human and equine, were in the air and then all down again on the ferocious earth, which sought to throw us into the sky forever. The growl of the beast overwhelmed me, and I saw horses skidding on their sides over the rubble of the court, and horses skidding over people and already the pink stone was smeared with blood.

84

My round, yellow horse was of the sort that shies by starting in place, making no motion but emitting a noise like a beaten drum. He is also so four-square that he is difficult to knock down. This is no credit upon me; his maker designed him so. We came down standing, and I felt his drum-heart beat between my legs. He plunged one step forward and the earth roared again, sending his hindhooves and forehooves in different directions. I heard a sound that I later recognized as a wall coming down behind us. If there was screaming it was drowned in the shrieking of the earth.

Before us was the wall of roses, closer every moment, though whether it was still upright I could not tell. The little old man was hanging from the vines; his hands were badly scratched.

How can a pavement of stone, underlain by stony earth, thrash like a broken-backed snake? I know of no way to study the matter. Again we were thrown, and we landed on the face of a horse, but still my terrified Daffodil was on his feet. There was a man under his hooves also, though the horse was trying desperately to avoid stepping on flesh. I heard something much larger than the wall come down nearby, and only then did I hear an echo of a single human scream. One more whip of the pavement threw us against the wall of roses, and without much thought for the matter, I plucked up the Sanaur of Rezhmia by his shirt back and threw him over the pommel of my saddle.

Portions of the tower fell on the broken stones behind us, exploding like bombs, and more fell to one side, and somewhere I heard a boom like a continent giving way and falling into an abyss, but the thrashing snake was dying, and in another ten seconds it was dead.

The courtyard was as ragged as the teeth of the mountains we had climbed the previous week. There was a red murk in the air as thick as bloody water. There was a perfect white rose blossom hanging on an undamaged vine above my head. Daffodil, with me upon him, was the only standing creature to be seen.

I thought to get off the horse, but so badly was he blowing and starting that it seemed he might die of sheer abandonment if I left him, so I pressed him among the crowd of fallen, looking for my friends.

Now the air was filled with living noise: living noise and dying. Now came the screams and the scrabbling and the protests of men broken and of horses with their hooves caught in their reins. I shouted for Arlin, but a scream drowned me out, and then I heard her own voice shouting for me.

It was unmistakably Arlin, and for the moment she had forgotten her role to the point where her voice was above contralto, and in the two syllables of my name (I am always "Zhurrie" when Arlin forgets

85

herself) there was as much rage at fate as there was fear, and enough strength that I did not have to worry for her life. I remembered the Sanaur of Rezhmia and put him down on his feet, where he could survey his devastated courtyard.

Instead he was looking up at me, his familiar/unfamiliar face now blank with shock. I leaned over and put one hand on his shoulder. "'Naur," I began (for the term "sanaur" when not used with "Rezhmia" means literally "my king" and I could not go so far as that), "I think it is over for now, though there will be strong rumblings. You have survived a great disaster."

He drew away from my hand and the shock withdrew, to be replaced by fury. "I have survived? I? What does that matter. What has become of my people?" As he spoke, there came a crumbling, a roar, and a boom as another weakened building came down, but the old king did not flinch from the sound. My horse did, however, and I had thought to give the beast some free rein and look for Arlin, when I felt a touch upon my boot.

The sanaur held my gaze, and he was not now only an old man with bloody hands. I saluted with the heel of my hand. "Who are you?" he asked me, for the second time.

I bent beside my horse's broad neck. "Pay no attention to what the Naiish said, except that my name is Nazhuret."

He kept his fingers locked into the top of my boot. "The only Nazhuret I know is dead these twenty years in Vestinglon. By treachery, I think."

I might have been more politic, but I could not call my politics to mind at the moment. In the middle of the wails and the dust and the rubble I told him "By treachery, most certainly, Sanaur of Rezhmia. But the teacher was not Velonya itself, but a man and that man is dead." I raised my head and I found Arlin, as much red as black with all the dust in her velvets. She was on her feet and all her attention was on a weal on the leg of her mare. I pointed at her. "Arlin of Sordaling ended his intrigues five years ago."

For the third time the sanaur asked me, "Who are you?" By now there were people running, limping, and crawling from all over the square toward his side. In the moment of privacy I had left I said to him, "I am that Nazhuret's nephew, half-bred son of Nahveh and of the Velonyan Duke Eydl of Norwess." I had to smile at the complexity of the expression on his face. "Now you know everything," I said.

He rubbed the dirt from his face with both bloody hands and shook off the soldiers who came to assist him. Into my ear he whispered, "If that is true, then it may be you are my heir!"

At this my heart plunged, as Daffodil's had plunged in the earthquake. "No, great 'naur. It seems you do not know everything, after all."

I found Arlin, who had seen me upright and so had no time for me, and I found the Naiish magician, who was gathering his ponies from among the wreckage. As there were now no gates to keep us out nor walls to hold us in, we led our beasts out of the fortress itself and pitched a camp upon the ornamental lawn.

The magician was taking off his woman's headdress, pin by pin. "Well, you have given me the story you promised," he said, and his voice started out high and ended low.

Arlin watched this behavior with wary humor. "We try to keep our word," she said. "Though I think we would have done fine without the earthquake."

Though we had suffered dozens of earthquakes on the road, many of which did damage around us, this morning's affair had become "the earthquake." It would not share attention with its lessers.

The magician continued to strip, changing female to male with every gesture, every piece of silk and linen. "I had planned to winter here," he said, placing a blanket over his privates as he replaced skirt and long trousers with a rider's ballooning breeches. (The Naiish, like most people who sleep in small spaces, are very concerned about their privacy.) "Now there will be heavy work and no food or heat to spare."

"You might find the sanaur will spare some of both for you," Arlin offered, twirling her knife. Inside the City, we heard a bagpipe wheezing in three-part time. There was actual laughter accompanying the music. People are endlessly strange.

"And maybe he will have me skinned. And you, too," the Naiish made this suggestion unemotionally. "Having announced you King of the Dead, snowman, it is appropriate of me to go elsewhere. Bologhini, perhaps. They could not have suffered as this place did, and besides, they are ready for quakes."

"You are afraid," Arlin said, and she prodded his arm reproachfully. "After all this, you are afraid to stay."

He looked at her and I could not see his answering expression, but the chiding humor died from her face. At last the magician reached out his hand. "Give me something of yours."

Arlin did not ask for explanation. She took out her dagger and gave it to him, pommel first. She did not tell him that this dagger had a reputation across all Velonya, as having ended an attempt against the Velonyan king. He took it, and he asked for something of mine.

I stared at him, perplexed, and he added, "Something that you have carried. Have treasured. Something to represent you."

I shook my head, able to think of nothing that fit that description. Of all possessions, I liked my horse best, but a horse was too troublesome to become a souvenir.

87

Arlin spoke for me. "Nazhuret has nothing. Nothing special."

In my humiliation I had an idea. I drew my dowhee from the pack. "Here," I said, and he drew back in exaggerated surprise. "Does a tiger give away his claws?"

I insisted that the thing was not special to me: that it was the image of any other well-made Felonkan blade, whether to be used for war or making paths in the forest. He took it silently and hid it and the poniard underneath his bedding on a pack saddle. On impulse I said to him, "Now give us your name, magician, and we will give you ours."

He smiled as he put the saddle on his pony, and even the smile was different from the smiles he had worn as a woman. "I have given my name to only one foreigner before, and that was long ago. But have it: Ehpen, I am called."

The name was two words of Rezhmian—"no safety." I asked for the rest, and he laughed.

"That isn't enough, Nazhuret? It wasn't enough for the other snowman either. Hear this. 'There is no safety in this life.' That is my full name."

He turned his face to Arlin. "Now give me another for you."

She stared past him for five seconds before answering. "I am Charlan, daughter of Baron Howdl of Sordaling in Velonya."

By his expression I could not tell if he had guessed her secret before this. "Tell no one that. No one here. Remain Arlin the eunuch instead."

"I was never a eunuch. Never that." The magician was mounting his horse and affected not to hear.

"Now you, without the poetry."

I answered that I was Nazhuret of Sordaling, nephew of the Nazhuret who was son of this 'naur's father, and that my father had been Duke of Norwess in times past. But I added that none of that touched me.

His bleary eyes blinked down at me. "None touches you? I'll remember that, Nazhuret, and lest it touch me instead I'll be on my way. No, I am not afraid, but with no hope of safety we can still seek our best comfort, can't we? And you—you are yellow-haired death riding a yellow horse."

He started along the road that ran by the sea, but Arlin shouted after him, "The other snowman. Might I guess his name?"

Ehpen squinted back and Arlin ran after him, or rather she limped, having been struck by more than one brick that morning. I followed.

"It was Powl, wasn't it? Powl Inpres."

Slowly the magician nodded, and then he booted his ponies on. He would answer no more questions.

I was astonished at her acumen, which seemed supernatural, but Arlin answered, "*He* said that to me more than once. 'There is no safety in this life.' It had to be Powl."

(You might have told us about the magician.)

I followed her back to our camp by the City, from which now came a smell of fire. "I never heard those words from Powl. Not at all."

Arlin grunted and poured more water over the dressings on her horse's leg. "Perhaps he never had need to tell you that," she said.

I could not stay out of that fortress, although Arlin lay with her swollen leg propped on a fountain (it was dry, as of this morning) and insisted this trouble was none of my business. And that I could be of very little assistance, knowing nothing of the place.

It was not real compassion that pulled me into the Rezhmians' long effort, or at least I don't think it was, but rather that sort of reflex that causes one to respond to a voice calling one's name or, for that matter, causes many men to gather and do nothing around one man who is digging in the road. There was such a feeling of urgency in the shouts and the answers of the leather-bucket corps, and the cries as new bodies, or even new living people, were discovered among the ruins, that I would have had to return to the city, even had I no arms to lift with, and only one leg to hop.

I came through the broken gate into that broken courtyard and saw no one and nothing save the bodies of a few horses, swelling in the autumn afternoon's heat. Everything was a-crumble, and all the big stones ran with cracks, but what amazed me was not the devastation, but that so much of the structure was still standing. It had been my personal conviction that the Fortress of Rezhmia had been flattened around me, but more walls stood than were shattered, and most of the buildings were as rectangular as before.

There was, however, a shortage of towers and spires, and amid the fires of the City the streets were flooded by broken pipes.

My ignorance of Rezhmia seemed to put me at no disadvantage, for there was opportunity to stand in a line with fifty other men, women, and children and pass sloshing buckets toward the smoke that billowed from a building so heavy in stone it seemed paradoxical that it could burn at all. Soon, however, our duty was taken over by a tank wagon with four horses that needed only four men to pump, and so I lent the width of my back to hauling stones away from the base of a fallen wall, in case there were people beneath it.

There were three people beneath it, two of them children, and though I have seen many terrible things, starting in a bad infancy, this sight was stronger than I. Stronger than my stomach, and as I stood puking bile and empty air in the privacy of a garden (wholly untouched by the earthquake but muddied by the floods) a voice behind me said, "This trouble is none of your business."

89

The voice was like Arlin's, and for a moment I believed she had limped into the fortress to pull me out again, but when I wiped my face and turned, it was to see a complete stranger: a man dressed in what might have seemed the canvas of a workman, if not worn so arrogantly, with a marvelous face and a marvelous necklace of gold around his neck.

His features were much like Arlin's also, although his coloring was only a shade darker than mine. He was tall and not very broad, and he leaned against the wall as a man usually leans against a garden wall, not as a man would lean on the day of a disaster.

He allowed me to stare for some moments: to stare and to wobble, I imagine, for my stomach had not entirely recovered. He then added, "Not that I question the efficiency you have been showing, but obviously you find the work more distressing than some, and others also have more at stake in uncovering their dead." Now I noticed that he was speaking Velonyie, and with a strong Rayzhia accent.

He shrugged himself off the wall and came toward me. The fading daylight glistened in the intricacies of the ornament around his neck, though there was nothing of special care or expense about the rest of his person. His fair hair was almost untidy, and when he put a hand upon my shoulder—to steady me, perhaps—I could see that his fingers were callused and discolored along the side. His air was both conspiratorial and reserved as he said to me, "You would be of more value to the City if you presented yourself to the sanaur, who has been asking about you, and of more value to yourself, if you simply rode away."

Now instead of sick, I felt only dizzy. I always feel dizzy in the presence of people who know more about me and my circumstances than I do myself. "Did the 'naur send you to find me?" I asked him, in Rayzhia, which seemed his native language.

He withdrew his hand. "No one sends me for anything. I send myself," he replied, again in difficult Velonyie.

I sat down on a stone bench and looked at the soggy ground, for this man was one too many things crowding into my head. Surely arrivals, earthquakes, and farewells were enough for one day. He allowed me quiet.

"Who are you?" I asked when I looked up again.

He had his arms folded in front of him. They were strong arms, but not burly. "Did you say 'what' or 'who'? No, you said 'who.' You are a person of native courtesy."

I bent and rinsed my hands in the wet grass. "I'm not known for being polite. 'Who' delivers more information in one question. Who are you?" Since he seemed to want it, I spoke in Velonyie.

"I am Dowln," he said, with some emphasis. "A snowman like yourself. If the term does not offend you."

I shook my head blankly.

"And I have something for you." He reached into a pocket of his stiff apron and pulled out something that he put in my hand. It was cold and heavy. As I lifted it into the sunlight, he turned abruptly and strode toward the dangling iron gate of the garden.

I saw that the thing was a ring, and precious. I chased after him. "No," I said. "Don't give me something like this. I can't keep it."

He didn't stop. "I made it for you," he said. "What else should I do with it?"

I caught up with him on the other side of the gate. "But listen. I will only sell it, when I have nothing to eat, or when someone else is hungry. Or for a worse reason. Or I'll give it away. Besides. . ." Here I forced him around to face me, though it was clear he didn't appreciate such violence. ". . . you can't really know who I am."

He looked at my face and at the ring, and he said, "Give it away, then. I make such things, and therefore cannot be sentimental about them." He shoved me away from him with such significance I had to let him go.

It was a ring of heavy silver, tarnished to a midnight blue except on the three raised wires that ran its length and took polish from the friction of the hand. Its stone was a sapphire of so dark a blue as to be black, and through it ran a star of six points, that caught the evening light and the red light of the fires and returned it in a cold silver.

Around this stone ran engraving, neither in Rayzhia nor Velonyie, but in the dead language Allec, and it said these words: I FIND MY LIGHT IN DARKNESS.

Altogether it was a work of great craft and beauty, but stern to the eye, and it had not been completed in one afternoon. Wonderingly I slipped it on, and it fit over the third finger of the right hand as no other ring ever fit me. I took it off my finger and put it into my deepest, most secure pocket, and left the Fortress of Rezhmia for the second time.

Never before and not since have I seen a sunset so bloody, for the red dust of the broken stone and of the roads filled the air. Every inch of my skin was caked pink, too, even under my clothes, with sweat creases and mottling that turned my stomach into red marble. It was difficult to breath, and Arlin's cough had returned under the influence of the dirty, smoke-filled air.

Because we had suffered the shock within the old city, and had seen it coming down around us, we had both forgotten the much larger Rezhmia City that lay behind the fortress park. Now it proclaimed itself to us, lit against its many hillsides by many blazes. We were no longer alone on the shaven lawns and by the green waters; weeping surrounded us. We gave away all our food.

91

Halfway through the red night hours, we heard cornets in the City above, and the citizens around us who could do so left their camps and ran to stand by the road. I went with them, more guardedly.

The sight was most dramatic, though I don't think for a minute it had been staged for drama. Four horsemen came riding abreast, holding torches aloft. After them came the cornetists; their faces and those of their nervous wet horses were pulled with worry. After these rode a few ranks of officers, flanked by more torch bearers, with the flickering light reflected in every button and blade. The crowd had begun to murmur.

There was no man there, I thought, who had not lost someone that day, and few of them even knew the tally. I felt extremely lucky, myself, being far from home, and I tried not rejoice over my state. The pedestrians were shouting two syllables, and not all together, which made it difficult to understand. Then my ears picked up the thread: it was "Reingish! Reingish!" that they were shouting. The minsanaur, the heir of the sanaur, was riding in.

The horses were all very grand: tall, fine-boned, and nervous. I could scarcely see the faces high above. I pressed forward, as eager as any proud burgher of the town, for I too had an interest in this man.

Here came a fellow in a grand helmet with plumes, looking slightly old-fashioned in his array. No—he was only a lieutenant by his uniform, and he carried two flags tightly furled and strapped to his saddle. Behind him was another, in scarlet (or so it seemed in the light of torches, moon, and houses burning) who had his saber drawn and held crossed before his body ceremonially, but another moment showed him to be only a captain. Next came a space, and then some anxious middle-aged men in civilian dress, then another space, and then a horse of so cold a color that, like my ring, it could transmute the red light into silver. It was not such a huge horse, and though all beasts around it trotted heavily and dripped at the mouth, this one still argued with the curb in its mouth and pranced diagonally over the road.

It reminded me so much of Sabia, Arlin's mare that was killed, that I almost forgot to glance upward at the rider upon it.

He was in size harmonious with his horse, and that was all I could tell. He wore no buttons and I caught no glint of blade. Then he rode into a band of torchlight and happened by pure chance to look in my direction.

There was my self, my wet and weary identity, encountered once on a mountain pass during an earthquake and then dismissed by all save the Naiish as hallucination. He wore civilian riding garb, very restrained and of very rich substance. His shirt was white, though flickering red in my eyes, and his hacking jacket some darker color. Upon the white of his breast hung a long, thin pendant. Or perhaps a dagger on a cord.

92

As he met my eyes, his face went from taut worry to wonder, perhaps to fear. I don't know what my face did.

"Reingish! Reingish!" shouted the crowd in my ears.

He pointed at me, and uneasily I saw that he wore on his third finger a ring of familiar shape.

I thought perhaps he would order me arrested. It occurred to me that he might order me slain on the spot. Perhaps he only wanted to speak to me. I certainly wanted to speak to him. But as we gaped at each other and his horse danced beneath him, the broken fortress in front of us answered his horn call, and a dozen men ran out to meet the party, crying a dozen messages at once.

His attention was pulled forward, and at the same moment I was pressed back by the shifting of the crowd. I saw the heads of a few horses, and once another plumed helmet, but they were moving on at a good trot and there was no more of Minsanaur Reingish to be seen.

That night, the ground rumbled three times.

The next morning, after a night of much work and little rest, Arlin and I bathed and I exchanged my Rezhmian clothing for the breeches, shirt, and coat of Velonya. It was not a frock coat I put on, for I don't own a frock coat, nor gentlemen's clothing of any variety or nation. Arlin dressed herself in the same blacks she had worn into the town, for having been cleaned at the inn only a day ago (only one day, yet a great age for the City) they were her tidiest.

I didn't like the thought of entering the broken fortress on horseback, for there is something of state and panoply on even the humblest horse. Daffodil certainly was the humblest horse, however, and I did not see how we could leave him behind and still expect to find him when we came back. If we came back. Besides, Arlin could not be expected to walk far with the bruise on her leg.

By the smell, there were parts of the inner city still burning, but by and large it showed us a more businesslike face today. There were teams of men shoring up brick walls with beams: some of the beams having been sacrificed from other structures flattened the day before. There was furniture scattered all over the pavement, some of it very neatly placed, and there were people using it, as though indoors had become outdoors.

I remember a family of two children and a toddler, scarcely more than a baby, who were gathered around a table in the street, while Mother heated their breakfast over a bonfire of wreckage. The youngest, who could barely walk, was waddling in circles around this poor encampment, as though possession by his feet could make the pavement into a home. As he looked up at me on the horse and our glance met, another of the innumerable shocks hit,

93

raising dust all around us. His infant face did not move, but tears began to ooze out of his eyes, like water from the cracks in a thawing rock.

We did not know where we were going; we thought we would ride until we came to something that looked like officialdom, or we found the opposite gate of the City. If it stood. We were in no hurry.

Officialdom is hard to recognize in a state of catastrophe. In catastrophe it partakes of the dignity of an ordinary building. The most impressive building we came upon turned out to be a church, with its domes collapsed and the golden triangle lying dented and propped against the pink stone wall. It was while I was surveying this damage I first heard my own name in my ear. Or almost my name: it was the words my name was made from, pronounced as the original.

Na Zhur'ett: King of the Dead.

It was an old woman in baggy dress and trousers. She had a sack around her neck, perhaps for the carrying of amulets, or small change. She said my name again, loudly.

"Do I know you, Mother?" I asked her, leaning from my horse so she would not have to speak so loudly. But she was not speaking to me, but *of* me. She looked beyond me, and pointed with her finger. She was chanting: "Na zhur'ett, na zhur'ett."

"Someone has spilled the beans," said Arlin, very uneasily. While I still stared, another woman came up, young and comely, and I thought intelligent-looking as well, until she also started uttering my name like some creaking hearth bellows.

"Why are you doing that?" I asked them, as reasonably as I knew how. My horse started to shy away from them. He was a creature of great good sense. In the next moment the two bagpipes were joined by a man who by face and feature had as much Velonyan blood in him as I, and all three were spouting together. We moved forward briskly, but the chant followed as people raised their heads from work that should have been more important than this nonsense.

"I'm beginning to feel jealous. What's wrong with the name Arlin?" my lady asked, although by her face she was more purely uneasy than envious.

Despite the rubble-strewn street and the crowd of pedestrians, we kicked our horses into a good trot. This did nothing to alleviate the problem, as any behavior smacking of arrogance inflamed these people's unaccountable admiration.

"That is how I heard them calling after the minsanaur last night," Arlin said. I answered, "There are many fewer of them, but still. . . This won't make an impression of humble sincerity, will it?"

Now instead of pointing at me, the people were pointing at a door in a wall. Both door and wall had been inlaid with shell and with turquoise.

94

Though half the work had been knocked out, it still made a pretty picture. The road ended before that wall, in a scatter of fallen trees in pots, and having arrived there, it seemed necessary we should get off our horses. Arlin would not take my help.

I stood before that door for a while, trying to collect myself in the belly of the wolf, while Arlin spread her attention slowly through the crowd, saying, "You shut up," and "Quiet, idiot" in meaningful tones. Her hand was on her sword and her words were finally effective.

The door opened. Behind it was that old man with bandaged hands: the Emperor of the City, Nation, and Territories of Rezhmia. He was not alone, on the other side of that door, but he was the one in front. The soldiers, gentles, and nurses that herded behind him had wide, staring eyes, like horses' eyes.

His vision adjusted to the sunlight, and then he spent a good while gazing at me.

He said "Our family has an invincible tendency toward shortness."

I stared back. Though I heard Arlin snigger behind me, it took me a long time to understand what he meant by these words. He himself was small, but I had expected that in a very old man, and not made any connection with my own lack of size. "Then the Sanaur of Rezhmia believes me?"

I spoke very quietly and no louder did he answer, "I believe that you are my kinsman. Come in, you and your friend who killed the murderer of my nephew."

Solicitous hands took our horses. I hated this, because the horse to me was all possibility of escape. Also, I had not until this moment realized how attached I had become to homely Daffodil, whose great barrel had certainly put an elegant new bend into each of my legs. Arlin was even slower to relinquish the reins, and she took some time right in front of the 'naur to point out the small tear in the skin of the black mare's cannon.

I remember that incident with unusual clarity, and perhaps because of that, I also remember the roofed court into which we were brought.

The roof consisted of a network of lathes making an arch, and running over these lathes, tiles of clay that overlapped without touching, making an enclosure of light without sun's heat, and air without wind. I found it marvelous that most of the shingles were still intact, and that the walls here showed no damage at all.

Up until that unsettled autumn, Powl, I had not studied the composition of the earth, except as it might relate to the composition of glass. It took disaster to awaken my curiosity, but since then I have come to see that during an earthquake, it is the substance of the ground as much as the structure of the building that determines whether it shall stand. It might have been the stony

95

anchor beneath that courtyard, which showed itself in humps and points above the level of the ground, that protected it. (Some of these sandstone prominences, carved into tables and chairs for enjoyment, gave the courtyard a sweetly gnomish air.)

I have concluded that structures on stone tend to live, while the same structures on good earth fail. Yet—and this is a large yet—the growl and the terror itself are passed through stone, and in a region of fat earth a quake either will not occur or will not spread far.

The 'Naur Mynauzet must have noticed my preoccupation with his outdoor furnishings. He stopped his progress toward the inner door and waved me to one of the sandstone seats. The herd came to a disorganized stop.

The chair had been polished and lacquered, presumably so not to leave pink stains on good clothing. I stood beside it, for I was not about to sit down in front of the emperor of all Rezhmia. I noticed that Arlin did not even approach the table, but stood at dark attention against a wall. She had been relieved of all her blades. For her, that must have been worse than having the horse taken.

"You will sit," said the emperor, in a voice that had no expectation of being disobeyed, and I did obey him. The seat was cold. He lowered himself down at the little table across from me, having to elbow back two nurses and a general who thought he ought to have help in the matter. He looked once over his shoulder, this father of a large family, and everybody scuttled to the far end of the court and stood as Arlin was standing.

"Nazhuret, nephew of my nephew Nazhuret, you will tell me how you happened to be here," he said, and I began by saying that I had come on a personal errand of the King of Velonya, for his ear only.

"No, you misunderstand me, young man." His eyes were sharp and of a greenish-blue color. He did not appear to need glasses. "Tell me how *you* happen to be here, or happen to be."

I was prepared for this, but that preparation did not make it less difficult. My own history is a story that was presented to me long after it could do anything to me but cause pain. As concisely as I knew how (I am not by nature succinct), I told him how my father, in the shadow of his arrest for treason, had given me to his brother to hide, and how Dickon had hidden me in the open: at the Sordaling military school. How the two people who knew my past (and that did not include me) died without revealing it. How I grew somewhat and learned some things and was at last discovered in the strangest manner by Powl Inpres, Earl of Daraln, who recognized me and who took me in hand.

As I related these facts, they sounded like someone else's story. They sounded like a lie.

I then told him how his niece and nephew had been poisoned by Duke Leoue, who then was granted my own father's patent. I expected this information would make the emperor very angry, but I had forgotten how many of those close to the throne of Rezhmia die of odd accidents or bad stomachs. What he said was "I'm sorry, boy. On behalf of our whole family I apologize." I was astonished to incoherence.

"Had I any idea of your existence, let alone the neglect and abuse you suffered, grandchild"—and here I had to remind myself that among the Rezhmian people all close relatives of two generations younger are called "grandchild"—"I would have entered the country in force to make them return you. I would have had you returned though it meant war again."

My tongue outran my tact. "Then, Sanaur of Rezhmia, I'm very glad you did not know of my existence. To have caused war between my mother's people and my father's. . ."

The emperor smiled, and seeing that smile I remembered that he was an emperor. I imagine that he never forgot it. "Yet, Nazhuret, we were in a very good condition to promote a war against Velonya at that time. Or at this one, for that matter."

So quickly had we arrived at the meat of my visit. "Yes, 'Naur, but why— now, I mean? Do you think you can conquer the North completely? No, you know you can't. I know the King of Velonya, and I have a strong confidence that this war you have prepared can only end in great losses for unimportant gains. Only a strong provocation should cause a nation to declare war in such circumstances, and I cannot see that there was any. . ."

". . . reason to begin a political argument so early in our acquaintance," the emperor finished for me. Smiling like an emperor, and like a grandfather.

I am not used to grandfathers. I let him silence me.

"I have a thousand things to do," he said. "And at least that many people to grieve for, now. But I will see you again, soon, and you can represent the other side of your family for me then."

The old man rose, and I rose with him. It occurred to me, only for a moment, that among the various forms of politeness I had learned there was none that would cover an emperor whom one could not acknowledge who was also a grandfather who could not be depended upon to acknowledge one's self. Only for a moment did this complexity concern me. I watched the man depart and I did nothing at all but look at him.

After him went the mass of followers, leaving only Arlin and myself, with a few maids trying to gawk inconspicuously from the far side of the courtyard.

And one other, whom I believe was not there until the last few moments. Standing in the center of the room, still dressed in his canvas work clothes

97

and glorious necklace, was the man who had given me the ring. As my mind recognized him, my hand was in my pocket. He stepped forward quietly amid the tinkle of the fountains, only to find Arlin at his side, not exactly blocking his way but making herself known. His eyes showed honest surprise as he looked at her. They were much of a height—about three inches taller than I, and their faces were alike as well. Two Velonyans of old blood: one golden and one black. The black one stood like a fighter, and the golden one like one who works leaning against a bench, but they were built much alike despite that. Perhaps the fair one had a shade more shoulder.

"So," he said, speaking past Arlin and to me, "that is why you asked 'who' and not 'what.'"

I tried to let my face answer nothing, which is difficult for me. Arlin, meanwhile, knew nothing about this man, for the events of the night had driven him out of my mind and I hadn't told her. Even of the ring, she was ignorant, but she is very good at letting her own face exhibit knowledge she does not possess. She met his gaze with a look of calm competence and secrets unrevealed.

He, in his turn, was staring like a man in front of a monkey, or a monkey at a man. He walked all around her, scratching his chin with his callused hand. At last he stood before her again and spoke very quietly to her, in Velonyie. "You're not a eunuch at all," he said, and if I had not been able to guess at his words, I would not have heard.

Arlin has a marvelous possession of herself. Without withdrawing from him one inch, she replied, "I did not say I was. Are you?"

He nodded to her but looked at me, and then at the cluster of maids, who now were pretending to clear out rubbish from the fountains. He crooked one finger, for in Rezhmia that gesture is not considered uncouth. "Please come with me," he said and, turning on his heel, he went into the building.

We had the choice of following him, or staying alone in the courtyard. Perhaps this fellow Dowln was sent by the 'naur to take care of our needs. Or perhaps not. He had a flavor of conspiracies about him, but I guess so did we, and Dowln also had a flavor of the solitary that argued against his being any-one's cat's paw.

He had recognized the unspoken lie of Arlin, and that was dangerous to us, but he also seemed content to let it lie unspoken (Forgive me the pun, Powl. I would rewrite, but it is the end of a long page). I remembered the gray wolf that Arlin saw and kept silent about, and the red trey that I saw and did not mention, on a snowy night many years before, and it occurred to me that the man who holds my secret also holds me. One can be held in pleasant ways and in unpleasant ways, and if I followed Dowln, I would find out. Arlin had already decided and was walking after the man. I followed.

98

After all, he had given me a nice present.

I do not remember the ways to his residence at all. If I had seen great damage, I probably would have. I do remember it was for a considerable distance
that we followed Dowln, and through more than one kitchen. People greeted
him with familiar respect, and they stared at us, though once or twice I heard
my name pronounced (not in greeting) behind my back.

There was a guard before the door of his quarters, which made it feel like
a prison, but the face of the man warmed so at the sight of the eunuch that
the atmosphere changed. Upon the door was the pattern of interlocked knots,
in gold inlay, that echoed the gold around his neck.

As we passed through the door, Dowln asked the guard if his wife's arm
had been set, and the guard answered that it had, and thanked the lord for the
bottle of pills.

Within were quarters spacious and spare and comfortable, according to
my simple standards. The place was clean, had plenty of light, frescoes on the
walls, and it was full of machines.

Arlin is clever with machinery, but I am passionate about it. I never even
approached the offered chairs, but attached myself to the first device I saw.
"What does this cut?" I asked him, fitting a small steel rod into one of the
holes drilled through the center pole of the thing. The saw blade came down
from above.

"It's an old-fashioned stone faceter, with preset angles. I can show you
more sophisticated sorts, if that appeals to you." He had brought out a bottle
of something—I cannot recall whether wine, water, or apple juice—and
stemmed goblets, which were spread in his clever fingers as I remember cards
spread in Arlin's clever fingers.

"It is not too different from a glass miter saw," I answered him. "If there are
improvements upon the idea, I would be very happy to see them."

Arlin had chosen a chair, and leaned her elbow on the table and her chin
on her hand. "Nazhuret is an avid optician," she said to the man. He gave her
a disbelieving glance and she added, "I am an optician also. We are all opti-
cians, where we come from." With her dry, ironical enunciation, she made the
truth unbelievable.

I could see that her words had confused him, and like Arlin, Dowln
had no intention his confusion should be seen in his face. He opened his
mouth to speak, but the earth spoke instead, and Arlin and he spent the
next few seconds keeping the glasses on the table. I held on to the
sturdy gem-cutter.

He spoke again, to Arlin. "We have not been introduced, and I have not
exactly—seen you before. My name is Dowln, jeweler to and personal slave

99

of the sanaur. Who or what I was before being captured at five years of age is
not really relevant anymore." He poured for her.

"My name is almost always Arlin," she said. "Who or what I was before I
escaped captivity at thirteen years is really not relevant anymore either."

Dowln slid into a chair beside her. "You were a slave? In Velonya is that
possible?" All this time the earth was shuddering beneath us, but everything
that might be knocked off shelves had been put away by now. I felt under my
hand the steel upright, singing in tune with the earth.

"I was a baron's daughter," Arlin answered Dowln, from inside her cup.
(She has no more manners than I.) "The distinction is a small one."

She put the cup down. "Why did the guard call you 'lord,' then? If you're
a slave. . ."

"Because I am his employer, and he is polite. And because I am a rich and
powerful slave."

She nodded, as he had nodded at her description of the daughter of a
baron being a captive.

I thought the brave performance of these two, ignoring the tremor in favor
of their own dignity, deserved some recognition. I clapped for them and then
sat down very carefully at the table. I do not know whether he knew why I
had applauded, but Arlin knew.

Dowln filled a glass for me. I think it *was* wine, but cannot recall the taste
of it. "Tell me, Nazhuret. Do you believe in dreams?"

There was always an instant of open-mouthed silence before this
Rezhmian/Velonyan eunuch jeweler spoke or replied to questions, just as
there was always before Arlin spoke. I must wonder now whether it was the
fact that both lived anomalously, and in much solitude, or whether it was
merely that he was not good in the Velonyie he insisted upon using. The
effect was to give an atmosphere of the portentous to the whole conversation.

I am an enemy of the portentous.

"Dreams? How could I not believe in dreams? I have ludicrous dreams,
almost every night."

"I mean dreams with messages. Dreams foretelling the future."

Now it was my turn to pause, though without intending dramatic effect.
"I have had dreams that seemed to. . . to rehearse the future, if not foretell it.
But I can't be sure there was real meaning in them, or put a science to that per-
ception at all."

He leaned back in his chair and laughed, and his voice, always high in
pitch for a man, rode up into the registers of a little boy. "Put a science to the
perception! Oh my friend, you are not what I expected at all. . ."

Here he became serious again. "Although I dreamed you once a week for
this whole year."

All notion of science flew out of my head. "What did you dream?" I asked him. "How do you know it was me you dreamed about, if I am not what you expected?"

He cleared his throat before answering. "It was never the same. One day it was an invading army that would steal me back to the North. One day it came to kill me. Once it was nothing but a voice, and a star in the dark, but always there was you in the thing somewhere, and always I woke in a sweat.

"By you, I mean your face, your coloring, your size, your voice. . . And your name. At first I thought I was dreaming Reingish, and had given him Velonyan hair for some dream-reason, but the voice is very different. And the feel of you in the mind."

The jeweler was playing with his goblet, running the foot of it in circles over the table, staining the already stained wood. "Sometimes in the dream you kidnapped me, and sometimes you killed me, or ordered me dead. Sometimes you had a woman at your left shoulder and sometimes black death."

Arlin let out a long sigh, and I could not read her feelings at all. She asked, "What about you, Dowln of the Sanaur of Rezhmia? Did you ever kill anyone, in any of those dreams?"

He did not look up. "No, I didn't. My skill is not in combat; my skill is in dreaming, and in his pocket, there."

Arlin was startled when I drew out the ring, as though there were some prearrangement between this strange fellow and myself. As I gave her the ring I said, "I forgot. I met this gentleman last night as I was hauling stones, and he gave me this. So many things happened after I forgot to show. . ."

Arlin had taken the ring, raised it to the light, stared into it and perhaps read it, and now she sat looking at nothing at all with perfect attention.

Dowln did not understand. "What are you looking at?" He touched her hand and then looked at me. "Is she subject to trances?"

"Do us the favor to use the male pronouns for Arlin, I beg you. And it is not a trance, actually. We call it 'the belly of the wolf,' though it would take a long time to explain why."

"I'm still here," said Arlin, and quietly she put the ring on the table. "You saw the essence of Nazhuret, if you made this."

His gaze rested on the ring as though it had no meaning or attraction for him at all. Perhaps, as it was his creation, that was true. "I was a true dreamer from childhood. That was why they gelded me. The belief is that a child who has this skill will lose it at puberty, so the sanaur cut me for the good of the realm." He raised his eyes for a moment: very fine eyes, only less expressive than Arlin's through being less dark. "What does your science say to that, Aminsanaur Nazhuret?"

"Don't call me that!" I spoke more sharply than was polite, but he laughed his little-boy laugh again. I was about to explain—if it can be explained—our peculiar status of having no status at all, but Arlin cut in with a more pertinent question.

"Did you speak of these dreams to the 'naur?"

His blue eyes shifted uneasily. "Of course I did. It is my purpose in life. Besides this. . ." He poked the black ring and I took it back off the table, putting it on my finger.

"And could the raising of forces in Rezhmia be based on your dream invasion? It would be very ironic if that were so."

"The sanaur does not tell me why things are done," answered the jeweler, seeming even more uneasy. "Why would it be ironic?"

I answered this time. "Because it's the Rezhmian militarization that caused us to be sent here. Do you see?"

He saw, and he rubbed his eyes with both hands against the sight.

No one else came for us, and so I supposed the jeweler was acting on the 'naur's behalf in affording us hospitality. Once during that afternoon Arlin expressed concern about our horses, and with the tinkle of a small bell, our host summoned a servant—Rezhmian in appearance—to find out where the beasts were stalled and make sure of their comfort. By this, as well as the presence of the guard, I was convinced that he was right in calling himself a rich and powerful slave.

Such a concept is foreign to a Velonyan, but then so is slavery. People are expensive to keep during our six months of snow, when there is more eating done than work. In Rezhmia the general emancipation that occurred twenty-four years ago freed all but the slaves of royalty, and most of those were manumitted or grew old and died before the time of our arrival. Dowln, with his double gifts, was a rare thing in the palace: a one-of-a-kind bird kept in a lavish cage, destined never to find a mate.

Of course, destined never to find a mate.

I asked him why he had advised me to leave, when we met in the evening under the shadow of the broken wall. He answered, after some thought, that he had thought it better if I left—better for me, better for him, and better for his elderly protector. (That is what he called the Sanaur of Rezhmia: "my elderly protector.")

He fed us fruit and cheeses on a worktable marred with burns and with splashes of gold and silver solder. When requested, he displayed more of his work: an eagle in silver with amethyst; a rose of five petals, in gold; two rapier hilts, one of which I recall as of onyx and knotted gold wire and the other of purple shell inlay, pommeled with a fragment of human bone.

I have never seen the equal of his skill, whether at home or upon travels, and his gift of art (a thing apart from skill, but dependent upon it) was consistent and perfect and very stern. Yet I had the sense that this man was not born to be living the life he was living.

The choicest machine in Dowln's factory was a large furnace that fed a very small refinery. I was allowed to unfasten the intake door of the great iron thing and examine the load of anthracite coal that fed it: stuff nearly gem-quality jet in its hardness. "I prefer to use ground oil, when I can get it," he said to us. "Then I change this orifice, here, which is threaded between the furnace and the smelter. But the army has requisitioned all stocks of oil, and good coal will do. It uses a lot of air, though. You should feel the draft through the hall, when I'm running coal."

When describing technical matters, Dowln dropped back into Rezhmian, and his conversation then seemed to gain spontaneity. Perhaps it was not the linguistic switch, but the subject, that caused his animation.

"Here. Look," he said, unbolting the top of the smelting chamber. I looked in to see the nozzle of the furnace, a thing like a hopper with a screen bottom, a steel rod running from one wall, and nothing else. The interior was not as large as my head, and colored the sad gray of metal that has been heated too hot, too often. "What do you think I do in this?" he asked me.

I remembered my second night with my teacher. "You're not the first person to set me a puzzle of this nature. I'm known for giving original answers. Original, not correct. Please tell me what it does."

Dowln took out a set of keys, opened a cabinet and presented me with a thin sheet of red glass.

I thought it was red glass, although I know no way to make glass take on so rich a coloring. The moment I hefted it, though, I knew my mistake. I am very used to the weight of glass, and this was heavier. I held it up to the window light, and I knew that this chip, six inches square, was a single ruby.

His face lit slyly, seeing my amazement. "It's my own process. I drop in a dust of carborundum, and keep the fire hot. What do you think?"

I gave it back to him, and told him I thought he was a great inventor. "And you ought to be the richest man in the world," I added. "To make gems!"

My outburst dampened his mood entirely. He looked down at the glaze of red in his hand, spun it on end in one palm, and then in sudden anger he sailed it onto the table, where it hit the wine jug with a sound of bells. Nothing broke.

"Why would I want to be the richest man in the world, Nazhuret? How would that improve my life?"

It seemed to me odd that a self-proclaimed beggar like myself would be arguing on the other side, but I wanted to know more. "The riches would be useless because you are a slave? Or because you are a eunuch?"

"Because I am human," he answered, and this verbal victory restored his humor.

"First I made sheets like that one: very nice for buttons. Next I discovered that if I shot the dust of carborundum at a fine post sticking out of the wall, I would get a shape more useful." Dowln displayed a set of earrings made of teardrop rubies. So true a red were they that one felt stronger looking at them, as though with an infusion of extra blood in one's veins, and when they were held up against the light they each created a dancing red dot on the tabletop, surrounded by a halo of brilliance.

"And these were a step forward," he said. I passed the earrings to Arlin, and the red dots danced over her pale skin and black hair. The effect was magnificent. "But only for cabochons and drops like these. There is something inexact in the crystal structure of my rubies. They will not facet well."

Arlin put the stones back into his hands and leaned over the smelter. "Had you asked me to guess its purpose, I would have said it was some sort of new stonecutter, gear-driven. But then of course the wire or rod in the middle would have to spin."

I was gazing at the rod idly, while wondering if I had just felt a quake at the edge of my perception. The machine did look like a saw, once one granted the necessity for such a large furnace to drive it. And I knew that jade is often cut using nothing but a wire, lubricated with water to keep it from burning.

The smelter, of course was always burning. "Dowln," I heard myself saying, ". . . if you did spin the rod, the crystal structure that accumulates would be different."

The jeweler stared at me. So did Arlin. Well they might, for my voice sounded odd. I had had what might be called a vision—not a divine vision or a philosophical vision but a mechanical one, and I was in a sweat because I would probably never know whether my idea was as perfect as it seemed to me.

Arlin grinned indulgently at my excitement, being the sort of person who is clever with things without being enthusiastic about them. Dowln went into a sort of trance, staring down through the hopper of his little smelter, biting a callus on one hand.

"It would be very interesting. The problem would be the gasketing, of course, but I could make one of high-temperature steel. I. . . want very much to try that," he murmured.

Over his words I heard steps in the corridor, and the crack of the guard's heels snapping together. A second later, those same heels fled lightly down the corridor, taking his two strong arms and his cavalry saber away from us.

Once again my senses reeled, not through movement of the earth, but through a cracking in my own identity, for I stood confronting myself, dressed in perfect, foreign tailoring and with hair dyed dark, but still myself. It was the Minsanaur of Rezhmia: the crown prince.

His face, looking at me, was taut with loathing, and with fear. I noted with a low satisfaction that the fear predominated. And I noted that the shock of our encounter was as bad for him—perhaps worse. After all, I may have had no idea I looked like him, but he had had no idea I existed.

"And this is what claims me as a cousin?" he asked the air, while looking straight at me. "This?"

I could not endure this ridiculous manner, and I asked, "To whom are you talking, Minsanaur of Rezhmia? The emperor's servant? My companion? The men behind you? If you are talking to me, you may use the second person directly. The familiar will do; I am no great personage." My answer was perilous, but I hate conversations that are both hostile and oblique. (One of these at a time is enough.)

"And you're insolent, too?" He put up a hand, like my own hand but better kept, as though to slap me backhanded. On one finger was a ring that glittered amazingly, though the late afternoon air was losing its light. I hoped he would not feel it necessary to finish the gesture. I could not predict what Arlin might do.

As earnestly as I could, I said to him, "No, great lord, I am not insolent; I only like to understand the conversation. And as for being your cousin, I don't ask you to acknowledge the relationship. I have no need of such, and I can appreciate that you cannot like it."

The raised hand sank slowly, reluctantly. For a few seconds he regarded us quietly, and for the first time I saw not mere temperament, but a quick, passionate mind behind all the Rezhmian pride. I wondered, inconsequentially enough, whether it had been difficult for him to grow up a crown prince and so short. Would that be worse than being a short nobody?

Of course Reingish had not been crown prince until a few years previous. There had been his father. I did not immediately remember how the 'naur's closest nephew had died.

I knew his other nephew, my mother's brother, had died of ground glass in his food, but that was Velonyan poisoning, ironically. We are not usually known as poisoners.

Reingish looked over his shoulder at a stocky man in civilian shirt and trousers. "Zhern, what do you think? Is it as I said?"

105

Zhern answered, "I have never seen so great a likeness between strangers, Minsanaur. Except for the hair, of course. And I don't think any of it is paint or padding. I cannot think where they got him."

I don't know whether they had forgotten I had ears, or merely that I was there. My first impulse was to answer that if I were going to change the appearance of my face and person, I would have chosen a more imposing model. That, however, would not be politic; the min'naur might consider himself a handsome fellow, and I had seen no sign of a sense of humor yet.

I also felt I was intruding onto a private conversation.

"I don't know who you think 'they' are, Prince. Arlin and I make our home in Norwess. I did not intentionally look like you. If I had had that in mind, surely I would have dyed my hair."

He smiled at that: a tight smile, but it improved his appearance. Was it my smile I saw?

Behind Reingish stood five men, three of them armed and one in a very decorative costume of red and gold. They shifted from foot to foot and their eyes never moved from their attention to their master. Intent as dogs. Uneasy dogs.

"Not proved, foreigner. Coming coiffed as a snowman has its own subtlety. But if you did not come to parade your illegitimate features, why did you make the trip at all?"

This conversation took place in the middle of the floor of Dowln's quarters. It surprised me that the jeweler had not offered the next emperor a chair, at least, even if the refreshment he had provided for us was all the food he had ready. The min'naur would reject the offer, in the mood he was in, but I had at least expected Dowln to try. While I puzzled over this, I answered, "We came as messengers, Prince. From Rudof of Velonya."

Reingish's eyes sparked and angry blood rushed to his face. It was obvious that he did not appreciate the king's many qualities. "Rudof's tame Rezhmian, is it? And they say the Velonyans don't keep slaves."

Myself, as a slave? As I heard this my mind filled with the history of every time I have been rude to, abrupt with, or simply contradicted my king. I put my hand to my mouth to stifle the giggles, and heard Arlin, whose thoughts ran like mine, clear her throat behind me. Before I could answer sensibly, the min'naur continued. "So then. What is it: this message you bring alone from the north woods to our city? Has Vestinglon decided to sue for peace before the war has even begun?"

Until this moment I had tried not to believe in the reality of the coming war, though it had spread itself under my nose from South Territory to here. Now it took me a moment to catch my breath, like a man splashed with freezing water. "The message," I said, trying not to be thought insolent, ". . . is for the Sanaur of Rezhmia."

For a moment I thought the man would leap at me, but instead he spoke very quietly. "And what am I, then?"

Arlin changed the tensions in her body. I knew she smelled violence. So did I. "You are the Crown Prince of Rezhmia, great lord," I said.

"But my grandfather is old, and leaves military matters to me." Reingish spoke more politely, more collectedly than I had expected. I nodded with artificial complacency.

"That is, of course, the wisest thing he could do," I said. I do not lie well. I don't mean my moral objections prevent me from telling falsehoods, like this one. I mean only that I am not competent at it. In this case, it didn't matter. I didn't expect to be believed. "And I am certain he will relay to you everything we have to say. He will probably even ask that I repeat my message in front of you. We will know as soon as the emperor has gotten the earthquake relief well begun."

I looked into a face of rage: white rage, hot rage, and the crown prince said nothing. His hand was around a pendant that had been hidden beneath his shirt and collar. I could not see it, but I knew it was his little dagger.

"I see by your glance at my decoration that you know me by my nickname. All the world does: Reingish of the red blade." He said this almost casually, and I did not reply. After some moments of staring daggers at me, his eyes began to wander over my shabby person. This examination got as far as my hand, and then the prince's face paled once more.

"Give me the ring. Let me see it."

I heard Dowln stir behind me, and Arlin shifted silently. I felt a great reluctance to part with the gift, even to the Minsanaur of Rezhmia, and even for a minute. But I do not value any item of adornment more than I do my life, and besides, I did not want to give way to attachments to objects. I tried to take the thing off, without success.

It might as well have been welded to my finger. I apologized to Reingish. "I don't understand, Min'naur. It went on easily enough." I couldn't even get the ring to twist around.

The prince grabbed my hand and held it to the light, saying, "It would come off with the finger easily enough, impostor."

Dowln was at my side, looking white and proud as the prince himself. "This man is the guest of your grandfather, Minsanaur," he said, and the three armed escorts of the prince made angry faces, and a noticeable clattering of steel.

Reingish gave no sign of having heard. He held my hand in a grip that ground the long bones together, but I don't think he did this out of malice.

107

"This!" He raised for inspection the ring and my hand together as though they were one thing. "It's an inauspicious stone and an ominous message. 'I FIND MY LIGHT IN DARKNESS.' Are you so proud of your wickedness?"

I looked at the stone, with its star of silver, bodiless, immaterial, and pure as mathematics. I felt a stab of pain, that it could be so misunderstood. "Darkness is not wicked, Min'naur. It is not even dark, really."

He dropped my hand and held his own in front of my face, with its blaze of brightness amid gold. "Look at this, foreigner, and know your own signet is only a parody, as you are a parody of me."

The ring was of the same pattern, though it was of gold and hence beyond tarnish. In the center of it was set the largest and most colorful diamond I have ever seen. It was like the egg of a small bird in size, and in shape. Around this splendor were carved the words, again in Allec: I AM THE SOURCE OF LIGHT.

I murmured my appreciation of the ring, heartfelt, but added, "I think the min'naur does the other ring a disservice. The meanings of the inscriptions are not very different."

Reingish was not listening. He, too, was lost in the play of light in the diamond. "The setting was made by my grandfather's dreaming dog, here. That was my mistake, I see. The stone is anciently in my family. It is one of our treasures, and this coarse snowman desired to destroy it: to cut it in two."

Dowln's face did remain guarded, but I could see the muscles in his neck tighten at being called "snowman." I remembered that this man chose to talk Velonyie with us, even though he did it badly. He said, "It has a bad flaw in the center, Minsanaur. When it was part of the orb, that didn't matter, but worn as a ring, it may strike something at the proper angle and fracture."

Reingish snorted and he stroked the ring affectionately with his left hand. "Diamonds are the hardest material upon the earth. I know that much. Here. . ." He held out the gem before me again. "Do you see a flaw? Any flaw?"

I looked into the stone and then peered across the table of its cutting, paying attention to the planes of refraction. I wished I had the loupe I carry in my backpack. "I do, Min'naur. It runs diagonally across the width of the gem. I would guess that this diamond formed originally as two adjacent crystals, which grew into one another."

He snatched the hand back. "So what do you know about precious stones, you beggar?"

After a glance at Reingish's face, I apologized again. "I am sorry to disappoint you, Min'naur. Although I am no jeweler, I am an optician, and I know how light is bent in different materials."

"This ring will outlive you," he answered me. Raising his glance he added, "And outlive the last slave, too."

108

So Dowln was the last of Rezhmia's bondservants. The last.

The last of everything becomes precious.

"It will if you don't strike it against anything," I told the min'naur, and he chose to take my advice as more hostile wordplay.

"Against your yellow head, you mean, snowman?" (He could insult my appearance no other way.) "Tell me when was the last time the might of the Rayzhia was broken against Vestinglon? It has been hundreds of years."

It had been only one hundred and ten years, as I learned in school, since Velonya reclaimed (or stole) most of South Territory from the min'naur's family. At that time the South was led by Parliz the Astronomer, who led his defense according to the triangulations of the stars. I was also an astronomer, but I had not been taught to put moral or precognitive meanings to the positions of the heavenly bodies. I did not know upon what military strategies the Rezhmians were leaning, for this war they were building, but I doubted they were those of Parliz.

Despite all of my stoic education and the training of my own picaresque life, this situation made me afraid.

Reingish made me afraid. I stole a moment in the belly of the wolf before I answered him.

"In Rezhmia," I said at last, "I see sweet pale grapes and fine green wines. And wheat. And peasants with round faces who sing while they work. War against the North will end this for at least a generation. Even if you win territories, and I do not think you can."

My calmness did not prove contagious. "So, northman who calls himself my cousin! You come here to counsel appeasement! So that our peasants' bellies might stay round and our wines good!"

I had not said "bellies," of course, but "faces." Nonetheless I did not correct the crown prince upon this. "It would be appeasement, great lord, if you were under assault. But Velonya has made no move against you, so peace is only common sense."

There was a great stir among the min'naur's five attendants, who glanced at each other and murmured half-sentences. I could see that my words impressed them as shocking lies, or shocking idiocy. It seemed that these men knew of such provocation.

In that moment the bottom was taken out from under me. Amid hardship and blood and wreckage, my firm ground had been the fact that Velonya had not provoked Rezhmia in any fashion, overt or covert. I expected talk of national birthrights, of hungry populations, or of the long, long dispossessed. What I did not expect was the natural courage of men who believe themselves attacked, as these five courtiers seemed to believe. That courage cannot be bent or outargued.

109

What I did not expect was for Min'naur Reingish to say: "I have seen the bodies of my people, gathering flies on the road. I have seen the villages burning!"

I have no magic way to tell if a man is lying. One might think I was at an advantage, face to face with my own face as I was. But I looked carefully at Reingish, and in my mind I tested his words, and I saw no reason to believe he lied. I was mystified, and so I told the crown prince. Then I asked: "How many villages have you seen destroyed, Min'naur? Were they north, at the edge of the plains, or along the road here? And did you have any evidence that it was Velonyan troops that did it?"

I hoped he would tell me. I wanted desperately some simple information, after coming so far on rumor. But my inquiry (perhaps not very respectfully put to the heir of an empire who already thought me a threat) produced only anger.

Oddly enough it was directed not at me but at Dowln. He pointed his finger at the blond slave's face, and I remember that even at the time I marked his gesture as one I should avoid making, for it only emphasized the difference in height between prince and slave. "You can disappear, you conniving lapdog!" shouted the prince.

Dowln kept marvelously calm as he answered, "You have already told me, Minsanaur, that on the day my patron dies, there will be no more slaves in the City. I never misunderstood you. But as for now, the sanaur is well and remains my protection."

The finger retreated, but there was a change in the focus of the prince's eye, from hot rage to cold. "Only if my grandfather knows, fool. If you all disappear, he can only presume, and quite rightly, that your treacheries swept you away together."

There were only four blades in the min'naur's party, one of the attendants being some sort of priest, but that was four more blades than we had. Unless I could reach the one upon which Dowln had been working, that with the wound-wire hilt. It had not yet been edged, but it would serve to turn a blow.

Possibly Arlin and I could take on four blades without weapons of our own, presuming Dowln didn't get too much in the way. But we were in the middle of a hive of enemies, and in a capital city of enemies; however could we find our way free?

While I thought these things, a speckle of small clouds passed over the sun, and the large workroom gave the netted impression of light under water, or of the light that took me and let me go again on the day I met you. I had a strange moment; a dislocation of mind; I cannot say more. Perhaps it was what people call a presentiment. It may be I was only feeling fear.

Dowln tried to step between Arlin and myself, to face the crown prince more closely, but we did not permit, so he was forced to call over my head, "Look into the hallway, some one of you. You will see the guard is missing."

Reingish snorted. "That mercenary. Of course he ran. He fears me."

"He fears you but he serves me," said Dowln, as though he were discussing the properties of gold as versus silver. "He is in the sanaur's apartments now, where his wife is chambermaid. He left with my prepared orders and with my token."

Out of the corner of my eyes I saw the face of the slave behind me. He was collected, yes, but he was white, and there was a film of sweat over his forehead. "We may be murdered, Minsanaur, but we cannot disappear," he said.

Min'naur Reingish thought. I could see his eyes flicker as though he were reading words in the air. The three other armed men shifted in place, but their hands did not leave their courtly rapiers. At last he said, "To kill you is not murder under law, slave, any more than killing a yapping dog. To kill these. . ."—and that finger pointed again, this time more effectively at me—". . . would be. . ."

Much more difficult, I said to myself, but only to myself.

". . . would be only a public duty. But I will spare my poor grandfather any further disturbance on this terrible day." He rubbed his sleeve over his face, and by the dark smears on the silk I knew that Reingish, too, had been sweating. The three hands on three rapiers relaxed, and Reingish turned to go, but then turned back.

"But I warn you, treacherous tool, I will make no peace with darkness!"

This time I did answer, as inoffensively as I could, "Why not, Minsanaur of Rezhmia? Every day does."

Reingish looked startled, but he was stalking out and did not ruin the dignity of it. When he was gone, and his attendants with him, Arlin turned to me and spoke her first word since the incident began. "That was a good line, Zhurrie! Was it spontaneous?"

I must have glared at her. "Of course it was." My attention was caught by something she pulled from beneath her jacket: a throwing dagger, small and sparkling.

"You didn't think I'd permit them to take everything, do you? This would have evened the odds considerably."

Dowln came closer to examine the dagger with his professional eye. "You would have killed him, then? The minsanaur himself? Well, why not? You, at least, are entirely Velonyan."

Before he could say more I interjected, "I think you misunderstand me, sir, if you think Arlin's loyalties are different from my own."

I stopped because out of the corner of my eye I saw a figure standing by the wall not far from the doorway. It was garbed—or "tented" might be the more appropriate word—in crimson robing with a dull gold undergarment. Its

111

head was surmounted by a hat that resembled the roof of the oratory in Norwess. Its face was smiling shyly and the hem of its garments were dusty. I recognized this figure as one of the attendants of the crown prince: the one without a sword. The priest.

I was mystified. "How did you get back in here?" I asked the man. "I didn't hear nor see you return."

"I didn't leave," he answered, and his voice was deep and lush. A player's voice. I was startled by the voice and then reflected that a priest's place is ritual, and ritual and theater are much alike. "I'm sorry if I was not welcome."

"You were not there a moment ago," stated Arlin, and the priest only widened his eyes, which in Rezhmia means the same as a shoulder shrug but is considered more polite.

Dowln gave a great sigh, as though the events of the last hour had finally caught up to him. He scraped a chair over the flags and sat reversed upon it, resting his chin on the high back. "Ngaul Eyluzh; since when have you been made a member of Reingish's inner circle?"

The man in red did not follow his host's example. He remained standing against the wall. "Since never, Lord Dowln. They merely overstrode me in the hall and I was swept up among them. I am, you know, not a sprightly walker."

Dowln rubbed the back of one hand over his jaw, and as I watched him, I felt there was something strange about the gesture. It was the lack of that small but unmistakable sound of abrasion that results from contact with most men's shaven faces. "I see. A common coincidence."

Eyluzh the priest shook his head chidingly. "Nothing is coincidence today, artifactor, and nothing is common. Almost one person in ten in the City is dead or badly injured. The floor of H'Appid Niaus is become a hospital."

Niaus's shrine is, I think, one of the architectural wonders of Rezhmia. Amid this city of pink stone it is the largest wooden building, if a structure woven of willow wands may be considered wooden. It stands four stories high, and each of the stripped withies that make it up has been dyed, either white with lime, madder-red, golden, or of a blue made from ground lapis. Supposedly the City was built around H'Appid Niaus, which is immensely old, as is the priesthood that serves it. When one willow wand fails, another of equal dimension is stripped and dyed and fitted in its place, so that while the entirety is ancient, none of the substance is.

Much like the human body, I reflected, that adds and subtracts, adds and subtracts, while keeping to the general pattern.

H'Appid Niaus breathed constantly, groaning, from wind and heat and cold, and the changing of the angle of the sun. Or so I had heard. And it seemed that its strength of many weak pieces had survived the devastation that flattened huge stones.

So did most of the weak human bodies in the City—survive, that is. The use of the shrine to care for them seemed fitting.

The priest in the gaudy robe withdrew his hands from the ends of his sleeves and he billowed a bit. I gather the pockets of the garment were reached from within. "Here we go," he said, and then blew his lips out in contradiction. "No. Those are my beads. Here."

His white hand, dwarfed by the mass of the fabric, held two objects: a slip of paper and a rod of turquoise, delicate as a graphite pencil. I was aware that Arlin's attention sharpened at the sight of the Sanaur Mynauzet's personal token. He delivered these things not into Dowln's hand, but into mine.

The note was short and the letters careful and tiny. IF MY KINSMAN HAS A TASTE FOR THEOLOGICAL DISCOURSE, KNOW THAT EYLUZH WILL OVERFILL HIS NEED. THERE IS NO OBLIGATION, BUT THE SHRINE SERVES GOOD FOOD. (signed) GRANDFATHER MYNAUZET

The others must have thought the message dire, the way I stared at it, and the rapidity with which I blinked. But it was only at the signature I stared.

I was four years old the last time someone had admitted me as a blood relative.

"You wish me to go with you and discuss the nature of God?" I asked the priest. "Why?"

Eyluzh spread his hands elegantly outward. "I would be honored."

I shifted my stare from the paper to the man. "But why honored? Such discussions are not my province. I have nothing to offer."

It was bad enough that the priest looked disbelieving, but when I looked from him to Dowln, the Velonyan seemed also to distrust my words, while Arlin, standing behind him, seemed to express that I was capable of talking endlessly about any and all subjects under the sun.

Eyluzh seemed more than disbelieving, however. He appeared really disappointed. "Then what subject would you like to discuss, O King of the Dead? I would like very much to aid in the entertainment of so sudden and strongly heralded a visitor as yourself."

I could not tell whether the man was sarcastic, gently ironical or merely overpronouncing my name. I gave him the benefit of doubt. "I would like to see the shrine itself, if I might, Ngaul Eyluzh. My conversation then can consist of gasps and cries of admiration, and I will thus escape contradiction."

The priest's eyes narrowed for a moment and he said nothing. I wondered if I had asked for too much, but then he said, "I think I can arrange that. You understand it will be at a disadvantage, what with the wounded. . ."

"We are all at a disadvantage now," said Dowln, perhaps to himself, and the priest turned his red presence around and started toward the door. I followed and Arlin after me, but Dowln, not rising from his chair, plucked at her sleeve and I heard him whisper: "It is very difficult to get permission from the abbot to allow a foreigner into the Appid. Eunuchs may not step into it nor yet touch the outer walls. They suspect our touch will cause decay."

I was not the only one to overhear this. Eyluzh's face filled with distress. "No, artifactor! You misjudge us. It is only that the strengths of your spirit are different from those of sexual man and not appropriate for H'Appid Niaus. We do not say inferior: only different."

Dowln's long pale face remained set. "Remarkable how those differences you detect never work to my benefit, priest. Not in religion, law, or life itself."

Eyluzh shrugged like a northerner this time, rude or not. "Remember that I am not responsible for the creation of any of these, Dowln: not law, not religion, and certainly not life itself."

I had the feeling none of this was being said for the first time. Arlin threw her black shadow between the men.

"Enough. It doesn't matter. I have no interest in fancy basketwork anyway, and Nazhuret does not need me to wipe his nose. If you permit, Dowln Goldsmith [and she relapsed into Velonyie, to please the man], I will remain here and distract you from work. We could play cards."

"Or just sit here and contaminate each other," answered the blond, smiling tightly. As we were passing under the doorway, I heard him add, for her ears, "They are not over-enthusiastic about women either."

As we passed down the cool stone corridor, lit only from clerestories and shining a dim russet from the color of the stone, I heard the jeweler's guard returning, accompanied by booted feet and the jingle of arms. We did not see the soldiers, since our paths had now diverged, but I was gratified that Dowln, despite his slave status, had the power to win protection from the highest subject in the land.

(Or perhaps it was because of it. Frequently our only recourse against abuse is that our suffering inconveniences someone else. That is a horse's only recourse, at any rate, and a slave does not have much better standing. I wondered if the emperor's horse would be called "Lord Horse" by the populace.)

I watched the turns of the hall with great attention, because I hate to get lost, especially withindoors. We went past three left-hand doorways, all closed, and then took the next turn, which had no door. Here the windows were at eye level and I was able to see we were a story above the ground. Below was a garden, of the usual Rezhmian tubs-and-flagstones-around-a-pond variety, but this place, by the earthquake's whim, had suffered great damage. The tubs were thrown and broken, the pond an empty hollow of stone and mortar, and the three-colored fish these people value so highly lay as so many gray husks on the pavement. Some of the fish had been as long as my arm.

My guide, more ornate than the red, black, and white fish, had not stopped with me, and I had to jog so as not to lose him. We went downstairs, again to the left, and then took a sharp right into a narrow hall finely inlaid with shell and coral, that was lit by torches—like something from the dark ages. As we passed along, the smell told me that the lamps were actually modern oil lanterns, fed—like Dowln's ruby smelter—by Rezhmia's tar and ground-oil pits.

This room opened out to an empty chamber of immense size, with spear-thin windows reaching thirty feet up toward heaven, and with spots of lighter color on the walls and on certain of the tiles, as though a decoration had been removed. The clean spot on the wall was in the shape of a triangle and that led me to think I was in an abandoned church. For a moment I felt a pang for the loss of our home in Norwess, that was an abandoned monastery, and then I was following my guide out of the pink stone and into late sunlight.

My first reaction to H'Appid Niaus was that its size was greatly overrated. It looked like a wayside shrine, painted in clean, sky-colors. The lines of its architecture (I am no student of architecture) went up and up, as though the whole structure was exhibiting the weightless nature of the willow wands of which it was constructed. Then I noticed the size of the courtyard that lay between the shrine and us, and the numbers of workers and the teams of oxen that were made small by comparison with the building, and I knew that the perfection of its design made both distance and size illusory.

Ngaul Eyluzh was watching me watch it. "Well. What does the visitor think?" he asked me.

I answered, "It has an effect like the stars. It reduces us to insignificance."

He laughed, but as though he expected that response, and he rubbed his hands together.

I had not uttered my entire thought, which was that I think it right and proper for the stars to reduce man to insignificance, but that I prefer places human-built to have a human scale, for the truth is that we are not insignificant at all.

I remember that the yard in front of the shrine was a crazy pavement, made crazier in the last few days, and that one spot of it was thick and sticky and brown with blood. It would have taken all the blood in a human body to create such a stain, and the carpet of flies that covered it gave a fuzzy appearance, as though it were a spot of crawling mold upon the rock. Eyluzh strode over this wallow of blood, giving it no attention, his red skirts scraping over and sticking to the stuff. The sight of the red silks pulling over the brown blood made me slightly sick.

Or maybe it was the smell in the hot afternoon air. There was the odor of a slaughterhouse around us, and I began to wonder whether the worship of Niaus involved animal sacrifice, when it came to me that a slaughterhouse, a battlefield, and a hospital all share the same unpleasant stinks.

The stairs were of the usual pink sandstone, but the wall before us was as strange as I had been led to expect. It rose fifty feet in the first story alone, and ranked beside it was a row of pillars, each an entire fir trunk, peeled, dyed, and inlaid in the shrine's colors, and connected to the building proper by "ropes" woven of willow, thicker than my leg and ornate of pattern. There was something both odd and familiar about this style of building, and after a moment's thought I realized that H'Appid Niaus was built like the houses of Bologhini, if one of those homely dwellings were raised to imperial size.

Above the second floor the walls swelled outward in what was doubtless more elaboration, of which I could see only the floor itself, serving as an awning for the entryway where I stood. That entryway led in funnel fashion toward the main doorway, that was perfectly round and woven into the whole like the rim of a basket. The effect of this was to make the pedestrian feel he was being led, pulled, or sucked ineluctably into the building.

We, however, resisted the pull and stepped through a small and more ordinary-looking doorway to the left. Once within, I heard weeping and other unhappy sounds, but at some distance. Here the smell was more intense.

The interior of H'Appid Niaus made the stone corridors of the fortress seem a marvel of simplicity. Not only were these smaller and lacking in the right angles that reassure visitors, but the interior walls were woven so sparely that some light could pass through, and so it was possible to pack more and smaller rooms tightly into the space (like the grain of a loaf of fine white bread). The stripes and speckles of light that touched upon each individual willow wand were echoed in large upon the walls themselves, so one did not always know whether he was about to cross a room or slam his nose upon a door two inches away. Hearing might have made up for this confusion of sight, but the porosity of the building made the sense of hearing equally unreliable. I almost lost the priest a number of times, and it seemed that H'Appid Niaus was intent upon convincing me that I was not only insignificant, but a dolt, besides.

I needed another sense, and so I unfocused my eyes, quieted my mind, and found one. I don't know exactly what my perception was, whether air against the face, echoes, or something more esoteric, but suddenly I had no trouble with H'Appid Niaus.

I caught up to Eyluzh, and it seemed he was disappointed that I wasn't lost already. Even priests appreciate petty mischief.

116

The rooms that opened out from the corridors were all closed by wicker gates woven tightly, and so I had the impression that there was only this tube of a passage, round and winding like the gut of a huge beast. The smell helped the image along. When the passage opened into the great assembly chamber, we were already at the back of the building and I could see the open top of the basket—the great door—at the other end, with bright light of day shining through.

The hall was high-domed, and the floor of it was not willow but pink stone, that reflected the shell and coral inlays of the wall. Standing in rows as straight as soldiers on parade or pieces on a game board were statues: twice life-height, each of them different. I could not make them out at this distance, but by the number and lengths of the limbs I suspected they were not carved in the realistic school. I spent little time examining these, for mixed among them, in rows of less order, were the ranks of wounded and sick, and the nurses that bustled among them.

Some of the patients were on folding cots, military style, and some of them were laid out on the floor itself. It was from this room that the groans and weeping had come. And from this room came the smell.

Eyluzh had already taken hold of my sleeve, to prevent me from stepping further toward the infirmary. "Alas, visitor, I cannot show you the hall today."

I told him I wished only to see how the people were doing, but he shook his head until his hat tinkled. "No, it is exactly because of them I cannot; the presence of uncleanness I have renounced."

I must have stared at the man, for he continued. "It is not that we are heartless, visitor. We have our healing orders, too. But my work is different."

When I hesitated again, he added, "And they do not need your help, my friend. They did not ask for it."

We climbed, and my orientation began to fail me for the numerous turns and the lack of windows along the staircase. I depended more heavily upon the sense or combination of senses I had discovered in the passages below, until it became easier to step with my eyes closed. I would have taken off my boots as well, to feel the texture of the tiles that crusted the wicker stair treads, but I suspected bare feet might be prohibited in the heart of the Appid, along with eunuchs and women and people in physical distress. Instead I rolled up my sleeves and let the air speak to the hair on my arms.

Now I could feel the breeze that had blown through the shrine yard, and which blew in reduced form through the huge basket that was the shrine. I made a little model of H'Appid Niaus in my mind, added the staircase, myself, and the blowing wind, and regained a perception of where I was.

117

We had climbed for some minutes and the priest was puffing like a porpoise in front of me. I heard this noise echoed from above and knew we had reached a ceiling.

I opened my eyes and blinked at the light pouring through a high-arched window. Wind made the woven shutter shudder against its moorings. I looked out and saw the Fortress City rising below me like raw pink mountains. Here and there oily smoke made ropes across the sky. The hall of fake torches was across the yard below us, and farther off stood the gate through which Arlin and I had entered the City only this morning. My self-conceit rose measurably; the building had not succeeded in turning me around at all.

Ngaul Eyluzh was trying to close the window, but the breeze fought him. I helped him haul around the big shutter and secure it, whereupon this high chamber became as dim as the rest of the shrine.

"Better!" the priest said. He dusted his hands upon one another. He caught his breath and looked at me closely. "Sometimes people get lost on their first trip into H'Appid Niaus," he told me.

"I believe that," I answered. "And for many visits after, too. It's not obvious."

"You did not get lost, visitor." His voice seemed to hold a little disappointment, but he turned away from me and led across a room the size of a good house in Sordaling, again all of willow and furnished only by one woolen rug and three wicker boxes. Eyluzh's sticky scarlet hem pulled against the imperfections of the wicker as it had against the dried blood.

Each wicker box was missing its top and half of one side, and had been piled with pillows. There was a tea service of three precious metals spread out on the rug between them. Eyluzh doffed his high hat, fell backward into a box, and let the pillows support him. I could see only his face and feet. "We test everyone with the maze and staircase. I am glad you did not fail it."

I laughed at him: his portentous words and idiotic appearance. "I'm glad I passed, too. I hate to ask for directions from strangers. But why test me? What can it matter that a nobody like me knows east from west?"

Eyluzh pointed a finger at me. I had thought the gesture was considered impolite in Rezhmia. "You are not nobody, visitor. Besides, we test everyone. Everyone tests everyone, constantly. Have you never heard of the War of Wisdoms? Oh—sit down. I don't mean to be rude."

I squatted on my haunches on the rug.

"No, no. In a chair, of course." He waggled that finger again. "Either chair."

I looked into the padded recesses and felt I had to draw the line. "No thank you, Ngaul Eyluzh. I'm happy enough on the rug."

His dark eyes were bright, like a bird's. "Afraid of closed places?"

I considered the matter and could not convict myself. "No, I just can't imagine feeling comfortable in a box of pillows. And I have never heard of the

118

War of Wisdoms." As I spoke I was thinking, with some feeling, that Rezhmia seemed to interpret everything as a matter of war.

Eyluzh must have read my face, for he smiled, and his round cheeks grew rounder, and his mouth, much like a woman's, made a shape like the bows of the Naiish. His feet (so obvious in the strange couch) drummed against the pillows in glee.

"Oh, my dear visitor! You misunderstand me. This discussion is not to make you unhappy. We play at our wordbattles as other people play checkboard. It is a way of passing the time and also. . . and also of discovering truth. And, of course, we are going to feed you: tea and sweet cakes."

His manner was so winning that my worry melted. I knew a moment's pang for Arlin, who had been eating toasted barley and wild roots for so long now. But Arlin preferred her food piquant; I was a child in my tastes.

"Ngaul Eyluzh, at last I realize that you are a comedian, under your imposing robes," I said, and Eyluzh gave me an owl stare.

"It took you so long? And I don't think the robes are imposing: only uncomfortable. To a stranger I must be a sight!" As I heard him, a wicker door butted open and a very small figure shuffled into the chamber with a tray. This tray was large and gold, and he set it down between us.

The cooking of Rezhmia puts our own to shame, old friend. It is not that we have a racial inadequacy. We have merely a short growing season. I counted seven different stuffed cakes on the tray, as well as three pastries. Some were obviously sweet, while others smelled wonderfully like dinner. Tears sprang to my eyes, for fancy cakes have a spiritual significance than nobody in this world understands but me. Beside all this glory was set a tall golden teapot with a spout in the shape of a stork's head and bill, and two ornate gold cups.

"Don't feel obliged to drink the tea," grunted Eyluzh, as his foot soles scrabbled and extended from the box with their owner following. "It's not a taste for. . . for northerners."

I am as typical a northerner as Arlin is a typical woman. I poured for both the priest and myself. Then I bit into a pastry.

Food never lives up to its smell, but it was still welcome. Eyluzh started right in on the sweets, and after he had reduced one to crumbs, he wiped his baby face with his baby hand and began upon me.

"Tell me, visitor. What is the name of God?"

I ceased chewing, let the question ring in my head awhile, and said in turn, "Your city is broken and your people suffering."

Eyluzh heard me expressionlessly, in the same manner that Arlin cheats at cards. He lifted his cup and swigged the hot tea, loudly. I imitated him, and the beverage tasted like the blade of a sickle that had cut weeds all day.

119

The priest tried again. "And how many are the faces of God?" This time I felt more in tune with the discussion. "How many died in the earthquake, Ngaul? How many lived through it? How many of these were your friends?"

He put down an empty cup. So did I. "Your methods are unorthodox, visitor. This is adversarial, like the courts of law, whose job is to find the truth."

I sighed and took up another treat. "I have never seen much truth unearthed by the process of law. Science gives you facts at least, and I am a scientist."

I blush that I bragged about that, but the sugar was going to my head in the pleasantest way. Ngaul Eyluzh grinned at me. He was bald under his headdress, as though the weight of it had squeezed off his hair. "I never heard of a barbarian scientist. Rezhmia is the land of science. Although of course I don't practice science."

"Why not?"

"The arts are more sacred. But let us return to our hoeing. Now you ask me a question."

I had not anticipated this, and spoke on impulse. "Tell me, Eyluzh. Who were you yesterday? Who will you be tomorrow?"

The priest's gaze sharpened, and he looked sly. "I was the same yesterday, and will be tomorrow. I have always been Eyluzh, and will be for eternity."

If the man had not said his own name I might have accepted the answer, for I remember eternity—at least sometimes. But because he claimed to take his name and face and maybe even his dusty robes with him, I was struck with pity, as though he had told me he trusted the pancake of the moon to feed him and the ocean to hold him up. Suddenly the air brightened and I saw a vision: Eyluzh the priest, or at least his robes, and the headdress and the bones that underlay his face, dry and rotten before me, covered with dust and busy spiders, the bony hand outstretched to take his life with him where life does not go. This was not a picture within the head. If it was of the imagination, it was of the eyes, too, and I stood in horror and sorrow at the sight.

In another moment it had faded and I looked down at the priest's living face, mottled and pale and gasping. I had not had my vision alone.

Then I was angry. "This country," I said, ". . . or at least this season. . . attempts to push me where I have no intention of going. Signs and portents. Circular prophesies. I do not accept them. They are. . . inappropriate. Worse! They are vulgar! Cheap!"

Eyluzh had gathered himself somewhat, though he still blew like a whale. He raised a chiding finger to me. "Still you cannot escape your destiny," he said with a shade of his natural complacence.

I lost my temper, which I rarely do. "Spare me!" I shouted. The young server pushed his head through the door and blinked at me. "Spare me these trite destinies. Meaningless word! What will be, will be: of course. Otherwise it won't be. You're chasing your tail when you speak of destiny."

I began to take hold of my own reins. I took a deep breath, which smelled delicious. I felt very strong, very ready for anything. "The truth is not hidden, priest of Niaus. It is open to all. Only we tend to look around us with our eyes closed."

My red mood lifted, and the pomposity of my statements rang in my ears. I giggled at myself. Eyluzh giggled with me. We stared at one another and my smiling face felt very stiff.

"I'm glad you set me straight about that," he said, and I had to laugh harder. So did he. He added, "It's a very potent drug and I'm surprised you're still standing."

It took me a few seconds to understand what he had said, and then I felt myself falling—or at least my viewpoint getting lower. My body felt nothing. There was a moment's panic and I remembered that I had left Arlin alone and done this stupid thing. Rise, I told myself: booted myself, whipped myself, and then I did rise again, but my body didn't.

To have died twice by the time I am thirty years old, I wondered, as I floated above this scene like a moth fluttering in a basket. This time there would be no Powl to reason me back again, for the priest had had every intention of driving me out of my body: this funny, prim little man, this priest who was not permitted contact with blood.

Ngaul Eyluzh was peering down over me, and I looked like a heap of linen and straw with small brown hands. The scuttling servant joined him and then my soul's attention began to waver.

"You gave him too much," said the servant, in tones no servant uses to a master, and the priest shook his head in confusion.

What was too much of a poison, as long as the victim be dead? More to the point, why was I fighting death, once already killed? When I had died before, I had not brawled on like this, striking with no-arms and no-legs against the fabric of my circumstance. This was not dignified.

But I was not feeling dignified, I was both outraged and afraid together.

Arlin. I had left Arlin. My no-mouth called her name, but to my fury she did not come and I did not go. I saw the weave of the ceiling, from within. I saw the shrine itself from outside in the free air, high up. I was a powerless phantom, and my notions of how life worked rose in rebellion: against strange and unjust saints and their cohort, against prophecy, omens, dreams, and suchlike superstition. My God was a God of optics, of long waiting, careful notebooks, and conclusions tentative. In this God of omens and destinies and cheap theatrics I did not believe.

Floating and fading, I began to think again, and even as the blue of the sky surrounded me and beat through my nobody, I became the man of science and I made an experiment.

"Dowln," I called, or thought or imagined. "Let your dreams be *for* something. Dream me down." I thought these words three times—not because three is a magic number, but in order to give my calling a fair chance.

The light that swam through me dimmed slightly and then more. I was in the workroom of the jeweler and before me sat My Lady Arlin, tossing an apple into the air and spearing it upon her dagger. She looked through me. Dowln sat behind her, one eye upon the door. I was sitting (in a manner of speaking) on the table.

"How long," she said in her hoarse, smoky voice, "is this dithering Yule ornament of a priest going to keep Zhurrie? He has a war to prevent, you know."

Her lean face, with its coloring of dusk and of clouds, had never seemed more beautiful to me, nor her skill at juggling more impressive. I was able to approach her very closely, far closer than my body's eyes could have focused without a lens, and I saw the pulse in her throat.

She did not seem meaningless to me as my own self had: not meaningless at all. Even the flick of the dagger that sent the raddled apple again into the air was imbued with layered purpose. Likely the difference I saw was that Arlin's body held life, while Zhurrie's did not. Or perhaps it was only that I would miss Arlin more.

She had not received an answer to her question, and her face stretched into a smile. "You don't believe me, landsman? That Nazhuret was sent here alone but for me, to stop this war? Or that he can do it? Dowln, you are a seer and an artist, but you do not know Nazhuret."

Still no response, so she turned to look at Dowln, and I, too, shifted my attention. Dowln's face was tense and white, and his eyes were not quite upon Arlin's. He was looking at me.

I was surprised, because I had not really believed I was there myself. "Get to safety. With Arlin," I said as clearly as I knew how. "The shrine was a trap. They will come for her next. Get out of here. Flee." When he merely stared and gaped, I added, "I like this less than you do! I am a man of science, not of apparitions!"

He knocked his chair backward and staggered toward us, one arm pointing. "Look, Arlin! Nazhuret! He is with us again. Something is very wrong!"

As though I had been summoned by his naming of me, I felt myself in human form, though I was no more opaque than bottle glass. Having hands, I sought for one of Arlin's, and took it. She gave a gasp and met my eyes.

I said, "Go. I am dead. The priest poisoned me. They must mean to kill you, too. Hide. Use all your skill and leave the country."

I didn't know whether she heard me. Arlin held to my arm-without-substance and I felt a grief I had never felt before. I would sooner have been turned into a cold stone upon her sword hilt, or a mute flea upon her person, as to be dead and silently drifting up away from her as she clasped my hand.

I could not stay longer; the two were in a rushing river all around me, that covered me over but touched me not at all. I held her hand against the force of it, but that lean hand had the flesh ripped from it and I was gripping a skeleton, and saying my good-byes to a mass of rags and bone. I let go and stared at my own hand, so glassy-clear, and then Dowln scrambled below me, also garbed in his own bones, and the staring teeth shouted, "Nazhuret. It isn't. . . I don't believe you are dead!"

Now the air was shiny green glass, molten glass, and the specter of my lady and my friend cartwheeled away into the distance. I stared again at my own glassy hand and shouted, "Oh!"

"Oh. That makes more sense," I said, or thought I said. I turned away from the vitreous river and it vanished like a picture on the page of a book, when that page is turned.

My memories of death are cloudy, like the memories of times before I could speak, but I remember that death was not trivial. It was not frustrating. It did not offend my human reason—if I still possessed human reason. This state was offensive.

It occurred to me that I had one tool that might serve me when hands and voice and even reason were gone. Powl, you gave me that tool, never naming it, nor telling me its use, and not knowing its use I had tried it out against all the exigencies of my life. It was good against anything: pain, failure, confusion.

I collected my bodiless self, fighting against the memory of Arlin's rotting dead hand, against her need of me and mine (so much more painful) of her. I waited with concentration and no set goal in the nothingness that surrounded me. In the belly of the wolf. I had no discomfort to distract me, save that of having no discomfort, and I was bothered by no thoughts. It was an immense contemplation, while around me I heard wailing and the buffet of air against my ears, as though I had fallen into the hell of winds.

Ngaul Eyluzh was peering at me, blinking. He had no hat. "No, he is not dead after all," he said.

"I knew that already," I answered him, but the force of my words or some other force threw me away into space and it required a lot of effort to maintain myself without panic.

"A man may be falling off a cliff, with nothing but death below, and yet be in complete control of himself," you then said to me. You were sitting on the stoop of the observatory. Your head was sunburned. You took note of Arlin's scowl to say, "I did not intend to diminish your sex, woman. In language, the male embraces the female."

"At his convenience, he does. What you say, Daraln, you intended to say. You don't do things by accident."

I remembered this exchange. It was out of the past. Arlin used to sabotage her lessons by being offended, as I used to do the same by distracting my teacher. I turned to tell her I knew what she was doing, but Arlin was not sitting on the grass, nor perched on the root of the oak.

Arlin had the sword—Dowln's sword with the woven hilt—in her hand, and she was in alert stance, her gray eyes black with attention. Behind her was a wall of inlay, the pattern lost in the dim light, and following her was Dowln, his flaxen hair shining. There was no Powl, of course. You had been a trick of memory.

I did not talk to Arlin, lest my words bounce me away again, but merely followed her down this unrecognized hallway to an arch that led to another like it. A woman in the pink-salmon silks of empire swished through, and Arlin flung herself down on the eunuch, flattening his yellow hair and linen beneath her night-colors. Her eyes did not leave the Rezhmian hen, who waddled out one door and in another. Arlin's sword was unencumbered and ready until the woman disappeared, at which time she allowed Dowln to lift his face from the paving.

My lady is a dreadful enemy. A magnificent friend. Dowln stared at her in shock.

He saw me beside them as he followed her through the archway. "Look," he whispered, plucking at Arlin's sleeve. "He is still with us. Look."

Arlin turned again, and her face was implacable, devoid of softness. I would have apologized, for offering such distraction, but Dowln's attention had already catapulted me high and away.

I saw my mother die, vomiting blood. I saw myself a squalling baby.

I saw the present King of Velonya, pale and taut-jawed, gazing down into the waters of his spring. Behind him was an old woman, holding the hand of a toddler: fat, carrot-headed. The child had a wooden sword, with which he hit the water. The father carried none. His shoes and trew were getting splashed. He has notoriously little concern for his costume.

I saw a great deal of air, and the earth far below, rounded and dark like a wooden ball. The sensation of falling was overwhelming, and my concentration faltered, making it worse. I reminded myself that I had no body at the moment, and if something as weighty as a mouse can drop from high places unharmed, then surely a man with no weight at all need not fear. I did not cease fearing: not entirely, but neither did I drop. The scene rolled away once again.

"He will do, he will do," said the face of Ngaul Eyluzh, from very close. "Though I do not know why he should have proved so susceptible to the drug."

The servant who was not a servant was squatting on the rug behind Eyluzh. "Often the barbarians are like that. Perhaps it is their coarse, simple diet, which does not accustom them to rich liquors and. . . and herbs of various sorts."

The priest was peering at something. Me, I suppose. "Not simple diet, Father. Simple brains." He seemed content with what he found in my face, for he said very forcefully, "Get up, fellow. Stand!"

I thought I might oblige him, rude as he was with his remark about my brains, for I had a strong desire to make everyone around me happy. An unusually strong desire. Still, I was being careful of my position in "the belly of the wolf." Quiet observation had served me well so far, despite the antics of the world around me, so I merely listened to his words as I had listened to the wind in the wickerwork, and perceived light, shadows, and the irritation on his round face.

The door behind the chamber opened, and through it I stepped, and stared down at myself. I mean, it was Reingish who came through. "Is he tamed yet?" the prince asked.

I am committing a dishonesty, in describing my observations to you in this manner. I cannot be sure these vignettes were experienced in the order described, or whether they were sequential at all. Interspersed among them were moments of flight, of forgetfulness: moments in which I lost control of the imbecile creature I was riding, named Nazhuret. I cannot fit anywhere in this sequence the image of the hart with the moon caught in his horns, though that feels most important, nor the sudden understanding I came to regarding the retrograde periods of Mercury.

I lost Nazhuret many times, but I guess that I did not lose my attention, for it was at a moment close-connected with the sight of the prince that I decided I must take more of a control over what had happened to me.

I had called my method of self-collection a weapon, and the only one that I possessed. I now remembered that I had another, that I had already used without recognizing it. I had used the method of science to discover what my no-body could do. It was very difficult to maintain both science and the clarity of mind I was finding in the belly of the wolf, so upon impulse I decided to essay a test. I would convert my meditation and my science into real weapons, which I would clench in my non-substantial hands for security.

I did not specify what the weapons would be, although I expected that self-collection would be some sort of shield and science the more active tool, that would therefore be held in the right hand. I was very surprised to find myself—or rather the linen-haired Nazhuret above which I hovered—holding in his left hand a short, thick sword of a style that our great-grandfathers would have considered antique, and in his right a round shield, glimmering in the evening light.

Science, even when the experiment goes as expected, always brings a little surprise with it. The three Rezhmians who confronted the body of Nazhuret drew away from my experiment smartly, and gasped. It had never occurred to me that other eyes would be able to perceive what was only a mnemonic device to me.

Nazhuret stood up, with sword and shield.

The minsanaur had no sword: only the red dagger around his neck that was the symbol of his hatred. He backed away and showed his anger to his own minions instead. "You fools! What good was all this? The bastard is more dangerous than before!"

The little fellow who had brought the tea was less afraid of his prince than of a sword of magic in the hands of his prince's double. He disappeared through the wicker doorway into the kitchen. Reingish strode after him, cursing.

Ngaul Eyluzh was made of stronger metal. He stood before the body I manipulated (my body) and he repeated the words "Do no harm, visitor. Do no harm."

He could have chosen no better control over me. I remember clearly the time when the whole world was larger than I, and had more capacity to hurt. Whether Nazhuret is dreaming or awake, he will not hurt anyone who pleads with him. But the priest had done me enough damage that I was not melted altogether by his pleas, and I pushed beyond him, seeking the stairs out of this high trap of wicker.

It seemed to me then that I might as well be playing twenty-guard, or some similar board game, for I hovered above and worked my clever little game piece with invisible fingers. Remotely. I knew the stairs were behind and to the left of Nazhuret, but it was a job to turn him around. When he did move, uncertainly to the left, the priest interfered again, and I was impressed at how adroitly Nazhuret moved sword and shield (science and contemplation) to ward him off. With no command from me. With no one at home.

Before my game piece could find the stairs, Reingish had slammed through the wicker door again, this time armed with a kitchen knife, and with this he came at the ensorcelled Nazhuret, with his magic sword and shield. I thought at the time that the prince's act was very brave.

It seemed I could only get in Nazhuret's way, so I let him handle the assault as he had handled Ngaul Eyluzh. The battle was no credit to either fighter, seen critically, for Nazhuret was not really accustomed to the use of ancient armaments, and of course he was not in his right mind. Reingish, however, was probably totally untutored in the uses of a carving knife. He probably didn't even cut the roast at table.

He attacked three times and received three wounds, the deepest one by ramming himself upon Nazhuret's sword.

Nazhuret had taken no wound, except that which had severed him from me. I wondered what it was, for the minsanaur, to look into those eyes that were almost his own. Did Nazhuret look mad, or mindless? If I were Reingish, it would have given me bad dreams.

At last the prince backed off, panting and bleeding, and Nazhuret made it to the staircase and put one foot upon it.

"Stop!"

Now Reingish was on his knees. "By the five hundred faces of God and by his thousand hands, I adjure you, stop!" Nazhuret paid no attention, but I did. Reingish was lifting his hand, and brilliance flickered in the air. "By the light that I carry and the light that I am, I cast dark into darkness! Begone! Begone! Begone!"

The light of his diamond exploded and took me with it, dazzled and dumb, into blackness. I did not know what had happened to Nazhuret; I left him behind again.

I was without sight, without hearing, without feeling. I was not without time, because time's anxiety surrounded me, and worse, I was not without "I."

This was not death; this was far more fearsome. There were memories in my mind, but they had no power to comfort—only to worry, to irritate. To frighten.

There was the thought that they had killed Arlin, and I—I was locked in a box between life and death and could not follow. There was the thought that Rezhmia had overrun Velonya as far north as Sordaling, and that it was my fault somehow, for being in the dreams of the sanaur's prophet. I thought that I had killed Dowln, as he had feared. I wished I had killed him much sooner. I wondered if all my friends and my enemies were long dead.

The heavy weight and agony of these thoughts was all in the word "I." No one ought to carry such a heavy weight, without material shoulders and a strong animal being to heft it with. I wished to God I might be rid of "I," now that Nazhuret was gone. I wished for a miracle.

God, however, has always been as unpredictable as Powl to me, and has answered me more with methods than miracles. I had learned my methods long since and now was forced to deal with them.

I used self-collection to pull my scattered being together in the darkness. When confusion washed over me I observed it, until I thought I knew more about despair than any man alive. Or almost alive.

Next, after solitary ages, came grief, which was less deadly than despair, but more seductive. I had known Arlin as a grown woman for almost six years, and the child she had been I remembered from my own childhood. I had known a few other women, for days at a time, but my black lady I loved as I loved no other soul, man or woman. And her loyalty to me was stronger than mine to her: unbroken since her thirteenth year.

Could she live without me? With whom else *could* she live? What other man could see her perfection? Whom would she *allow* to know her perfection, disliking most of mankind as she did?

Could she die without me? Dead or alive she would look for me; neither in death nor life was I to be found. I thought I heard my lady's voice calling in the featureless dark. I kept as calm as I could, for Arlin's sake. I heard her again.

There was a flash—of light, or hope, or something. Perhaps it had been there unnoticed for a long time. It was not above me nor below. I took different attitudes to it, trying to see it as a horizon, as a rope, as an adamant in a necklace, and then I disciplined my experiments. I postulated that the shining was from the diamond of the minsanaur that had thrust me into his hell. I tried to climb it.

I stuck myself to the lance of light and went higher: brighter. I was succeeding, but after all I doubted it was a diamond, for it was too linear. Suddenly I knew my hypothesis had been wrong. I was climbing the star of light coming from the sapphire on my own hand. (There is no loss in being disproved, in science. The gain comes from having an answer at all.)

I was sitting on the wickerwork staircase, my two hands raised above my head in a mimic of rope—climbing. The light was lower, but a glow of silver came out of the blackness of the stone on my finger. There was no one around me at all.

I almost lost myself in the intestines of the building, because it was made to be an illusion, and besides the light had changed. Then I remembered to close my eyes as I ran. It became an exciting progress, and I left some skin and blood against the woven walls. From the distance I could hear people shouting, and even a heavy chanting of many voices, that sifted through the filter of wickerwork so that I could not understand anything said.

128

Space slapped me as hard as any of the walls. I opened my eyes and stumbled into the great hall, where the sick lay still and the healers stood listening. There was no sound louder than a whisper. Being no priest, I stepped across the sandstone floor to the closest bed, where a man lay smelling of broken guts. His face was green and his eyes frightened. Not of his injury, I thought.

I asked what had happened, in my best idiomatic Rezhmian. He answered me: "War."

The courtyard was filled with people standing in small clumps, seeming to my dazed senses to reflect the clotting blood on the pavement. I ran without any thought save to find Arlin, and I retraced my steps to Dowln's workshop, only to find it locked.

Of course: I had seen them flee the place. I had seen them in a dream, a drug-dream, a fantasy, but I had no sense or memory to go by now except that drug-dream, so I followed the vision of a corridor past the big archway, past scurrying women, past tubs of roses, past a child's funeral, where his small body lay under the heavy brocade wrap, crushed by yesterday's disaster, and men all around me shouted and called and dragged the heavy clanging arms of tomorrow's disaster. I brushed by soldiers, but none of them stopped me. I heard the sound of my own name, but I was not certain whether it belonged to my recent drug enchantment or to the present moment.

The light was failing, and I was lost. I needed to find Arlin, and I ought to find the sanaur who had declared this impossible war. I held myself upright by the trunks of two potted apricot trees and tried to think how to accomplish either of these goals.

I had never been to the sanaur's personal chambers, or to those of his intimates. I presumed they were in this building, for we had seen him in the doorway only yesterday—and then his pet jeweler was here. But there was no proof of this.

As for Arlin, in my delirium I had only seen her in the passages. I had no idea where Dowln would take her.

In another moment I realized that Dowln would take my lady nowhere, because no one could lead or drive Arlin, nor any student of yours. She would decide where she was going, even to the last extremity. And where would she go?

Like me, she would feel she ought to find the sanaur.

I was leaning on the saplings, and they bent with my weight. I could no longer forget that I had been poisoned and still felt somewhat sick. It occurred to me I could vomit behind the huge pot and feel better for it. It occurred to me more strongly that I had to piss.

Remember, you forbade me to piss against buildings, let alone in them? You said it was unhygienic and encouraged the dogs. Here I had no access to civilized facilities and the windows were too high for human aim. I voided into the pot with the apricot trees, and was only half done when an old woman, dressed in apricot color herself, shuffled up behind me and ordered me to desist. It was too late for such an injunction, and I continued to piss on the tree, feeling more humiliated than a man sick and amid catastrophe ought to feel.

I apologized in what words I could find and explained it was an emergency.

"It is an emergency for everyone, lad," she answered. "But we are not all peeing on the bushes."

Something about her accent drew my embarrassed face toward hers and I saw this was an old dame of some quality, with a bruised face and one arm wrapped in linen. Although her words had been sharp her eyes seemed human enough, and as she saw me swaying she stepped forward as though to catch me.

"Brace up now. We've all suffered in this," she said, less angrily but still tart. I nodded and did not put any weight against her elderly frame. "Tell me, lad. How many did you lose yesterday?"

I felt an impulse to laugh and quashed it. "Lost literally, Grandmother. I have lost my companions since noon today and I have lost the sanaur's chambers completely!"

She nodded, winced, and held her broken arm more still. "You can't get there through the main hall anymore. That's your problem. Follow me."

The old lady set off in the direction I had been going and I picked up my weapons and followed, adjusting my steps to hers. She gave a wide stare at the antique sword and shield that I was dangling from my fingers to appear as harmless as possible.

"Those come off a wall in the earthquake?" she asked me, and I answered, truthfully, that I did not know.

Again I heard Arlin call my name, but the old lady did not respond to the sound. Perhaps she was only hard of hearing, for the call seemed very real and not magical at all. I felt a strong desire to dodge past my guide and run down the sandstone corridor, calling in my own right, but I could not tell where the voice came from, and I might go wrong as well as right.

I wanted to pick the old lady up and carry her, as once I did a farmer's daughter in the fields of Satt Territory, but her goodwill was everything. I followed behind her little feet and heavy skirts, while the last daylight died and I knew something terrible and important was happening without me.

I heard running feet down another corridor, echoing from everywhere. There was a shout, which faded.

A man came by in the opposite direction, lighting the wall sconces one by one. He moved very quietly, and very slowly.

"Once you have grandchildren, it is easier," she said over her shoulder. Her lined face was black and white in the lamplight. "They may kill one of your children, or even all, but you will have some to carry on."

I asked her who "they" were and she answered, "Anything. The earthquake. This war. Great-grandchildren are even better. Once your grandchildren begin to bear, you can stop worrying." She turned and peered at my face.

"But you're a child yourself. Not old enough for your own children."

I replied "Oh, I'm old enough, Grandmother: well old enough. I don't have any children, though."

The old lady turned away and sighed lustily. "Just some mother's worry yourself. That's what you are. Just another worry."

It hardly seemed a fair accusation. My mother must have worried about me severely for the first few years of my life, but then she went beyond worry, and for the most of my youth I worried no one but various instructors. And myself. Yet the old woman's complaint drew feelings of unease and regret from me. My heart was beating heavily. I touched the belly of the wolf to find composure.

This time I was sure the voice was Arlin's and not a souvenir of my delirium. I asked my guide if she heard anything, and she answered, "Oh, they're digging up walls, still. They'll be doing that for weeks, I imagine." She looked around again, lost me in the dark, and took a grip upon my sleeve and marched me on.

She did not hear what I heard, but I soon began to hear what she did, and it did not sound like shovels to me.

"They are fighting, I think, Grandmother. Can you tell me where?"

The old lady shrugged, perfectly calmly. "There will be fighting, with this war after all." I wondered if she had understood. I decided to push past her, for the sounds of violence themselves might lead me to Arlin.

But there was something about this half-heard battle that did not seem like Arlin. That dull clang of metal was of blade brought hard against blade. There were the grunts and bellows of men using their weight against one another, crudely. My lady did not fight like that, nor did she allow any hulk of a man to use such weapons against her. Arlin's battles were silent except for the light ring of the saber. And the sound of bodies falling. I did not rush past the old lady after all, and that was my great fortune, for she pressed her good shoulder against a narrow, leather-padded, and inlaid door to the left of the hall, and I followed her into a long chamber and the presence of the emperor.

He was at the head of a black table scattered with papers, looking very shrunken and small in a black leather chair. Behind him stood three guardsmen in attitude of defense and four others lay dead around them. The mosaic floor of sandstone and turquoise was earthquake-cracked and slippery with

new blood, and I saw myself standing by a door at the other side of the council room, assaulting the sanaur's men with a dowhee.

It was an astonishing sight, and it came on top of too many astonishments.
For a long moment I could only stand and watch myself, thinking that I was
not free of the enchantment after all, and a body that was mine was still moving independently from me. Independent and wicked.

Nazhuret smashed aside the blade of one more of the guards and disemboweled the poor man at his master's feet. Seeing this I was freed from my
paralysis, for the blow was heavy and crude and did not use the dowhee in its
strength. This was not how Nazhuret, body or mind, had been taught to
fight. I turned to assure my elderly guide that this fellow attacking the sanaur
was not the lad she had helped along the halls, but she was no longer beside
me, nor anywhere in the long room. It was as though she had never been.

The sanaur stood, pressing back against the table. "You do not fool me,
Reingish," he said. His voice echoed among the stones and the hangings of
the room.

"I don't need to fool you, Grandfather. Just the men in the hall who see me
flee and find your body. I'm your bastard grandchild from the North: a stupid,
treacherous brute."

The little old man did not flinch. "You describe yourself well, Reingish,"
he said.

The prince was a very good fighter, even with a weapon as strange to him
as a Felonk dowhee, but I saw that his power against the sanaur's men was
their awe of him. I saw a man thrust at him and allow the thrust to fail and I
saw that man die for it.

I was running toward that black table, but there was only one soldier
standing. The sanaur drew something from his belt: a dagger, I presumed.
Whether it was for his nephew or for himself I did not know. I shouted,
"Reingish! Reingish! You have failed. It will do you no good to kill
Grandfather now! Run or suffer the penalty!"

Reingish sprang back and lifted his eyes to me briefly. He spat like a cat.
The last soldier standing was worse distracted than the prince was, and I saw
his head skitter under the table before his body fell, fountaining blood.

There was only the table between the prince and myself, but there was
nothing at all between the prince and the emperor. To my surprise, the old
man threw the dagger in his hand, which was not a throwing weapon at all. It
hit the minsanaur hilt first in the face, as he was lifting the dowhee to strike.
As the blade rang on the stones, the door behind him slammed open and Arlin,
a black shape with dead-white face, stood facing the image of Nazhuret.

"No!" I began to shout, and then choked back my words, for I knew the
danger of distracting anyone in Reingish's presence. Her saber was in her

hand. He smiled at her, softly, intimately. I wondered if I smiled like that. Casually, he raised his arm to wipe blood from his face; he raised the arm with the sword in it.

Arlin stood unmoving, her gray eyes black, and then her saber struck for the prince's neck.

For a moment I thought it was over, for Reingish stood staring at her and around his throat ran a tiny, mathematically pure line of red. As he stepped back and into guard I saw that he had been very fast, and Arlin had only scratched him. It had been a terrifying scratch, however, and his eyes blackened with respect for this "eunuch" who had done more to stop him than seven of the emperor's chosen.

So she knew him, I thought. By the tiny pebbles of color that made up the eyeballs or by the subtle difference in hair or stance she knew this Nazhuret was not the real one.

The prince struck in turn: an abrupt, unconventional flip of the tip which would have fooled most soldiers of Rezhmia or of Velonya. But in countering a dowhee with a cavalry saber, Arlin had more experience than any fighter living, and she turned the broad blade past her face and slipped it away.

She had done as much against me a thousand times.

In fear and in enjoyment of my lady's expertise, I leaped into the air and struck one palm with the other fist. I did this silently, for my fear was much greater than my enjoyment, and when I saw the door behind the combatants swing open, revealing Dowln's face, so pale, so strange-eyed, so steeped in enchantments, I froze in the fear that Reingish would use the jeweler against Arlin. The emperor's eunuch had more sense however, and he faded back into the corridor. I noticed that his blue eyes had remained fixed upon those of the little emperor, and I wondered how he could love him so—the man who had ruined his life and his manhood.

It was not a question that bore investigation, since at the moment both Arlin and I were at life's last risk for this same emperor. At least he was my "grandfather."

In my moment of inattention, Reingish had found the thrown dagger lying on the tiles and used the sanaur's trick to throw it at Arlin. A dueling saber is not held with the heavy grip with which a farmer holds a hoe, and the shock of the knife hitting the round hilt caused Arlin almost to lose her weapon. In that moment Reingish struck and I saw blood on my lady's hand and running down her face. Without knowing how, I was on the polished table and sliding toward my own image, screaming in rage.

Then, pouring out of the door where Dowln had stood were more soldiers, in dress no different from those who lay in blood. By the angle of their attention, however, I knew these were Reingish's men, and my slide toward the prince became a cannonball over his head. I heard a blade in the air behind me, but did not know even if it had been directed at me. The men pressed back again without decision, but I had come down sliding on the wet, red paving and one leg folded under me as I came at them, groin-level, with my head unprotected and unprotectable.

As there was no point in trying to regain my feet, I careered on, like a child in snow, and feeling the presence of at least three swords coming down at me. I slid past them all, by luck alone, and my ancient weapon opened two bellies and spread a red stain over a third.

I was on my feet again, but I had blood in my eyes: blood and guts, and the stink of it in my nose. My body chose this time to tell me that it had a monstrous headache.

The wounded man crumpled and his eyes asked for me to ignore him, which I did. The two who were opened on the floor merely lay across my way, staring at the ceiling, waiting to die. There were two more but I was choking on bile, and my museum-piece sword was sliding in my grip.

I heard the voice of the sanaur call the men in his uniform to drop their weapons. I heard Reingish curse him and then I heard Arlin bellow out at the bottom of her voice, not my name nor even that of Velonya, but the words "Norwess, Norwess!"

A dukedom destroyed long before I learned I might have inherited it: gutted like these poor men. A realm I visited as a wary trespasser, and which I had never desired.

But my lady has a streak of romanticism about her, where I am concerned. And she sounded in a great good mood.

I saw her turn Reingish's blade from the emperor one more time, and there was a spark at contact. I drew my attention back upon my old sword, which was, somehow the belly of the wolf made material.

The belly of the wolf was always hungry in the nursery rhyme, and so I let it attack the two remaining soldiers. I took the hand off one, and he stood screaming, and the other ran away down the back corridor.

Behind me was a clatter and I saw Reingish's dowhee skidding around my feet. Without thought I bent to retrieve it and then I had a blade in both hands and a shield up my elbow.

Reingish had lost his weapon and his men and all his chance, or so it seemed. Arlin backed off a small step to allow the emperor to decide his fate. Delicate of her, I thought. But Reingish was not weaponless; he had his little red knife, symbol of all his hate. I saw it in his hand and then he was attempting my trick one better. He leaped—he seemed to leap—upon Arlin, but as she ducked it was apparent that his feint was only to get her out from between him and his grandfather. He hung in the air like a bird, like a plains eagle with his one sharp red talon descending toward the old man's throat.

It was the sort of moment that freezes in the mind. I remember being astonished at the tininess of the blade, and noting that there was something different in the ring on the hand that held it. The stone was gone from the setting. But though I was frozen, Arlin was not, and my lady split Minsanaur Reingish open with her saber, from midbelly to behind the legs. His innards and he fell separately to the floor. Upon Arlin.

I pulled her out. She was coughing. I had bile in my mouth. Already there were flies. For a short while there was no one else in the room except Arlin, the old sanaur, and myself.

She spat her mouth clear. "It reminds me of the monstrous pig, which you had to slaughter in Rudofsdorf. Remember?"

I looked up. "Indeed, it is monstrous." One of the soldiers, as I glanced at him, trembled and died. "It is a slaughterhouse." I met the eyes of the emperor, which were wet, and they glanced from one dead Rezhmian to another—not his heir, but at the soldiers—blinked and shed tears.

"Why did it have to be you?" he whispered. "Twice in two days, and now he who was almost your twin. Is this what my boy foretold to me? Is this the promised ruin, rather than the earthquake? Why you?"

I stood up, helping Arlin. Now a few guards scrambled into the council room, and a man in the salmon color of the aristocracy. They found us all talking amid the blood and bodies, and no weapons raised, so they stood in horror without decision.

"Why me? Because he was almost my twin, Sanaur of Rezhmia. And he took my identity in order to commit murder. And anyway—I couldn't let him assassinate you."

The little old man gave me a glance of birdlike intelligence. "Why not? Did you think I would be less inclined to answer your government's belligerence than he? That's not the case. Or that he would make a more fearsome commander in chief? That's definitely not the case."

"No, Sanaur!" Arlin spoke with minimal courtesy. "Nazhuret behaved as Nazhuret *will* behave. It is his nature. In. . . certain ways he is a simple man."

The sanaur began to pick his way out from among the steaming, broken limbs and bodies. He had largely escaped being soiled. "All the more reason," he said, rubbing his hand over his thin eyelids, "that I will not make you my heir, though you are eligible."

I choked in pure surprise. "Sanaur! Of course you won't do that. My loyalty is. . ." and here I had to stop and think, for all the events in the past two days had made me lose sight of the fact that I had no declared loyalty to Rudof, and had insisted as much many times. To the face of the king. Here we had been acting almost as the sworn representatives of the North; it had seemed appropriate.

". . . my sympathy is for Velonya. It raised me. I have almost a Velonyan mind."

"Almost?" Now that I had denied any interest in the power it was his to give, the old man showed me a warmer eye. "You certainly have not a Rezhmian mind."

"I have not a mind for statecraft, that is sure, Grandfather. Had I now just been attacked by my own heir and traitorous soldiers and rescued by two strangers out of my nightmares, the day after an earthquake that crumbled half my city, I would not be thinking of the political necessity." He glanced at me again, as though suspecting he had been insulted.

"No, Nazhuret, you're right," said Arlin, and she put her hand on my shoulder. "You'd be thinking of the eternal meaning of things. Or else you'd be digging buildings out. Or playing marbles with orphaned children." She turned her face to the emperor and said as though to an equal, "Nazhuret spent his youth in poverty and all subsequent years in the search for truth. The dukedom of his betrayed father was offered to him and he turned it down. Why do you believe he would then lust after authority in a nation of strangers?"

The sanaur peered fiercely at her, one hand on the door out of the bloody chamber. Many people in the hallway bowed to him, wide-eyed. "You are not a eunuch at all, are you? I only thought so because you are so much taller than he. Northman tall. And because of the sword. Women in Rezhmia do not carry swords. But by your—I will say the word authority—over him, I believe you are his wife."

I bowed. "This is My Lady Charlan, daughter of Baron Howdl of Sordaling Province, great 'Naur of Rezhmia."

"Not his wife." Arlin corrected us.

After the long, measuring look she received, Arlin added, "I never said I was a eunuch to anyone. I never said what I was."

The old man smiled and passed through the door. "No, and we were too polite to ask. No mind.

"You both have saved my old life, for its few more years. I thank you. Now my time is not my own, but these people will see to your needs."

He walked alone down the hall.

While they were bathing me I got sick, and then I fell asleep. I woke up in a panic that I had let the moment go: the moment when the 'naur would at last talk to me. After all we had been through, after the privation, the confusion, the violence, and the irritating air of predestination, still we had not been allowed to speak our little message of peace to the Emperor of Rezhmia.

I woke up in a well-padded bed, under silk covers. I woke up with a dizzy headache and I woke up angry. I was blinking at the face of Dowln, and he was lifting my head to a goblet.

My mood was terrible, and so I said, "You shouldn't do that. You shouldn't lay hands on me when I'm not aware. I've been a fighter all my life and you can't tell what I might do."

He put the glass to my lips, and what it contained was surprisingly bad-tasting. "I thought of that," the jeweler said calmly. "But Arlin said you never exploded that way. She said you tend to wake amiably."

Thus convicted, I finished whatever was the terrible draught. I did not feel amiable. Despite his protest, I got out of bed.

I was dressed in silk—to my embarrassment in the salmon—pink silks of Rezhmian royalty. The color looked odd against my always sunburned skin, and my sunburned yellow hair.

"You were given a potent drug which is very effective at controlling people's actions. Or at killing them. I'm glad you survived, but you must not push now. It is damaging."

I needed his help to stand. "Are you glad I survived? Though I have been the ogre of your dreams?"

"Not only that," said Dowln, and then he added, "Your weapons, Nazhuret. I found them and cleaned them."

"The dowhee?"

"No, the ancient set. Look." He attached my hand to a bedpost and left me for a minute. When he returned he had in his hands the old sword and shield, but they glowed of gold and of steel and of bronze. Set into the boss of the shield was a blood-red garnet and at the pommel of the sword was a clear ball of beryl.

I stared at these dumbly for a moment, but the medicine was working quickly and I began to laugh. "These are what I invented? I made these out of poison and my own mind? Who would have credited a half-sized snowman with such skill?"

Dowln glanced from me to the weapons and back again, determined to be respectful, however I behaved. "The workmanship is good, and very old," he offered. "I cannot tell whether they are Rezhmian or from the North."

"Science," I stated, holding out the shield. "The workmanship is very good indeed. It took many people to build this shield, though I invented it yesterday. And contemplation. . ." I waved the sword in the empty air. "That, I suspect, is more ancient than the other." I put both down on the messy bed.

"They were an experiment of mine," I said, and then staggered off to void my bladder. Not in a planter pot, this time.

Dowln took Arlin and me to see the emperor again, and I was aware that this was the meeting for which we had come so far, through privation, earthquake, and treachery. All this for a little conversation, where I might plead Rudof's cause and my own. I was tired, but my head improved by the moment. Arlin's eyes were sunken and shadowed, but she preserved that air of dark inscrutability that was her own.

At the entrance to the 'naur's chamber I almost turned on my heel and walked out, for the place was draped and decorated with the weaponry and armor of Velonya as it might have been with the heads and skins of animals. Against the inlaid wall were dozens of sabers and pikes, which leaned like tentpoles, all scuffed, battered, or broken. An ugly pile of harquebuses rose from the tiles, dirty and in disrepair, and all about hung the uniforms of men, rusty with dried blood. The old emperor looked more fragile than ever as he sat upon the barrel of a three-pound cannon, in his hands a lieutenant's field jacket, ripped, burned, and discolored.

My temper died back when I realized that he did not consider these sad things to be in the nature of trophies. He was turning the filthy cloth in his hands again and again, as though it would drop a secret if properly handled.

"Which division is this?" he asked me, perfectly calm. "I used to know all these things, but your king has modernized so much. . ."

Neither Arlin nor I answered. Her lean face was white, which is the sole way she displays her anger. The old man peered up at us without embarrassment. "I am not asking you to betray your red king, grandchild. I would only like to know.

"All these things, these dozens and dozens of sidearms and swords and artillery, were gathered after the battle of Kowleseck. Kowleseck is perhaps a hundred and fifty miles north of here."

"I know where Kowleseck is, Sanaur of Rezhmia," I replied as evenly as I could. "But I know of no modern battle fought there."

My "grandfather" sighed at me. "So wise and so ignorant. That makes a difficult combination, you know? Velonya attacked Kowleseck in the early summer: first of the big raids against our cities. Our civilians."

I felt my feet had been swept from under me. Arlin braced herself and looked distrustfully at the man whose life she had saved. "I surely am ignorant, Sanaur of Rezhmia, if there have been raids against your cities. But I know they were not accomplished by King Rudof. Look elsewhere."

He cocked his birdlike head and let the uniform drop. "Reingish, you mean? That was my original thought, Nazhuret—it is so odd, calling you by your uncle's name. I suspected that young adder myself. But not even Reingish could commandeer an entire regiment of soldiers of Velonyan body and Velonyan face, mount the officers on square Velonyan horses and supply them with modern Velonyan army weapons, and set them against towns that were destined to be his own.

"And also it made no proper sense, for Reingish could have had me killed a hundred times with less effort than this, and set about inflaming the public without interference. That would not be so difficult, at least in the City, for the folk within the walls are always more belligerent than the peasants—perhaps because they do not do their own butchering and have no experience with the reality of blood."

His rheumy eyes glanced from one death-garment to another as he spoke, and I believed that this old man had a strong sense of the reality of blood.

"Possibly it was not Reingish, then," I said, "but I am convinced it was not Rudof of Velonya either. I know the man and he does not send troops against civilians. Under no circumstances."

He got up slowly. The last two days had been no easier on the emperor's body than upon mine. Arlin offered her arm and he took it. "Well, lad, that may be true. In fact, I will say it is likely true from what I hear of the King of Velonya. But it doesn't matter in the slightest, for the raiders are from the northland and it is the northland, not young Rudof, against which we have declared war."

"You have?" Tears stung my eyes to hear this, finally, although I don't know whether they were of grief, despair, or simple frustration.

"Yes. And we move out the day after tomorrow. It must be quick." He looked at me and then away again. "You see, Nazhuret, if Rudof cannot control his barbarian rowdies, then Rezhmia must do so for him. And I. . . I cannot wait for the men Reingish has suborned to unite in a new pattern against me. Also, there is always a period of danger after the death of an heir declared. Two of my grandchildren were assassinated last night: one in this very building—don't sympathize, I scarcely knew the one and despised the other—but I have a need to direct Rezhmian energies elsewhere, and to be elsewhere myself."

"The emperor is going to ride with his army?" asked Arlin, losing her inscrutability for a moment and staring at the old man who looked—as old people will—breakable as a newborn bird.

He smiled grimly. "Not ride, exactly. Bounce around in a dark and stuffy carriage surrounded by nursemaids," he answered her. Then his smile died.

"The interview is over," he said. "Go home now."

I don't know if I blinked or merely dropped my jaw. "But Sanaur of Rezhmia, I have not. . . I think there can be another solution. We can save so many lives. . ."

"Can we, lad? I think not, and I have lived with the responsibility for over twice your years. I think what we are going to do is to lose a generation of

young men to the flies. And so will Velonya. That is how history and the
nature of man have arranged it. War is not always avoidable or best avoided."

The emperor grew more forceful and more bitter as he spoke. His hollow
cheeks darkened. As I opened my mouth I realized I had no answer for him,
and that what he had said to me was almost what I had said to you, Powl, that
beautiful summer day.

"Though it is always evil," added the emperor. He waved his gnarled hand
at us as though shooing children out of doors.

"Go now, Nazhuret. Prince Nazhuret, although no heir to me. And Lady
Arlin—enemy though you are I create you also Princess of Rezhmia (in your
own right, as foolishly you are not married to the boy). Take good horses and
not the asses that bore you here. Ride out of the City as quickly as you might,
for you are in danger as enemy aliens, and in more danger as Rezhmians
standing so close to the throne. Get along. You are dismissed!"

So strong was this fragile man's power that we almost ran from the chamber. He called us back at the door.

"I have released my slave," he said, and his voice shook. "The last slave in
Rezhmia. If you would do me one last favor of many, please. . . please take
him home with you."

A servant woman closed the door in our faces.

I did not know whether we were being honored or simply made prisoner,
for a good dozen Rezhmian cavalry flanked us and followed behind as we
were led from the fortress and the outer city. Our saddlebags were filled with
fine linen and wool and that preserved food that Rezhmian cooks have made
an art for the eyes as well as the stomach. The horses upon which they had
mounted us were not our horses but the southland's best: tall creatures built as
lightly and strung as tightly as fiddles.

Repeatedly I told the officer in charge that these were not our horses, but
he might as well have been deaf.

Repeatedly Arlin cried to them, "Where is Dowln? The jeweler. The
sanaur said we are to take the jeweler. . . ," but for her the company was
equally deaf. Her ferocity in this matter surprised me; after an hour of frustration she stopped her prancing horse sideways on the sunken road and
blocked the passage entirely.

"Dowln the prophet, the jeweler," she shouted at the milling cavalrymen,
and she dared to draw her saber. "By the emperor's command you will deliver
him to us!"

No City man could claim not to understand my lady's accent, nor her
intent either. The troopers rolled their eyes and whispered. The lieutenant
who led them grew darker and angrier by the moment, and I remembered

that Arlin had pulled such a stunt only a few days ago on the streets of Rezhmia's outer city, to allow me room to stare at a sign. I wondered if any of these men might be the same as the soldiers she had so insulted the last time, and I doubted she could get away with such effrontery twice. The officer gestured curtly and one rider pressed forward. I loosened the ancient blade from where it was strapped to the saddle pommel. I could put my hand to this less obviously than I could reach behind me for the dowhee. My nervous horse I backed beside hers, so that she would not be side-on to attack.

Before bad went to worse we heard someone approach at a trot.

The rider was wrapped in a cloak of white linen. He rode no horse at all, but a white mule, very tall and fine-boned. He let the hood of the cloak slip back from his shining hair and gestured to the beasts he led behind him.

"I suspect you value these creatures," said Dowln. "And I suspect strongly that they would meet with no respect in the emperor's stables: especially on the eve of war."

I looked into the unimpressive face of my yellow horse, which stood six inches shorter at the withers than the one I now rode. Arlin's dull-black mare put her ears back to all of us in general, and a few of the cavalrymen giggled.

"I am late because they did not want to come with me," said Dowln. The white mule put its ears back at the Naiish horse, and the effect of that was more spectacular."

As though the laughter of the cavalrymen had broken a spell, our companions no longer felt obliged to keep silent. They began to joke with one another, and if we were the butt of the jokes, at least we were not at swords' end. We broke into a good trot and then a canter as we progressed along the main avenue to the west, and it seemed it was the responsibility of the pedestrians to get out of the way of our hooves. When we passed under the gallows sign for the inn King of the Dead, it was not I but Dowln of Velonya who stared and whitened and lost all impulse of motion. The horses behind slammed into the croup of his mule, which squealed and kicked.

The little horses were no longer rough; they had been clipped closely of their new winter coat, with only their leggings and the part of the back that is covered by a saddle to remind me how bearlike they had been. Still they sweated and blew to keep up with the long-legged racing beasts of Rezhmia.

"Those would travel better inside your saddlebags," said the lieutenant to me in great good humor. I did not understand the idiom.

"He is saying," said Dowln, whose mule had no difficulty with the speed of our travel, "that your ponies are only worth slaughtering and salting away." The tall eunuch shot a worried, protective glance at me. "It would be a common opinion, here. That's why I stole them."

Arlin is the horse lover, but my own anger at this suggestion surprised me. I held tightly to Daffodil's lead rope and it occurred to me that half the old brute's problem was that he had to run with his head tilted unnaturally high into the air. On impulse I drew my dowhee and sliced through the rope. My short, inelegant yellow horse—built so much like me—tucked his head and ran much better.

"You don't know this horse," I said to the lieutenant, ". . . what he has done and where he has been with me."

The lieutenant laughed. "No, I only know where he *should* go."

I had expected some outburst from Arlin, but maybe she agreed with the Rezhmian. Maybe she had never liked these rough creatures with their short legs, their beards, and their strong opinions.

I felt a certain despondency as we careered through town, scattering local merchants and local dogs. First there was Arlin's affection for the angelic Dowln, whereas before she had liked no one on earth besides you and me, Powl. I am not even sure about you. Now there was this lack of concern for the honor of the ponies that had carried us through earthquake and war.

Though Arlin had said nothing, she had watched me cut the horse's rope, and smiled to see the beast heeling free like a dog. She did the same, and when I next glanced to my left, Arlin was standing in the saddle and her fancy horse was rolling its eyes and emitting stiff little bucks.

"Observe, fellow," she called out—to the lieutenant, I presume. Her mount began to shoulder in as the tension on the reins was removed, and it shook its fine head and bucked again. I pressed my own horse against it, so that it was locked between the black pony and me. I saw Arlin start to count, bouncing on her toes, but we were approaching a turn in the road, and after that we were scrambling around a dung cart, so Arlin sank down and grabbed the pommel until the way was clear again.

"One, two, three, sweetly girl, sweetly," she called, and with the word "sweetly" she was in the air and then balancing on her toes upon the black mare's broad hips. She patted her in front of the withers and slipped forward. Next she untied the mare's headstall and handed it over the back of the empty saddle to me. While all this happened, the Naiish mare kept her ill-tempered ears pinned and her lower lip pouted, but it was strictly a statement of opinion on the horse's part: no excitement, no panic at all.

Arlin got a cheer from the cavalrymen, but her tall horse, so suddenly left without a rider, reared and balked and struck my own horse with one shod forehoof. The free horse backed through the lot of us, with the booms of huge horse lungs being slammed and the curses of riders feeling their legs pinched. It escaped backward and plunged into the market, where it scattered dried fish and oranges. One of the riders swung back to retrieve the horse.

Arlin was ahead of us, slipping the saddleless black mare between the frightened passersby.

"It is a good Naiish horse," I said to the lieutenant. "It follows the rider's weight and small signals from the legs." I tried to sound mild and uninvolved while I was surging with an unholy fire of victory. Petty, petty victory.

Arlin had her arms crossed. She spun the horse around and brought her toward us, dancing flying lead-changes over the cobblestones.

"I think," said Arlin to the lieutenant, "that they are of slightly more use carrying the saddlebags than being carried in them." As the trooper returned leading the other horse, which pranced and pulled and rolled foolish eyes, Arlin added demurely, "Oh, have you brought me back the *extra* one? That was kind of you; I was wrong to let it get away."

I could not see the officer's face, but I had no fears he would order us slain for Arlin's stunt, and I did not care what the man himself thought of us. However, I turned in the saddle and saw Dowln, his face half-shrouded in the linen hood, and in his beautiful eyes was awe and adoration.

This fellow was in love with my lady, I realized, and she. . . she was at least attached to him. I felt my face go cold and white.

No woman had ever loved me but Arlin. I had performed the act with a few others, and they had seemed to enjoy my company, but not one had ever claimed to love me.

And Arlin had never loved anyone else.

She took a place in the first row of the company, between the humiliated lieutenant and Dowln. I let my horse's natural desire to follow push me back among the troopers, who were laughing and making gibes among themselves, happy as any stupid men at the start of a war.

The yellow horse beside me lifted his head and rested his heavy jowl upon my knee as we trotted out of the City. A few times he sighed.

Now that war was declared, it seemed the orderly militarization of Rezhmia fell apart. The soldiers in the streets were not going anywhere and the civilians shouted louder than ever. The city air was full of the smells of roasting meat and hot metal; I could hear the smiths hammering from all sides like the pulse in my abused head. I lagged, and only occasionally did I see Arlin at the head of the troops, her gray eyes shining as she shared her barbed wit with Dowln or the lieutenant.

Things seemed so very bad: war, natural devastation, poison, abandonment. . . I gave up on my own abilities and let my Rezhmian horse carry me on; it at least had spirit. When our escort stopped and turned before me, I was mildly surprised to find we had run out of city and were once again in the paradise of mountains, sea, and grapevines. There were as many men toiling in

143

the harvest as had been before war was declared, and they sweated and
strained in exactly the same fashion. The same people were selling the same
new wine out of the same great jugs we had bought from on the way to the
City, and the same flies buzzed in the fruity smell.

"Go whichever way you please," said the lieutenant to me. "Cross-country
or along the road. The road is much shorter, but I'd recommend the less traveled roads. Wearing the royal color does not make you an aristocrat or even
a Rezhmian. Not in the people's eyes."

Hearing this rudeness from the fellow who had been assigned to guard our
safety only deepened my despondency. If there was such contempt in an educated man of the emperor's guard, then war had been inevitable. I wondered
if he knew that my lady and I had each saved the 'naur's life. I wondered if that
knowledge would have improved matters.

Evidently he had not bothered to speak to Arlin at all, for she had pushed
her horse (she was on the tall one, again) through the crowd and between the
man and myself. "Dressing in a uniform and sitting a saddle," she said in a parody of the lieutenant's tone, "does not make one a patriot. Or a fighter. Or
even a human being."

He had his sword half out of its scabbard, and even his inferiors knew that
act was unwise. After a few seconds with his gaze locked into Arlin's, he chose
again and kicked his horse back toward the City. His company, without command, scrabbled after him, but two or three of the cavalrymen sneaked a
salute, passing us. Others grinned in a friendly manner. I decided then that
they knew about the 'naur.

"The lieutenant was Reingish's man," said Dowln as his mule trotted
energetically to keep up.

"Then what did the 'naur mean sending him to guard us?" I asked. "Does
one give the fox the job of feeding the chickens?"

He gave me a tight smile. "He was Reingish's man because he is ambitious
and practical. He could be trusted not to murder us now for the same reason.
And because his men are ambitious and practical, too."

Arlin circled back around the road, unsatisfied with my progress. "Is the
yellow horse slowing you down, Nazhuret? I'd like to get to more broken
country before we camp."

Dowln said, "I think you expect too much, my friend. It is surprising the
man can ride at all, after what was done to him. Generally a man drugged with
access root dies within the day."

Arlin laughed at him. "Not Zhurrie. Besides, sick or well, Nazhuret can be
traveling when I fall down with exhaustion, and all others gave up the day
before." Having said as much, she frisked her horse forward along the good

road, and my own elegant animal whinnied and followed. The yellow horse sighed a few more times.

Dowln stayed back with me, evidently worried about my health. His fine face, so like Arlin's, looked out from the linen hood and he waited for me to say something.

I did not. That was my small act of spite. I ignored the eunuch jeweler who was so worried I might be sick. Also, I said to myself, "I have two things you don't, fellow. Rich, tall, and handsome as you are, I have two things. . ."

I almost said it aloud, I am ashamed to admit, but I knew my Arlin too well to be confident of my superiority, for although she has all the warmth of a woman, she has also a very original taste, and appreciates what the rest of the world scorns. She appreciated me, after all. Perhaps Dowln had something of more value. Or two things of more value. I didn't know.

After a few minutes, Dowln let his mule catch up to her horse, and I was left alone to brood. It occurred to me that it had not yet been twenty-four hours since the priest had slipped me the drug. Perhaps I would still die.

That thought cheered me a little bit.

As it happened, I felt better by evening, though my eyes had developed a difficulty in focusing, which made the suburbs of Rezhmia City into a soft green blur. I had to wonder whether this effect had been with me all the hours since my poisoning, and I had been too miserable to notice. If so, that meant I had fought the assault on the emperor at a great disadvantage. Now I did not care that I could not see Arlin and Dowln trotting before me on her black beast and his white. They were much of a height, those two, but she sat taller because her horse outreached his mule. Their backs, also, looked much alike. Velonyan. Not like me.

My own horse stumbled over something, and that something stumbled out from among his hooves, shining white in the fading daylight. I stretched up my eyelids and wished for a good lens, but then my vision—although not my head-cleared enough for me to see that pale gray face, round as the stained gray moon and grinning at me. It was a dog I saw—a long, furry dog, or else a wolf, for I had never known which the beast was—and I had met it originally the night I killed a man for the first time. It did not belong here, on the sweet sea coast of Rezhmia, amid a buzzing of bees where the peoples' hands were stained only with fresh wine. It had too much hair for the climate, if nothing else.

I straightened, not wanting to look anymore, but the question of the dog would not leave me, so I thought I would ask the soldiers riding behind if they had seen it. Then it occurred to me that the soldiers had spun around and frolicked off a number of hours ago. I had to wonder who was making all that noise of hooves behind me, so I turned.

There were three of them, dressed in coats that I thought were like the undyed linen of Dowln's cloak. Their horses were dim. I opened my mouth and engaged my voice box to speak, but there was something too odd about the middle man. It needed all my will to make my eyes center on the widening red stripe down his middle and at last I saw it was a huge rift in his middle, out of which his inner organs spilled out: the white, sausagy intestines, only slightly broken, the somber, slick surface of the liver, and the improbable green gallbladder. His skin was dry and gray, exactly the color of my dog's pelt. He looked like an old pomegranate that someone had opened on the chance it was still good. In my horror I turned from him to ask his neighbor what the man meant by riding out in this condition, but that fellow had no attention to spare for me; his hands could not handle the reins properly because he had no hand and no blood in him either. Still, he offered me no insult. He didn't look at me at all, nor did the one broken open, and so, instead of looking at the third rider, I simply fell off my horse.

I was in a camp off the road, with a nice little fire and a tent over me that I had not known we possessed. Arlin had my head in her hands and was forcing a cup between my lips. It contained the miserable substance Dowln had given me in the morning, but since it was Arlin giving it, I drank the stuff without objection. "Did you see any of them?" I asked her. "Or the dog—the wolf. You saw the wolf in Grobebh?"

Her large gray eyes did a subtle dance, following her thoughts. "Yes, Zhurrie. I know about the wo—your dog. I didn't see him. I didn't see any of them. I never do."

The taste of the draught was terrible. I turned my head away, in case my stomach might reject it with her so close. I heard Dowln kneel beside us, and he asked, "What did he see, out there?"

Arlin's voice was reserved. "Nazhuret is. . . followed by ghosts, sometimes."

Dowln gave an intent sort of sigh. Like that of a scientist in the midst of observation. "Yes, of course. He is the king of ghosts, isn't he?"

When he said that, they were all before my eyes again, and I thought I would certainly vomit against the wall of the tent. My body was so stiff it felt like wood, but Arlin put her cheek against mine and her arm over me.

"Oh, go fuck yourself. If you can," said my beautiful lady to Dowln with such vibrating anger in my behalf that all my unhappiness was carried away. I squirmed around, and she wiped dirt and tears from my face with her dirty velvet sleeve. "I don't know myself, Arlin," I said to her, "why these things come to me. Dead men and wolves. Death itself. And my parents, whom I did not remember, with a baby that pissed on my shirt. Remember that stain? It was real, wasn't it? Or was it?

"I don't know anymore what I am. These damned signs and portents. Or am I just crazy? It would be a relief to know I was crazy, my love. You could tell me what to do and I would follow behind and do it. I look so much like a born servant. It would be a relief."

She pushed the hair from my face and whispered, "I'm sorry, Zhurrie, but you can't have that. Freedom took you first." She was crying. "You are the servant of your own freedom, and I can't save you. But I can tell you," and she turned my face around to meet her gaze, ". . . that you are Nazhuret, who ran away from Sordaling military school and missed his graduation, who has kin on both sides of the border, and who grinds lenses for his living. A very poor living, too." She kissed me and added, "And you are my great, high passion and unlawful lover."

The draught must have been working now, for I felt myself sinking into honey: bright, glowing honey. "Then I can endure anything," I said. I think I said, "If you still love me."

Her pale face hung over me softly as an owl's flight. "Love you, Zhurrie? But it is you who are angry at me, as I remember."

I could not deny this; I was too confused. "Why am I angry?" I asked, for information's sake.

Her face withdrew slightly. I could see she was thinking. "Because I raised my sword against you—or Reingish impersonating you—in defense of the Rezhmian emperor."

This was very difficult, for a man in my condition. The honey made it easier, though. "But you knew all the time it was Reingish. The eyes. . ."

"I couldn't see the color of the eyes at that distance," she said. "And he had gotten everything else fairly well. He moved differently, but I had. . . reason to believe you were not yourself. I didn't know, Zhurrie. I didn't know if it was you."

Now I understood, or understood at least as much as the honey allowed. "So, you would have killed me to defend the Sanaur of Rezhmia?"

I heard Arlin laugh, and felt the warm air in my ear. "I went to kill, all right, Zhurrie. But I knew that, if it were you, I would not succeed."

I was astounded at this reasoning, and after giving it thought, I strove to tell Arlin that she was wrong, for you, Powl, our teacher, once had to beat me in danger of my life, merely to get me to punch you solidly on the jaw. Even if I thought all good depended upon it, I would go into a fight against Arlin a handcuffed man. But I said nothing of this. I said nothing at all, for the drug and the honey had buried me in its gold.

It was Dowln who decided that we should strike across country next day. I had to press my horse's shoulder in front of his mule, to get a glimpse of his face above the linen cowl. "Have you much experience at traveling cross-country?" I asked him. "At traveling light?"

147

At traveling at all, is what I meant.

For a moment he considered whether to be offended; he tautened his face and lifted one eyebrow toward his high hairline. The expression was so much Arlin's I must have stared.

"I have ridden north as far as Teykattel Port in Sekret, after amber," he answered me. "And I learned some of my smithery in the Felonk Outer Islands. Also, of course, I go west to Warvala every few years, to buy jade and opals. I know roads that go more directly to Velonya than does the sea road."

Sekret? The far islands? I let this new image of Dowln the traveler ripen in my mind. "I lived in Warvala for six months," I said at last. "But I did not frequent the sort of crowd that buys jade and opals."

The fair face stared out of the curve of its hood, like a moon not yet full. He looked at me with blue eyes that grew flat and blank as he spoke. "But they traded something, didn't they? I see you at a table with four others. They are drinking wine, but there is more to it than that. You are talking in two languages and making them laugh, but there is more to it than that. I see you with a barrel above your head. I see you taking a knife from a drunken man. But there is more to it than that. . ."

I must have shuddered because Dowln's mule flinched, but he himself did not. "I was a barman at the Yellow Coach," I said. "And a translator, when that was needed. And a peacekeeper."

The mule's sudden motion had caused the flaxen hood to slip off the flaxen hair. Dowln's face looked as though he had never endured the sun, and around his neck was the intricate, solid ring of gold. It shocked me to see it.

We were climbing a hill: very rocky. As usual, Arlin led. I heard the clang of his mule's shoes against stone and I smelled sparks. "The 'naur freed you, Dowln. Or he told me he had. Whyfor the collar?"

He shrugged and did not look back at me. "When it was time to leave I could not find the key. I don't know where I last left it."

"The key to your collar was in your own care?"

"Of course," he replied in his stiff Velonyie, looking straight ahead. "One wouldn't care to take a bath wearing such a thing. . . And I was late enough, you grant me, with your ponies and their gear."

That bright little circlet slid and snarled on his shirt with the mule's bouncing trot. It was a heavy chain of complex linkage, and I could not take my eyes from it: symbol of a man as property.

"I have the tools to cut it off," I offered at last. "It would only take ten minutes."

He chuckled. "Longer than that, Nazhuret. This collar is hollow and lined with steel cable. I made it myself; I should know.

148

"At the moment, it's all I have. Besides, my prince, what matter?" At some signal of his, the mule pumped its lean hocks with more vigor and caught up to Arlin's black Rezhmian horse.

Her mount was a stallion (perhaps by some last irony of the sanaur's and perhaps by her own choice), and as I paid some attention to his mule I found it to be a she-beast. She wiggled her long, elegant ears at the stallion. Mine was a humble horse and needed some encouragement to catch up with the other two.

Why would a man forge his own collar, and anchor it on steel?

We rode fast: very fast. I have ridden that smartly once or twice in my life, on a horse of the king's stable, carrying a message of the king's household from Vestinglon to Inpres. Still, never had I pushed for so many hours altogether, not even when Arlin's mare carried the two of us together from Rudofsdorf and my teacher's life seemed to hang in the balance.

I felt a great compassion for the Naiish ponies. Like them, I am short-legged and sturdy: not made to travel far and fast. By now they were both released, for they carried no gear we were too afraid to lose. Arlin and I possessed no such gear. At times I thought we had lost one or the other, because Arlin's black and my old Daffodil would disappear for a half hour at a time. We were among the vineyards, now, and I thought that such creatures as our ponies might be easily snagged by the locals. Perhaps they would be better off stolen, unless stolen for the stewpot.

Each time I began to give up on one of them, however, it appeared again. Daffodil was no longer a horse of unusual color. He was a gray: black sweat and white froth intermingled, lit by gold where one or two hairs stuck out from the rest and dried. His breath made the booming sound of a forge fire, when the bellows are at work, but he stayed with us. Horses fear being left behind. I could feel the heart of the Rezhmian horse banging between my shinbones, and he was so slick and shrunken by sweat the saddle could be kept on only by my own balance.

At last, near twilight, we were made to slow by the increasing traffic. "Tabyuch," called Dowln over his shoulder. "It's a wine center: very popular among visitors in autumn. We may find some mobilization here, but there's no way to go around."

We found some mobilization; we found the little city's streets solid with the dried-blood-color uniform of Rezhmian infantry. We could not turn corners on horseback without shoving some poor recruit off his feet and perhaps under the feet of the horses. The mass of the recruits (or more likely conscriptees) were new to the uniform, and behaved as random clogs in the flow of traffic. Some of the men without uniform were also obviously in the army. If there were any tourists there for the harvest, they were not enjoying themselves.

We shouted and bellowed to one another. I remember thinking it odd that the smallest person in our company—myself—should have by far the deepest voice. Night fell long before we found a place to rest, and the horses' coats were stiff with dried foam; I pitied them and us as well, though my head was much better today and I had not succeeded in dying. There was an overcast, with a red tint to it from the dust still hanging in the air and once, as we approached one more inn that would have no space, a heavy tremor rang the earth beneath us. The horses were too tired to spook, but I felt the large heart of the beast jolt with my own.

Arlin had been leading, as she had all day, and she was using her gift of invective to win us a slow way through the streets. Her voice, always used at the bottom of her register, began to fail her, and as it grew darker the black shape on the black stallion grew invisible to the milling men who were at least as confused and weary as we.

"Let me go first," shouted Dowln, pressing his mule against her. "I'm all in white and so is this thing I'm riding. They will see me."

Arlin gave back gratefully, and our march immediately doubled its time. An open swath appeared behind Dowln's mule, into which I urged my own horse, closely followed by Daffodil, who was taut with dehydration, glassy-eyed, and seemed to have put his chin upon my knee for the night. Rezhmian soldiers and the burghers of Tabyuch were darting smartly out of our way with glances of immense respect, and I saw to my amazement that the eunuch slave had a whip in his hand, a small ivory and leather whip, with which he lay at the populace left and right in a most practiced manner over the head of his mule, which seemed to approve.

"How can you do that?" I asked him, before thinking whether it was politic. He misunderstood my question entirely. "It's not so difficult. The mule has been trained to lay its ears flat along its neck when the whip comes out. It isn't startled."

Even in my exhaustion I was fascinated and repelled that a man who had been (in Velonyan eyes) so humiliated by life should feel it justifiable to flog innocent citizens on the road. I remembered his insistence upon speaking his birth tongue with us, and his lack of proficiency in it.

"If you think this trip is taking you to your real home," I muttered aloud, "you have a surprise coming." Fortunately he did not hear me, or never mentioned it.

Still, we went very fast once Dowln took the lead, and came to a street upon a gardened hill where the quality of the buildings caused me to feel I

150

would be asked my business at any moment. Here there were fewer milling infantry, but quite a few cavalry, troop and officer alike. "There will be good stables, here. Too bad, but the horses will need some money spent if we are to ride this hard again tomorrow." I glanced at Arlin, for in this remark Dowln had hit her harder than any slight against her family. And she did stare, and her face did look moon-pale in the light from a tavern window. I thought (so assured was I of my lady's regard) that I might offer Dowln a word that evening, concerning Arlin's feeling about her horses. I also thought I might be too tired to spare the time, and as I considered the question, a small company of horsemen in the emperor's green filed down the street in great discipline, leading a half-dozen prisoners.

Some of these were clearly Velonyans. One looked remarkably like a native of the Felonk Islands, complete with dowhee sheath on his belt, but most of them I could not see. One prisoner, though, was on ponyback, and led another Naiish-style pony behind her. I knew those dirty skirts, and I knew the intricate headdress, and I knew very well those eyes, half brown and half silvered with age.

He knew me also, and he looked at me with great interest and surprise but no pleading for favors. I kicked my horse up with Dowln's mule. "I must get him out of there. That. . . that woman. I must get him out of there."

Dowln glanced sideways at me, eyes widened in alarm. He thought I was raving, and it was a reasonable conclusion. But as I pushed my horse forward, he came with me and was in front of me when we stopped the cavalry.

To my relief, he did not use his whip against the officer. Instead he shouted, "I am the emperor's slave, Dowln the prophet, and maker of Adiamant, the minsanaur's ring. This old woman of the Red Whips: we must have her from you." As he spoke he pulled from his head the linen cloak, and the symbol of his powerlessness caught the light of a close street-lamp.

The company came to a difficult stop, and some of the prisoners on foot suffered for it. The lieutenant stared perplexed, or perhaps stunned, while the lesser horsemen shifted in their saddles and did not fear to murmur among themselves. I saw a hand reach for his sword's hilt.

Dowln seemed not only oblivious to, but above all their doubts, and he showed no fear. I thought it better to have a sword between him and danger, however, and besides—I had led us to this contention. I pushed the mule behind my own horse.

The company gave back, and the lieutenant made a deep salute. I saw a dozen pair of eyes glistening at me under lamplight, and after a moment I noticed that their eyes were on my ring—which was certainly not named Adiamant—and that its own starburst was shining as the full moon shines through a rent in curtains.

At a snap of the officer's fingers, the ponies were led out, and I looked directly at Ehpen, the Naiish magician, once more in his woman's garb. He seemed calm as always, and reasonably entertained by the way things were going.

"You've changed again," he said to me.

I had no energy to ask him in what way. I was tired, I had been drugged, I was dressed in foreign silk: so what? "I thought you were going to winter in the City," I said. "By the direction you are now going, you must have headed away at great speed when we left you."

He snorted. "There is no benefit in a broken city," he said. "There is no benefit to a stranger in a war."

I looked from him to the cavalrymen of Rezhmia surrounding us: men or boys not much larger than I and years younger. "Is there benefit to an old friend in a war? To a family?"

Perfectly calm in his captivity, surrounded by the sabers of his enemy, he shook his belled headdress and answered, "I leave that to you to decide, Nazhuret, for this war is yours. It is both sides of your blood."

White eyes glinted in the darkness as they who thought me Reingish heard me titled "King of the Dead." The old magician in his female role folded his hands together over the pony's saddle.

I remembered one Red Whip rider who had withstood the persuasions of our military to defend a traitor Velonyan who had only paid for his services. That Naiish died unbroken, and he was only a simple rider.

This was Ehpen, the magician of the plains eagle horde. He would enter the fortress and not return, unless we could intervene. I found the lieutenant and looked him sternly between the eyes. "The prophecy requires hi. . . requires this one."

They did not think of refusing. My old magician was pushed out to us like lint from a bellows, with his ponies and all.

"What prophecy is this?" whispered Dowln into my ear. In Velonyie.

"Surely you must have some sort of prophecy with this old woman in it," I answered in the same tongue.

Didactically he said, "I deal in dreams, not prophecies. And I have had no dreams about an old woman with bells on."

As the magician left the sorry group of captives, all eyes followed him: some sad, some resentful, and one man purely despairing. In indecision I entered the belly of the wolf and I heard myself shouting, "No! No! I know it. These must be scattered! Even here on the street, they must disappear. Go! Flee lest the prophecy overtake you all!"

In a riot of feeling they scattered, and I drove my weary horse into the center of the troop with no great care for the cavalrymen surrounding me. My

arrogance overcame them, as had that of Dowln, but his was natural and mine
the result of ridiculous inspiration.

All the prisoners were gone, and though one or two of the troopers had
watched them go, none had tried to take them back. The magician was gone,
too, into nowhere with both his ponies. "You lied," whispered Dowln, sounding quite hurt.

My antic mood had not left me, and his words stung me into further
baroque action. To those among the cavalrymen still close enough to hear, I
called, "You obey me because you think me to be Minsanaur Reingish. You are
wrong. Reingish is no longer with us, nor is the ring Adiamant." I held out my
hand showing the black ring and its star of blazing silver. "This is not it. 'I
FIND MY LIGHT IN DARKNESS,'" I read to them and then I pulled off my
kerchief to expose my sun-whitened hair. "I am not Reingish but Nazhuret."

They fled. All the troop horses plunged away, knocking pedestrians right
and left. Some screamed. Even the lieutenant was gone from view, and the
intersection was much quieter.

The mule's picky little steps caught up with my horse again. "It was your
prophecy, then, that made you do this thing? Not mine but one of your own."

I glanced back in surprise. It seemed my absurd babble had convinced him,
and I wondered at the quality of his own visions, if he could be so gullible.
But he had seen me in his dreams, and he had seen Arlin. "I had no prophecy,
Dowln. As you first said, I lied."

He trotted behind me dubiously. "But the next part. About who you are.
That was no lie."

Arlin, who had been flanking the cavalry troop (in case of difficulties), now
pressed up with us. "No, it was all true, but Zhurrie made the most of it. He
has a gift for rhodomontade, when he needs it." She spoke smugly as any wife
over her husband's claims to fame, and I glowed complacently as any husband.

Dowln was not done with it. "But what you said—and my ring on your finger, shining in the night. I did have that vision. Of you as you were just now.
That's why I made the ring. It must be important."

I hated this. "Sink your visions on an anchor," I said, and the subject
was dropped.

The inn he found for us was very nice. The dinner almost made me weep.
After eating, we all slept like the dead, and I was king among them.

It began to rain in the middle of the night, or so I gathered next morning from the soggy appearance of the street outside. Our inn room, too, had
a soggy feel to it, as did my knees, that had spent too many hours hugging
a horse.

Dowln was awake first and I let him have first cry upon service. He bathed in front of the tile stove, with a Rezhmian disregard for modesty. I remember that naked he did not look so much like a lean woman: so much like Arlin. His gold collar stole the first light in the room, and when he lifted it up from his collarbones, I saw it had left a ring of scarring around his neck.

I wondered what we were to do with him.

"Where will you go, in Velonya?" I asked him, using the mumbling voice that usually will not wake my lady. "Have you family somewhere?"

He dried his face in a towel before answering, and I thought perhaps he was weeping, but when he looked at me he seemed cool enough. "If I had, Nazhuret, I would go anywhere but to them. What soldier of Old Vesting would welcome the return of a son like me?"

"A soldier like me," was my answer, and I meant it, though I distrusted his dreaming-gift. He did not reply to that, but he said instead, "I am charged with seeing you home to Velonya. After that is done I will have no further interest in the place."

It was in my mind to ask him how this attitude meshed with his insistence upon talking in his parents' language, and how he had introduced himself to me so forcefully as "another snowman," but the other surprise he had just offered buried that question. "You are charged with seeing *us* home?" It was Arlin speaking, her voice growly with sleep. She was sitting up in bed, her hair in her face. "I remember being told it was we who were supposed to take you north."

The damp towel sagged and slipped down his body, catching in the chain-work of the collar on its way. As Dowln stared, I heard the rain against the window, cold but peaceful in sound. Out of the corner of my eye I noticed that the plaster under the window was water-stained. On impulse I touched it with my finger and left a mark.

Dowln sat down at the foot of the bed. ". . . to take me north?" His eyes went from confusion to anger to dreary amusement. "By the sanaur, I suppose?"

I answered him, and he sat there unblinking, looking through me. Dowln was hardly older than I was. Amid his dreams, treasures, and prophecies it was easy for me to forget that fact, but now in this uncertainty, and in the uncertain light, he looked no more than a boy.

"Well. That is certainly like old Mynauzet." He continued to stare past me—at the rain-clouded window, I suppose. "Which do you think is true? Did he expect you to protect us, or us to protect you?" I asked him, mostly to smooth over the betrayal I felt in sympathy with his.

"It's probably both," Arlin said, scratching her black head with both hands.

Dowln gave a little smile, taut and chilly. "Knowing the sanaur as I do, my friends, I would bet money that he had a third idea in mind, that he shared with none of us." His expression grew even sharper and his eyes came into

154

focus as he added, "Perhaps he has filled me with false information, so that if you take me to your king he will be led astray."

"I doubt you would tell anything to damage Rezhmia or the emperor," I said to him. With his grin unchanged, he answered, "I don't imagine myself immune to strong persuasion. Few men are."

This idea did more than surprise me; I was angry. "You don't know our king either, fellow. He would never harm an envoy."

Now the grin changed. It became less painful, but more malicious. "Can King Rudof afford that kind of gallantry, Nazhuret? When he might save the lives of hundreds of his own men, or even the women and children?"

"It doesn't work that way," I stated, but I have to admit that I was thinking of the single survivor of the Naiish raid, five years ago, and how his cries shocked the camp.

Arlin cleared her throat. "It doesn't matter, Dowln. We aren't taking you to the king, but to our teacher. If we can find him. And you may believe that he is one of the few you mention, who are immune to strong persuasion. Or any other kind."

He glanced from one of us to the other. "What sort of teacher is this? Of sciences?"

I answered readily, "Of sciences and more. He. . . he made both of us what we are."

Dowln's blue eyes, lit from the side by gray window light, fixed on mine and I saw the black pupils expand to fill the eyes and then diminish again. "Him. Yes, him."

He got up from the bed and pressed his face against the beading glass. It was cold, and he was still naked, as white as marble. "Yes, I will see him before it's over," he said, and he picked up the clothes he was going to wear and turned his back to us.

I glanced at Arlin, to see what she had made of all this, but she was sitting upright in bed, as naked as Dowln, her gray eyes black, her face intent, and her mind in the belly of the wolf.

The rain was daunting, but to remain in the town was dangerous, especially after my masquerade of the previous evening. There came a number of small tremors while I washed, and when the servant came with our breakfast tray, he was skidding his hip against one wall to prevent toppling over in the next disturbance. He was a boy—too young to be snatched by the mobilization, I thought—and by the set of his face I knew he had not grown any more accustomed to the earthquakes than I had.

On the tray was a beautiful assortment of late green grapes and early red apples and oranges and chestnuts. And pastries of three or four kinds. It was

the most abundant moment of the year in one of the most generous cli-
mates, and this was the traditional harvest breakfast of the well-off who visited the vineyards, where Rezhmian soil met the equable winds off the Old
Sea. Such an unexpected luxury for people in our situation. We had come
to the palace and gone from it, and had eaten only leftovers and poison.
Now here, in the gray and the driving rain and between long rides, we got
the good food.

"It won't happen again," said the boy, putting his work of culinary art upon
a table and spreading out plates and glassware.

"We won't eat like this again?" I asked earnestly. So many people had
engaged in dreams and prophecies around me that I was quite prepared for
the busboy to reveal my future.

He showed a moment of adolescent contempt for my stupidity. (Here was
one who had not mistaken me for royalty.) "No, sir. I mean the earthquake.
Professor Aganish of the Institute says that these are the last vibrations of the
war-day quake, and that they will not hurt anything else."

"The war-day quake?"

He had finished his table-setting and left in the center of the table a
stained copper bowl of grape leaves, just touched by the colors of autumn. He
adjusted the decoration until it was perfectly symmetrical and said, "That's
what they're calling it." He took his gratuity without expression and left the
room, spinning his empty tray in the air.

Arlin and I were well into breakfast when Dowln strode in, his face white
and glistening with rain. "The ponies are gone," he announced. "Stolen during the night."

Behind him stood two men, one of them obviously a horse groom and the
other the hosteler himself. The latter wrung his hands and grimaced for us.

"Not the good horses, mind you, and not the mule, but the ponies."

Arlin and I got up without a word and followed them out. I remember that
my lady was carrying a bunch of pale grapes, which glowed in the morning
light like dewdrops or like fish eggs against her black sleeve.

The party of us had the satisfaction of staring all together into two empty
stalls sprinkled with horse manure. The hosteler made apologetic noises while
reminding us that he was not responsible for things stolen. Arlin sighed and
went to see whether our saddlery was intact. When she returned she told the
flurried hosteler and the outraged head groom that it was all right.

They stared, and so did I. "How—all right?" asked Dowln. "They weren't
much but you may need the money they would have brought at sale."

Arlin leaned negligently against the stall door, the very image of a cock-
sure young idler who knows more than you do. Her hands were playing with
a feather. I looked at the feather.

"It's all right," I said. "I know what happened. There won't be anything else missing." As the hour was getting on, I went back and finished my breakfast.

Dowln questioned us again and again as we climbed the vine-covered hills on wet and laboring animals, on our relations with the King of Velonya and with our teacher. Explaining was more difficult than was the climb.

"We are not soldiers," I told him, and when that wasn't enough to be accurate, I added, "We don't fight at anyone's command."

My wet silks clung as close to me as my skin, leaving me steaming and with the feeling of being naked on the back of the horse. Arlin's black, quilted velvet was soaked and heavy, but the individual drops were trapped in the nap, giving her jacket of crystal. Dowln's linen was scarcely wet; it shed the rain.

"Everyone fights at the emperor's command, in Rezhmia," he said. I heard Arlin cough, and I cursed the weather.

"Everyone fights at the king's command in Velonya, too," she answered him. "We don't, because it is inappropriate for people of our teaching. If the king doesn't like that, he can always have us hunted and hanged."

I thought she coughed again, but it was Dowln's laugh. "And would you permit yourself to be hunted and hanged if it were the king's wish?"

"Yes," I said, and "No," said Arlin, together.

By midday the rain had eased up, but the road had gotten worse, and the vines gave way to rock. By the position of the brightness in the clouds that marked the sun I guessed we were approaching the mountain ring and the city of Bologhini. We got off and led the beasts, except for Arlin, who went easier by driving her stallion from behind while holding to its tail. I tried this, but it was awkward for me, while Dowln expressed no desire to take such liberties with a mule.

We all suffered, pumping our stiff bodies over the stones, but I did not hear my lady cough again, and the horses, free of weight, fairly dragged us forward. The afternoon was downhill, which was lighter but more dangerous, and Arlin's stallion took a slip and came down on his chin, nearly smashing her left leg under him.

Again Dowln pressed for answers, shouting over the stones and through the rain. What arts did we study, who was our patron, and whence came the money to keep us? Arlin had relapsed into her usual silence, so it was up to me to bellow back, "Optics! We studied optics and astronomy. And languages. Arlin learned some medicine, when the teacher felt inclined, and of course we learned to fight. . ."

(The art you scorn most and teach best. We learned to fight.)

157

"But you said you won't fight," answered Dowln, controlling his mule with effort. The beast had decided it had had enough running and would now walk. Its decision was unalterable. (Dowln's voice had begun to give way that afternoon. Contrary to my ignorant expectations about the vocal power of eunuchs, he spoke neither shrill nor strongly, and I don't recall that he ever sang a note before me.)

"I said we won't fight on command," I answered. "And more than that: we would be useless in an army. Our skills are solitary. By impulse. Instinct, perhaps." I had never had to describe our eccentricity so openly. I felt everything I was saying to be wrong.

"What you appear to be, is temperamental. Art without discipline." Dowln shook a wet finger at me, and now it was Dowln who was coughing as he rode.

I lost my temper as I rarely do. "'Temperamental'? Perhaps. 'Without discipline,' I will not grant you! And as for our patron, our monies. . . Know this, you horse-faced Rezhmian dreamer: everyone and no one is our patron, and our monies are what we can beg! We are beggars, fellow! Beggars and simpletons who have just lost a baby and did not want to be sent sick and grieving into a catastrophe of the earth and of treachery in the country of the enemy!

". . . and that's what Rezhmia is to me, 'grandfather' or no. The enemy. I want to be home!" Then, to complete the circle, I began to cough.

Dowln looked closely at me, under his pouring hood, seeming completely unoffended by my outburst. Arlin trotted up and stared as well.

"Zhurrie! Are you really angry for once, or is this also a public entertainment, like being 'King of the Dead'?"

"I'm really angry," I said, and at that statement I was suddenly angry no longer, but only weary, cold, and very disheartened.

In the dome city, they told us that if we had been there a few days previously, we would not have had a chance at a room, for the city was mobilizing. (I wondered whether Velonya, too, was mobilizing. I hoped so, and I feared it.) One day later and we would have been out of all luck again, for they were expecting the Shoreland Infantry to pass through, going west. As it was, Bologhini was empty, and we had our choice of good rooms and fresh food.

Arlin ate without conversation and went to bed early. I was aching, but a long way from sleep, so I went to the bath house to breathe the steam. After a few minutes, Dowln joined me. He did not use his towel to dab sweat or to cushion his head on the bench, but instead he stuffed it under his golden collar, to keep the metal from burning his skin. In the dark he smelled differently from most men. I tried to analyze the difference, but the room was scented with orange oil and my nose is no scientific instrument.

"She says you dislike almost no one," he whispered after a quarter of an hour. "But I feel that you dislike me."

"Don't say 'she,'" I said, and I peered around as though the empty room might not be empty. "Not in public."

"All right. Arlin says. . ." He left the rest of his statement hanging in the air.

I was too tired to be embarrassed, and too tired to deny for kindness' sake. I took a steamy breath and told him: "You do things I can't like. You. . . twist the fabric of life with your 'visions.'"

"You don't believe in visions?"

"I don't approve of them. I think they are a path going nowhere. I think perhaps you started this war."

He laughed at me. "If I did, Na-Zhurett, then you did too, for you *are* my vision."

I ignored that. "And you whip people on the street. I find that terrible. You are arrogant with the poor and harsh with animals. And you love my wife."

"Now we have it," he said, and sighed, and rested his long Old Vesting chin on his knobby Old Vesting knee. "Though she says she is not your wife."

I did not feel ready for this exchange. I poured water over my head. "There has been no public avowal: so what? A legitimate child of mine would be in danger. . ."

"Evidently, any child of yours is in danger," he said. His eyes were pale in the firelight like a dry winter sky, and I could not be sure I saw sympathy in them.

"But you don't deny you love her, I notice."

He showed his teeth. Perhaps he was smiling. "No, I've always been a little bit in love with death."

"There!" I pounded the bench. "That's what I can't stand about you. Arlin is a person, with different sides to her, and a history all her own!"

Dowln pointed his finger at me. "Don't call Arlin 'her.' Not in public."

I almost got up and walked away from him, but I wanted him to understand. "Listen. I knew her at the age of thirteen years, when she escaped her house and played in the markets with me, riding the swan boats on the river and getting into trouble. That is what a person is. Not a mere vision, word, concept. Even if you were to title her 'perfection,' it would be a diminishment from what she is really: eyes and mind and twenty-eight years of life."

Dowln nodded, as though I had merely agreed with him. "I'm not ignorant, my friend. Nor stupid. But I also saw her with Reingish, and equally with all those things, she is death."

I flopped down on the bench, the towel over my eyes to shut him out, but he continued talking. "But you have no reason to be unhappy because I love your wife. She loves you. I have never seen such a passion or such a loyalty. To me she is kind, as she would be to a horse."

Now it was my turn to laugh. "There. You don't know that Arlin is never kind to men as she is to horses."

"Well, I am not a man, am I? Perhaps she has never met a eunuch before and thinks me some sort of beast. I don't object. And you should be gratified that I love her, like any man who owns a jewel that other men covet."

I waited before answering, and the peace of the hissing fire and the firelight dancing on the rows of benches quieted my mind. "I don't want to own anything other men may covet," I said to Dowln. "And don't say in front of Arlin that I own her."

Then I did get up, rinsed, and went to bed. It was our last bed of any kind for some days.

The mule was useless to us now. It had lost confidence, or at least its temper, and it would not move under saddle. Dowln was compelled to sell it to the innkeeper for much less than its worth and to buy a horse of less sensibility. We were further delayed because it had to be a horse that would fit a mule's saddle. Luckily the back of a racing animal is much like that of a mule. (Perhaps this is not random chance. I was missing the good sense and comradeship of Daffodil already.) Dowln was mounted, and possibly overmounted, on a bay gelding not long retired from the five-mile track outside Rezhmia City.

For a while we kept to the road by which we had first approached Bologhini, but when the teeth of the mountains opened onto the plain, Dowln pointed us south of the way we had first come, where no path lay over the dead grass and autumn-dry scrub, and said this was the straightest way to Warvala: safety for us and the beginning of the royal courier line. At first I thought this was another of his visions, but he showed me the compass in his saddle pommel and the map in his waxed bag.

Now the eunuch led, on his fresh and anticsome horse, and I was surprised by the coolness Dowln showed while being flung around in the saddle. A man who usually rode a white mule would not be expected to deal with such mischief, and in the continuing rain besides. Again I could see Dowln rising in Arlin's estimation, but as the hours of rain hit us and the horses slipped upon slick ground and floundered in sandy ground and the whimsical wind of the flatlands buffeted us north and then south, I lost interest in personal worry.

I had said to you that I wasn't sure war could be avoided or should be. Now I was appalled at such arrogance. Such ignorance. Now there was war, and I had failed to stop it.

What now? We were pounding along as though we had a real message to deliver: as though lives would be won or lost by our speed, but surely King Rudof had put spies and messengers in place long before he had sent us. Were we running to save the North, or to save ourselves from the army that followed?

"How far behind do you think they are?" I called to Dowln. As he leaned to listen to me, the dark day was lit by lightning and his horse objected and Dowln hit the ground.

I caught the beast, cursing it, and helped Dowln back on. Even doused in mud he looked fair, tall, and noble. Like Old Vesting. He made no fuss about the tumble, and did not waste temper on his horse.

"The Hainaure Cavalry? They won't make this sort of time. A week, easily. But the Shoreland Infantry is before us. They may have reached Zaquashlon by now."

This filled my cup of misery. I felt the wet cold through the woolen shirt I had put under the silks. Rain dripped off my hair as though from so many downspouts. Arlin turned her horse to us, not to check upon Dowln, as I had thought, but to ride a while with me.

I felt obliged to give the man his due. "He handles that asshole of a horse pretty well, doesn't he?" I asked her. "And he's not one to complain."

She sniffed, not necessarily from scorn. "He's all right. I wish he would trade with me; I'd appreciate a horse like that. But he has some sort of superstition about riding a stallion."

We were riding slowly enough to chat, because the bay had bruised himself a little with his stunt. "Maybe he feels people would mock him for it," I whispered to her.

"We wouldn't," she replied. "And if he wanted, he could make some really naughty jests about me on top of this boy." She slapped her stallion's beautiful, soggy neck. It made a sound like mud pies. "And yet he's so mannerly, Dowln could easily handle him."

"Could I?"

Arlin laughed and turned her face to me. Her hair was full of rain gutters, too. "Of course you could, Nazhuret. You can handle almost anything. You have let this blond changeling intimidate you. I don't know why."

I didn't inform her. I was considering a three-way switch, whereby Dowln could have his gelding and Arlin her racehorse, when she emptied my mind entirely by saying:

"I don't know. I might decide to fight in this war."

I was no longer cold. I was sweating. I asked her what she meant. "Powl would warn us not to try. That it would be useless for us, and fatal." I heard your voice, old teacher, across the years and through the rain, and I repeated your words to Arlin. ". . . Do not touch the police, the military, for you will wind up hanged."

"I believe it now, after the last five years. The more we try to help, the less we will be understood. No good to them and deadly to us."

Arlin trotted a few yards before answering. "I said 'I,' Nazhuret. Not 'we.' And about Powl. Do you think he himself isn't already planning battles with the king? Or with those old alliances of his, of which he spoke?"

"Old alliances? Oh, yes. And odd acquaintance. I remember, now. I thought he had meant us, by that," I answered her.

She shook her head forcefully. "No. He was talking about his own strength, apart from us. He has tools that we. . . that even *you* don't know about, Zhurrie. 'Powl' is only a part of the Earl of Daraln."

I had known that, but not dwelt upon it. "What Powl teaches us to be, we are, Arlin. Powl himself may well be something different. What's that to us? He is the carver, not the carving."

"We are not the same carving," she said very gently. "I'm sorry if hearing this upsets you. But hear me, my true knight. I will fight for Velonya."

"My true knight." Arlin called me by those awesome words rarely. Each time she did it was as though the sky opened to receive me. This time, however, it was only rain that went through the opening in the heavens, and my heart did not rise at all.

Another thing you said to me was regarding attachments, which you feel will tie my hands and warp my understanding. Of course you're right, but sometimes it is impossible to be completely right and sometimes it is merely foolish. If Arlin chose allegiance to rule over allegiance to our teaching, she would not go to war alone.

I rode lonely and full of dread, and I took the opportunity of the rain to weep a little. I included all the dead in the red city in my weeping, even my cousin Reingish.

The rocks gave way to the plains, and the horses under us showed their true usefulness. I believe we were three days crossing over what had taken us so long before.

The saddlebags grew lighter, for the animals ate with the sullen single-mindedness only a man who has worked with his body could appreciate. Dowln's replacement horse had become Arlin's, and it kept the most flesh, having had fewer days of hardship behind it. Mine, which had been hers, suffered most, and I became obsessively concerned with preserving the stallion.

Arlin told me I did nothing wrong as a rider, and as I learned most of what I know not from school or from you, Powl, but from her, I could only trust her word. But still the poor creature grew so thin the girth would not tighten, even when I stopped and made a little knot in each of the fibers in its weave. I had to hold the saddle on by balance, and between the natural sway and the lack of padding on the stallion's withers, he soon developed a bare patch and then a sore. I threw away the saddle and rode bare on that very bony back.

My own body also hurt, although I'm sure not as much as the horse's did. My fingers on the reins stiffened and locked and ached at night as they never before had. (But they have since, in wet weather, or at a change of season.) The insides of my thighs were a bloody bruise.

On the second night I saw a patch of blood, some dry and some shining, on Dowln's saddle, and for a moment I had the alarming thought that his castration scar had opened again, more than twenty years afterward. I then remembered he had had even less riding to harden him lately than had I.

I called his attention to the stain, and without expression he pulled a rag from his gear and began to dry the spot. The rag was dark already with dried blood. "What should I have done?" he asked me, his voice like his face. "Asked to stop?

"We are probably now even with the infantry marching along the sea road, and tomorrow, if the spirits allow, we will be in the town of Warvala. Then my duty to you will be over."

We camped only a few dozen yards from a stream, and Arlin was carrying water in a pot and spilling it on the horses' backs, so that the salt of their sweat would not irritate them. The beasts were hobbled instead of picketed. (They were not going anywhere by choice.)

"What is your duty?" she asked him. By her voice, she was the least tired among us: but Arlin had been born to ride.

Dowln sighed and settled onto the turf. I saw that his blousy Rezhmian riding breeches were stiff with blood, and even his linen cloak was speckled. "To see you to Velonya. Just that."

Arlin's eyes were bright and pale in the starlight. We had no fire. "How are you to do that, emperor's man? If we meet soldiers. . ."

"Then I am the emperor's man. An extension of his person, in fact. Do not dismiss the importance of that."

The shining eyes narrowed. "But do not presume too strongly upon it either. We are not at court."

Dowln laughed, showing white teeth. "I knew there was something different about this place," he said. "So that's it. It's not the court." Arlin laughed in reply.

I was flat on the ground with no desire to do anything at all, so I saw them both outlined against the blackening sky, and I remember the scene very well.

Arlin came and sat beside me, but she was not done with him. "What about the Naiish, sword-maker. What value will you be if the Naiish catch us again?"

Dowln's eyes went wide, and then distant. In the severe light of the stars, his blue eyes were the same as Arlin's gray ones. He sucked in his breath and held it.

"My value is, corpse-maker, that with me the Naiish will not catch you."

She did not take this appellation as an insult.

On the next day my stallion's heart began to go wrong. He would utter a "whuff" and I would feel the music of a crazed drummer between my knees. He did not slow down, but his head began to sag, and to sway left and right as though in a confused wind. I relayed all this to Arlin, but it was no surprise to her.

"He's too muscular," she answered, looking down on the horse's neck. One could see the muscles, as well as veins like hands of fingers reaching, clearly under both hide and hair. "He is good for a day or two at this speed, but for spanning countries you want a horse with light bones and neck. Not as impressive, but like my. . . like my. . ."

". . . like your Sabia," I finished for her, because now it was Arlin who was weeping: weeping as though she'd never yet wept for the mare at all. Or for the baby.

Because of Arlin's upset, and my concern for her, and Dowln's physical misery we didn't notice as we passed into a loose herd of buffalo. At last I looked up and saw one horned head, and then two, and neither of them offered to gore us or to flee. My speed-dazed brain decided they must be domestic. Ahead were many more of them.

"Arlin," I shouted. "Clear your mind! Naiish! Naiish!"

She looked up at me, her face wet and resentful, and then in two seconds her eyes had unfocused and then hardened again, and grief was behind her.

"Keep riding," screamed Dowln. "Keep riding and don't change your direction left or right!" It was as though he had a detailed map of time, as well as of the north marches of Rezhmia. I hated him for that, but I kept riding.

As we reached the center of the herd, the animals began running from us, lowing nasally as buffalo do. I remember one calf that had difficulty getting out of the way. It seemed that its horns, slopping this way and that, overbalanced it at speed. It fell three times while I watched. Wild buffalo must have more coordination, or there would be none left.

When we came out of the buffalo's dust, I saw the unthinkable before us. Two of the long brush-built houses that make seasonal homes for the Naiish people blocked our way. Between them was a Naiish well and only ten feet of passage, in which many of the people had gathered to see what was disturbing their cattle. This congestion of people was only eighty feet ahead.

"Ride, ride!" screamed Dowln, like an angry old woman, and he took out his damned little whip and beat our horses about the hocks with it.

I cursed the eunuch as I have rarely cursed anyone in my life, but the horse had the bit and we were passing the well.

By God's grace, I think we didn't kill anybody.

There was shouting behind us, and after a minute there was the sound of hooves, but we passed by a few tents and some frightened cattle and we were alone again on the rough grass.

The stallion's breath sounded like mad flutes.

After a half hour, Arlin pulled up her racehorse and my mount was not so crazy as to want to gallop alone.

"We've lost him," she said, and turned in her own steps. "Dowln."

I had not thought the pursuit that effective. I had not heard a single arrow, but my anger at Dowln, which had heated to conflagration, chilled instantly to be replaced by worry.

We found him in five minutes. His horse was trotting heavily, its chin an inch from the grass. "I fell off," he said, and he smiled through a split lip. His beardless cheek was a criss-cross of scratches. "But I had the sense to get away before doing it."

"Let me clean that face for you," I said, but he pushed right past me.

He shook his head. "I'm not stopping again." He kicked his horse into a canter.

We came into Warvala before nightfall, and to me it seemed an act of magic, so unexpected it was. I had not realized we'd crossed the border. The town looked very familiar, but also very busy. As I sat in the main street, recalling the way to the Yellow Coach (where I was sure we would find hospitality, if only in memory of my usefulness in times past), the stallion I rode died under me, and almost crushed me in falling.

I rolled to my feet and stared at the beast, still beautiful in its parched lifelessness. I remember that somehow in its agony it had gotten its tongue over the bit, and that seemed to me the most pitiful part of it all. Arlin reminded me I was still holding one of the reins.

A dead horse always draws a crowd, though everyone has seen a dead horse before. Out of this crowd marched a little man, about my height, portly and with his hair combed sideways over a bald dome. "Say, you can't leave that here," he said.

There is also always someone to say that in such instances, too. I have heard it said, in those words and in that tone, about the smashup of a laden lumber wagon. As though the teamster could put the huge logs over his back and march off. . .

I was in no mood to hear those words right now.

I was thinking I did not know how long this accident would slow us down. I was thinking we had probably only some hours' lead on the Rezhmian infantry moving up from the South. I was thinking that such a fine stallion had doubtless had a name, and that I had never learned it and now never would. I decided these thoughts were inappropriate to the moment, and so instead I looked at the short, swaggering citizen in front of me. He ran away.

I was almost used to streets full of soldiers, but it took me aback when I saw the sky blue and white of the Velonya Royals that surrounded us. I strode through them, and perhaps it was the expression upon my face or perhaps it was something Arlin did behind me, but the soldiers made way without incident.

The Yellow Coach was where I had left it. There were two prettily dressed guards at the door who were not intimidated by travel stains or temper, so I shouted for Alshie, the landlady. After a half minute of waiting, I turned to go around to the back, but the guards stepped away from the door and it was not Zaquashlan Alshie who faced me, but Rudof of Velonya.

"I stopped here upon your recommendation," he said, with the broad smile of a man who is amused, and expects to be better amused. "But I didn't really expect to meet you here." His green eyes took in our dirty, dry condition and more besides. His smile disappeared.

"You aren't here by accident, are you? You came looking for me. By the three faces, Zhurrie, your gifts are supernatural!"

I answered, "I've heard just about enough lately about the supernatural!" Arlin gave a nervous guffaw and I realized that once more I had begun a conversation by insulting the King of the North.

The king laughed also, and it seemed a strange sound for a leader at the edge of war. Men *do* laugh in such times, but it is a very special sort of humor, all barbs and edges.

I stood as closely to him as I could and whispered, "How much time do they give you—your spies? It can be only hours."

Rudof stared at us, his fresh face going white under its freckles, and then he dragged me off my feet and into the common room.

It was Arlin who told the king about the advance of the Shoreland Infantry in the South, and of the emperor's Hainaure Cavalry on the plains behind us. She spoke much better than I could have, seeing anger turn to desperation and then horror in Rudof's face. While the king was still dazed, she explained that the Rezhmian heir, Reingish of the Red Knife, had died in an attempt upon the 'naur's life, and that the old man himself was "leading" his cavalry.

King Rudof began to pace. As he moved he felt along the plastered, beer-stained wall beside him, like a blind man feeling his way. "I heard about an earthquake," he murmured and then said louder, ". . . a catastrophic earth-quake. That's all I heard. I was certain that meant we had all winter. In fact, I didn't expect an attack at all. They have no cause: nothing to stir the people. Especially if the young madman is dead."

So I told him about the roomful of sad weaponry the emperor had shown me, and about the raids.

Now the king glared at me and showed a bit of his temper. "There have been no raids. Do you think I would do that? And if I did, that I would lie to you about it?"

This was complex, for although I did not think he would send soldiers to burn peaceful villages, I thought it likely that if he *had* done some such thing, he would lie to me about it. I thought it best to leave the question alone.

"I think that something did happen, and that the emperor told me the truth as he understood it."

Rudof shifted his hands from the wall to the long benches, but he kept moving. "You think he told the truth. But he's your relative—family, isn't he? I wonder where your loyalty lies." He pointed an accusing finger, and I saw the hand was bloody with splinters from the old wood.

Arlin pushed between us. "That was unworthy," she said.

I was irritated too, and beginning to stiffen up. "I am related to the emperor. And to you. To about the same degree: second cousin or something like that."

The king straightened in pure surprise. It must never have occurred to him that my being the son of Norwess meant we shared a great-grandfather.

"And as for my loyalty, it is to my own conscience, as we have discussed before. My time, however, has been taken up by the King of Velonya in no easy manner for the last little while. And no matter what my descent or my motivation, thousands of armed Rezhmians will be at the border any hour now."

Rudof sank onto a bench and lay his damaged hand palm up on the table. "That's really a pity," he said distantly, with a groaning sigh. "Because I'm here in Warvala with no more than two hundred useful soldiers behind me." He began to pick at the splinters with his other hand, which was far too large and callused for the task. His fingers went slick with blood. "So what do I do, Nazhuret? Challenge the emperor to single combat?"

I sat down on the other side of the table, but I had nothing to say. Behind the bar stood the very Alshie whose attention I had been trying to draw, and though she met my eyes she was too intimidated by the company to gesture a hello.

Arlin remained standing, her face in the square of light thrown by the open door. "Powl," she said, and her face twisted sideways in a grin. "Where is the Earl of Inpres when we need him?"

The king looked up intently at her, and for a moment their faces were mirrors, different only in color. Two long, aquiline Velonyan faces. What had become of the third Velonyan face: the one worn on an other-than-male body, and concealing an other-than-Velonyan mind with other-than-human abilities? I had lost track of Dowln when the horse died under me. I feared he might come to trouble in Warvala. If he tried to use his little white whip on the Zaquash locals, for instance. . .

I stood. I almost went out the door to check on him, but this conversation was so crucial. Perhaps it was hopeless, but it was crucial nonetheless, and besides, even Zhurrie the Goblin is not fool enough to walk out on the king.

The king's grin had straightened itself, as though he'd found something wholeheartedly amusing amid the hopelessness. "Powl *is* here! I don't mean in body. I haven't seen him since I asked him to locate you, back in middle spring. I have only had letters since, and the last one over six weeks ago. No, I mean all that the earl has to give us is already here. I have spent over half my life receiving Powl's lectures on history, government, ethics, military strategy, and. . ." Unable to put a name to the rest of his education, he fell silent and shrugged, looking for understanding in our eyes.

"And you, card cheat. What do you have of him?"

(The king had called Arlin "card cheat" for the past five years, though I don't know that he believed she really was one. It was his way of dealing with a woman who was not a woman—whose eccentricities had saved his life. He had never played cards with Arlin, I am sure.)

She turned her face back to the shadow. "Have of him? Five languages. An experimental pharmacology. Geology, optics, and of course, systems of combat. Plus. . . the other."

Both of them looked to me now, but I was not ready to speak. I was thinking of the way you introduced me to my own death, and midwifed me back again, and how I had sat one day, shivering and alone in the autumn rains, under red maple leaves and pale oak, and seen each individual raindrop fall free into its own eternity. I was wondering why that sort of magic communicated so perfectly to me, while Dowln's bright and horrible dreams put me into a fury of pique.

"What have you learned, Nazhuret?" the king repeated. "Put your offering into the common pot."

I could think of nothing that the two hadn't said except that last thing which had reduced them both to silence. I said, "I learned that mirrors mean nothing. That we can only know ourselves by looking at the world—and especially the people—around us. And each of us performs that service for the world in return; we reflect it back to itself.

"That understanding is the root of all science. Of all philosophy. . ."

". . . of all sitting tied in a chair, facing a brick wall," added Arlin, out of our long common experience.

King Rudof leaned back and put his two long legs and his two large feet on the table. He scratched his carroty beard stubble with both hands and smiled the sweet smile that caused courtiers' hearts to jump. "With all that on our side, my friends, what chance has the emperor's cavalry?"

Of course, only minutes after that moment of understanding we were in a bitter quarrel, for two of your three faces, Powl, were of the opinion that the King of Velonya had to ride home at top speed, while the king himself believed that the Bill of Parliamentary Limits, signed after his coronation six years before, made the person of the king expendable in times of war and, therefore, free.

"This is not a chessboard," he said. Repeatedly. "It is not a game at all, and if it were, it would not end with the death of the king."

"Not death, sir," Arlin corrected him. "Capture. In chess it is capture of the king we wish to avoid. In war, also."

The couriers had gone out: those on horseback and those with wings. Had we been in civilized regions, many hours would have been saved by use of mirror-stations. I regretted sharply not having used my training in glass-grinding to help the Zaquash people install such code-towers. They would have been useful for other things than announcing invasion.

But large mirrors are expensive, and they need regular cleaning and constant protection. Codes need trained operators, and who would pay them?

I let Arlin and the king have at it, and I stood at the south end of Log Street and looked for dust rising from the horizon of the plains.

Once it had taken me three days to walk from here to the border. I wasn't hurrying, then. I had crossed this much territory between dawn and midday, on the stallion whose body had been hauled off the road while we were at the Coach. I could see the flat track the barrel of the horse had left, and two rounded ruts left by its near-side iron shoes.

No dust on the horizon. The earth was too wet for rising dust. I wondered how much of the earthquake had been felt up here. I wondered whether the infantry had crossed over the border, and whether some horseman or pigeon had been dispatched from the pink city at the same time we had been, to tell the North it was at war.

169

The horizon was not still any longer, but the movement was singular, and it evolved into the shape of one horse and his rider. The man had dropped the reins and was flapping his arms as though he wished to lift body, saddle, and horse together into the air. On second glance, he was beating his weary mount with sticks in both hands. The animal's neck was straight as a rod and carried no higher than its chest. I could almost hear its breath blowing.

This apparition came not toward the corduroyed Log Street, but east of it, and a scattering of soldiers on foot ran past the last warehouses to meet with it and stop it. The horse's hindlegs gave way for a moment, but it did not fall as my horse had. I wanted to know what the man had to tell, but no sound traveled to me, except for the characteristic loping footsteps of King Rudof.

"I have an heir, Nazhuret! Tell her—uh, him, that I have two children, and the oldest of them a son! I am infinitely more replaceable than—than this card-cheating Arlin, for instance!"

I wondered if at this moment I had told the king how Arlin had saved the life of the Sanaur of Rezhmia, he might not have seen her as far more replaceable.

She was equally excited. "And ask him how old this heir is, who is expected to take the reins of power in case of his death?"

I did not "tell" Arlin, nor did I "ask" the king. We all knew that Eythof was six years old. A little skinny boy with brown eyes, red hair, and a stutter.

"Your Powl is regent," Rudof answered the question I hadn't spoken.

For a moment I was without speech, seeing my teacher, with his elliptical language and eccentric ways as the pilot at the helm of Velonya, and then I asked a very rude question. "How did you get the queen to agree to that? I don't believe she. . . that she approves of the man at all."

King Rudof blinked and hesitated. He decided not to get offended, but he was stiff in his reply: "There was no legal need for her approval."

No approval and no knowledge of the plan either, I'd bet. What a situation: a bomb with a long fuse! I swallowed my next question, which was to have been "How did you get Powl to agree to *that?*" and I pointed beyond them, to where an emissary from the group which had received the rider was stamping through the puddled alleyways toward us.

There were two men I recognized: one being the first minister of the last parliamentary government, whom I had heard was "head of the loyal opposition" in this one. The other man caused Arlin to freeze, then to slip into a position half in front of the king and half in front of me.

King Rudof thought he understood. "Don't let the colors prejudice you, my friends. This is Maleph Markins, and he is not much like his father."

170

Arlin answered calmly, her voice very different from the grate and growl of her argument. "We met young Leoue this summer, sir. Someone had been trying to kill us, you see."

"I heard you lost. . ." The king's green eyes shifted from her face to mine and he fell silent. So I knew you had told him about the baby. Until I saw the young duke in his bumblebee colors, I had almost forgotten that problem myself.

"It may be he. . . ," Arlin continued. "We never found out; this war got in the way."

Young Leoue's far vision was not the equal of Arlin's or mine, but his reaction, when he made us out beside the tall king, was at least as noticeable. He stopped so suddenly the excited soldier behind him slammed into his back. His mouth hung open.

The head of the loyal opposition scrambled up onto the road and to the king's side, completely out of breath and white-faced.

"Terrible news, sir! A vast cavalry is approaching us from the South; ten thousand Red Whip riders, only hours away."

The king put his hand upon the man's shoulder and smiled at him with real enjoyment. "You must believe me, sir! They're coming!" said the parliamentarian.

"But I don't," answered Rudof. "I don't think there *are* ten thousand Red Whip riders in existence, Minister Pel. I suggest what you see approaching is the army of Rezhmia, bound upon invasion."

The king got his little moment of satisfaction as he put a hand behind each of us and presented his source of news. It would be the last such moment in a long while, I feared.

The king wasn't leaving, though he sent a number of civilians flying northward, Minister Pel included. He said he felt that to flee the City of Warvala, leaving the citizenry to possible rapine, would be a wickedness that no political good would be able to erase.

I suggested that it was his own presence in the town which was bringing it into danger, and he agreed, but said a flight now would be too late to correct matters.

We encountered the messenger at the Yellow Coach. He turned out to be a Zaquashlan who had ridden out to take wild deer or buffalo on the plain, and come within sight of this nightmare encampment without any of them seeing him. He described it as being composed of a few thousand riders, and broken in two separate wings, which if they continued as they had been, would flank the city between them. He had seen no very splendid pavilion, such as one would expect around an eighty-year-old emperor, but he had seen at least two Naiish clan standards: the Boar of

Five Horns and the Old Horse. There had been singing, too, and the idiom was Naiish.

This was confusing. Men who glimpse an army and then run almost always overestimate number, and I could not imagine the emperor traveling amid only a "few thousand" troops.

"They've tamed the Red Whips!" It was the young duke talking. He had overcome his shock at seeing us and sat at a table by that of the king and shoveled in a supper of bread, greens, and thin beer. I thought either he was the sort who didn't care what he ate, or his tastes were as monastic as his appearance.

"You can't tame the Naiish people," I answered him and the king together. "They claim the plain is neither Velonyan or Rezhmian but Naiish, and who can contradict them? Who has ever displaced them who tried?"

"We didn't," said King Rudof, who was eating the best cut off the joint as though nothing awaited him this evening save his pillow nor the next morning save his bath. But he drank thin beer, like the duke.

Arlin had finished her argument, and having lost, she ate with silent intensity; I can't remember what.

I do remember that I had a piece of the Coach's famous raisin pie. (Alshie makes an astonishing raisin pie, and when I went to the counter to beg a piece, she acted almost like the woman who had paid my wages, years before.)

"Of course we didn't, sir," answered the duke. "They have no affinity toward us. They are Rezhmian."

It is a universal misunderstanding, at least among Velonyans, that the Naiish and the Rezhmian people are of one bloodstock. Most of my life I had believed so, as well. Yet there was something about the language of young Leoue, about his way of reasoning, that reminded me strongly of his father, who had hated me for the shape of my face and felt no embarrassment for doing so. I felt cold to the bone.

"Don't say that, my lord, in the presence of a Rezhmian—especially a Rezhmian soldier. Nor to a plains rider. If there is a blood relationship, it is not obvious from within."

"Sir" was good enough for the king, but Leoue would naturally be called "my lord." It is a peculiarity of our modern aristocracy that the man of highest respect is called by the title given to every respectable burgher. The nobility, who had less to lose than the king, held on to their privilege more tightly.

It makes of conversation a sarcasm: especially when it was me calling old Leoue's son "my lord." Yet I had no choice, save to remain silent, and at this moment, silence was dangerous.

172

"Forgive me, sir," I said to Rudof, "but you must take this messenger's story with some salt."

"I do," he said in turn, and glanced sidelong from me to the duke. ". . . And I'll salt my food myself, old friend. I need no help."

My journeys caught up with me; they overtook me in one moment, while I was reflecting that the house of Leoue and I had exchanged roles, and now King Rudof was chiding me for leaping down the young man's throat.

And Rudof himself was no fledgling anymore. If I had almost thirty years under the belt, then so did he. He had been king for six years and it was all his business. So I fell asleep.

I woke with the king's jacket thrown loosely over my head, and a feeling I had committed an error. Arlin, across from me, was asleep with her hands wrapped around herself and her eyes open, in the belly of the wolf. I have never met anyone, North or South, that had that trancelike facility, save Arlin.

The duke was still sitting beside her at the table, though he had flung off his woolen jacket with its military colors, and looked more like a student than a great bumblebee. "I think you are mad, sir. Forgive my impertinence, but I think you are God-touched to go into disaster tonight, and I do not wish to encourage you."

I saw the king's face: amused, irritated, obstinate. It seemed a very Rudof mood. He noticed I was waking and immediately poked me the rest of the way. "All of Powl's students are a little mad, aren't they, Zhurrie?"

I was being seduced by the king, as I had been before, more than once. I resented it. "As far as I know, sir, I am the only mad one. Powl was careful in that way."

The duke could not like hearing us talk about you, since his own father had considered you the source of all the nation's degeneracy. (What an accolade!) He said nothing of his feelings, however, but merely asked the king to repeat his plan, for my reaction to it.

Rudof poked me again, and grinned charmingly, but I was not comforted by that grin. "Of course I will, Leoue. But I'd hoped his skills ran to hearing in his sleep. No? Or you don't want to admit it?"

"No!" I spoke too loud, and tried to wipe my weariness off my face, but the grains of grit were so thick they made a noise, and abraded my skin painfully. "No, I was sound asleep, sir. What? What are you planning?"

He looked down at me with the same air of schoolboys conspiring that had first led me into danger with him, and he said, "I'm going to capture the Sanaur of Rezhmia, Nazhuret. I will negate the entire invasion by capturing the king. Chess—you know?"

I might have answered as the duke did, that this was madness. I certainly agreed that it was madness. I might have decided at that moment that Rudof

173

could not be turned aside, and it was too late to run safely, and that it was better to go out in a spark of brilliance than be hunted into a corner. Both these
answers would have been acceptable to the man who was the king. But I chose
honesty, and I said, "I think you will fail, sir. I think you will win nothing, and
be taken for your trouble. I think if you are willing, there are enough people
in this town who will hide you, and see you safely north, regardless of occupation. I myself will stand by—"

"I wanted you with me in *this*! I am going, not fleeing, Nazhuret of
Sordaling! My only question is whether you come with me or not!"

I remember not only the king's always-memorable anger, but also that
Leoue flinched as King Rudof titled me "of Sordaling," as though he had
called me something else entirely.

"Four days ago," I answered, speaking slowly so as not to be caught by that
anger, "Arlin and I saved the life of the Sanaur of Rezhmia against an attempt
by his heir, Reingish. Arlin, in fact, killed the min'naur."

"I guessed as much," said the king. I don't know whether he was telling
the truth.

"Of course four days ago we had no notion that the old man had decided
for war. I don't know what difference that would have made. You said it; he's
my family. What sort of weapon would that make me in your battle, my king?"

Rudof's eyes were brilliant as the sun through leaves. "Weapon, Nazhuret?
Have I ever asked you to strike a blow against anyone?

"You are what you have been to me for five years—a lucky piece. Pure
superstition. I only invoke you when human help seems useless, like now."

I looked from my mad king to my lady, who was so deep into the belly of
the wolf as to look more than mad herself. In fact, Leoue was the only one at
the table to show human rationality, for I felt my own reason slipping away.

I swung my feet over the long bench and stood up. "I have to walk a
while," I said, but I ran.

The last time I had been in Warvala, it had been early winter, and Arlin and
I had been almost desperate with cold. I had gotten work at the district library,
putting in order the Allec and Rayzhia collections, but Arlin had paid most of
our keep, with quick fingers and some trained playing cards. For my sake she
had avoided the Yellow Coach. Now as I splashed the wet wooden streets, with
the familiar wet smell of winter closing in, I wished so clearly for that time to
be back again that I almost drove myself demented. I stood at the porter's door
of the library—one of the few brick buildings in this half-civilized city—and
imagined I was going to work, filing books misfiled for the last twenty years.

I broke out of that delusion with my foot on the bottom stair, and I suddenly knew where I was going.

174

"I only invoke you when human help seems useless, like now." I had been horrified by the king's idea of me, as I was horrified by the reality of Dowln. I was looking for Dowln, because human help seemed useless, and I expected to find him where you would find a jeweler.

The first shop I came to was already boarded up. The second, across the street, had a heavy wagon in front of it, and that was loaded with furniture and children. The burgher driving it looked Zaquash, and in the local dialect I called to him.

He answered me in fine Rayzhia: "He said you might be here. I'm not sure he understands we are leaving. I told him, but I'm not sure he understands."

"Well, you never know, with Dowln."

He pointed at the door and gestured I should open it. Then his horses hit their harness with a rattle of bells and the family was off.

Inside the house were a few tables and an empty display case, fronted in very good glass. Upstairs, all the bedding had been stripped from the beds, except for one, within which Dowln was nested. His tall Old Vesting frame was too long for the Zaquash bed, and he was curled like a hedgehog.

He had bathed, and washed his hair. I envied him that, and I envied him his sleep more. His blue eyes were moving behind the translucent eyelids. I felt a great reluctance to wake him, for I was deadly tired myself.

Dowln was looking up at me. I lowered myself beside him. "You were dreaming?" I asked him.

He shrugged out of his blankets. "I'm always dreaming."

"They're gone," I said. "The whole family." Then before he could respond to that, I continued. "Tell me, dreamer. Should I go?"

He didn't wonder where. "Why ask me? I am the emperor's man. As no one else in Rezhmia, I am his."

The feather bed was seductive. I rubbed my face in my hands. "Yet I don't think you'll lie to me. Should I go?"

He sat up, using the cold to bring him fully awake. "You also hate my gifts."

"But I no longer doubt them. And I have nothing else. I cannot see how this town. . . or my king. . . or Arlin and myself can survive through tomorrow. Not with any human help."

His face, so pale normally, was touched blue, by cold or emotion. He looked at me, black-eyed, and then Dowln ran to the window and vomited bile convulsively.

I was astonished. I put a blanket over him until the spell was past, but he shivered hard for five minutes, then shook his head, stood up, and dressed in fresh clothes.

He looked down at me again, as composed as he had been in the ruined City. "Very few whom you know here will survive tomorrow, unless you go with your king."

175

I took him by his bony wrist, to thank him, but he trapped my hand there. "And also, unless you take me with you," he said.

I know that when our suicidal little procession left Warvala, I had been washed and given new clothes, but though I have sat here at my table these ten minutes trying to remember, I don't recall where I bathed or what I put on. I doubt it was Rezhmian finery, but I am not certain even of that.

Arlin dressed in black, and she rode a black mare I had never seen before. The king dressed in dull russet, and that was the color of his horse. Dowln, who had been introduced to the king only as our guide, was cloaked in gray, the color of the horse he had been lent. We looked like children's toys, dipped into buckets of paint. Simple. Simple-minded.

Young Leoue was with us, dressed almost as black as Arlin, and three others of the king's personal guard followed us splashing through puddles as the light faded.

The stars were astonishingly bright, and as I believed I was looking at them for the last time, I tried to forget the geographical patterns by latitude and the astronomical patterns by level of light. This was very difficult for me; science reared its head and gave me ten stars of the third magnitude and seventy of the first, as well as the constellation of the Goose, just touching the northern horizon with one wing.

The plains are splendid for star counting: not like my occluded native forests, which I would not see again.

It was very cold, and I remember feeling I could bear the rest of this idiocy if only my fingers were not so chilled. And if Arlin were not here. I was also irritated by the noise the guardsmen made—they who were honored to be in small company with the king and probably did not believe they were riding out to die. They shifted and creaked in their saddles, and tinkled their spurs, and spoke among themselves in a ridiculous sibilant whisper.

To my slight surprise, King Rudof was irritated by them also, and about an hour past sunset he sent the three back to Warvala. So I guess they did not die.

That left three of us who had been stealth-trained by you, Dowln (who was inexplicably good at being quiet), and Leoue. The young duke had had his father for a teacher: that man so much my enemy. He taught his son stalking very well. As well as you taught me. So we prowled toward the cavalry of Rezhmia silently, as though stealth could make any difference in the end.

When we saw the glow against the clouds in the sky, we buried our horses' reins in the soil. It was an anchoring that would serve until the beasts got hungry, or afraid. It was enough. They would find their way home.

176

The king led.

We walked over miles of short grasses, old but too wet to crackle under-foot. It seemed we had dismounted too soon, because the fires were higher than we had thought and the encampment farther away. As we topped the next rolling down, I saw the fires themselves spread out before us, filling the near horizon. They were impossibly many, like all of Velonya's midsummer bonfires gathered on one hilltop. In the middle were some flames that might be proud of themselves, but for the most part the fires were paltry: not mili-tary issue. Together they all made a pattern (I speak fancifully) like the sun wearing the crescent moon as a skullcap. The sun's skullcap was on the other side from us. No more was visible.

I relayed what I saw, for among us my vision was the best. Arlin, mean-while, had stood on tiptoe and then lowered herself to the grass, turning right and left and sniffing like a dog. "I smell blood," she said. "At first I thought it was the sea, but it's blood. Blood and guts."

Rudof snorted once or twice. "Maybe it's a dead animal, somewhere down-wind. We are too far to smell anything from the camp."

I did not want to contradict the king unnecessarily, but Arlin's nose is as reliable as my eyes. I could smell nothing, but I tested the air. "Wind's coming from the South, sir. From the Rezhmian camp to us."

"Maybe they overtook a herd of bison or cattle and slaughtered them for tonight's meal." The young duke's voice shook. I wondered how much fight-ing he had seen, if any, and why he wanted to be with us in this dementia.

Arlin very haughtily informed him that it is not the custom for armies about to go into battle to slaughter large animals: at least not in public. It is then that soldiers are most aware of the similarities between the bodies of beasts and our own, and least inclined to watch entrails spilled upon the ground. Leoue took the contradiction meekly enough, but I could feel his shivers through the earth.

Dowln gave nothing toward the discussion, and I was glad, because I had learned to be frightened every time he opened his mouth. When the king led us forward again, Dowln was close behind him. I cut in between the two.

"I hear them," said King Rudof. He flattened himself and spoke into the grass: much better than whispering.

Arlin sank down more gracefully. In the same manner she said to us, "Isn't it fine that each of us has a special sense or skill, better than the others. We are like the five old men in the parable—the king has the ears, and Zhurrie the eyes, and I can smell a stink anywhere. . ."

Leoue was close by my right side and I saw him flinch.

After a moment of thought I realized his misery was due to Arlin's words. He thought we were making ourselves special at his expense. Even the way he stalked with us, out to the side and behind, reminded me of the wolf in the pack whom no one respects, who hunts with them on sufferance.

Why had he come? Did he hope to win the king's favor? The king was throwing himself away, so there was not much to win.

There was the slightest of noises behind me, and I looked around to see Dowln, tall and thin like a mile marker, obscuring the stars. He had remained standing while the rest of us had followed the king to the ground. His pale eyes, reflecting pale light, were calm and self-possessed. He did not feel it necessary to imitate our actions.

If he was not his own man, he belonged only to one other. I thought: he's a slave, but he's the emperor's slave, and his humility is another man's arrogance.

And I was a beggar, but I was a beggar protected by the king. I felt a strong compassion for young Duke Leoue, who would face the whole Rezhmian force believing that a beggar had more honor than he did.

"I need no more remarks about my ears," said the king, pointing a long finger at Arlin, whom he liked deeply despite all disagreements. "'Large ears make a deep soul.'"

"'Long ears make for obstinacy,'" she answered. "Witness the donkey."

Now I heard, too. The sounds were Rayzhia, but where generally that language is a series of hisses and growls (to the Velonyan ear), the sounds I heard were shrill and abrupt. And then there was wailing.

"Perhaps a religious rite?" asked the duke, and I hoped no one would snap his head off for his ignorance. No one did.

"They're grieving. . . someone," said the king, raising his head again to look. "They must have hit opposition already."

I heard Dowln lower himself to the earth and sigh.

We waited until the sounds had died down: until the bottom of the night. Despite my woolen jacket—there! I have determined that I was wearing a woolen jacket—I was chilled and stiff. My mind was more upon Arlin than upon my own death.

I remembered her as she had been in the spring, when her pregnancy had first begun to change her. For a while she was sick: not just in the mornings, but at times all day, but then she blossomed like a flower, at the same time the first flowers were blossoming. She smiled a lot, and her saturnine personality lightened as much as I had ever seen it. Now she was black night again, with a calm coldness her training had only purified.

Another man would have done his best to keep his lady out of this nightmare. Another man would have wound up crippled or killed by Arlin, trying. Myself—I don't know whether I could overcome and bind a fighter of Arlin's standard, but I know I could not beat Arlin herself. Besides, she was one of your students, Powl, and so her freedom was inviolable, even if it was only her freedom to die.

I was almost equally sick about the king, not merely for his own sake but for that of Velonya. There was no one else so perfect for the role of leader of our nation: no one else who had the personal power over men and yet who would let himself be chained by increasing law. There was no one else who was taught by you.

But because he was another of your students, and because he was king, I could not leap upon him, bind him, and drag him back to Warvala. I thought of it, I felt the ropes in my hands, I almost hallucinated the act as a young man may hallucinate copulation, but I did nothing. Instead I sat in the belly of the wolf, and waited, and shivered.

It was a silent wait. Arlin was deep in her own contemplation, and the king (to my surprise) was engaged in a similar meditation. I hadn't known he had been taught the art. The young duke sat with one knee up and his face taut with discipline, and Dowln—there was no guessing the mind of Dowln.

We moved again when the king decided. Half the fires were out, and the sounds from the camp were muted. We walked upright, trusting our eyes were better adapted to dark than those of soldiers sitting around campfires, and that we were more alert than the average sentry.

We were wrong, for the first figure we saw we had almost overrun, and he turned and sniffed the air even as Arlin had done. She was behind the man and she stood at least two hands taller. She put one hand over his mouth and slit his throat with her dagger. The man had a bow and she took it. This whole act astonished the king and Duke Leoue, too, but neither dared make a sound.

"That's odd," said Arlin in her deepest, quietest voice, but she did not explain. We went on.

Almost immediately the stink went from something to be noticed to something to be avoided. It was fresh death: slaughteryard, not rot. First we found a horse, reduced to a barrel-shaped lump on the ground, and next his rider. After that the ground was dotted by corpses.

They were all Rezhmian. Astonishingly—all Rezhmian cavalry. There was another sentry, whom Arlin took through the throat with an arrow stolen from her last kill. He went down cleanly.

"She is mother death herself," said Dowln in my ear, with no emotion. So angry did this make me that I took the tall fellow by the collar and knocked him to his knees, which put his face not far below my own. I uttered one or two incoherent threats and in self-disgust I let him go. He rose up again with no more emotion than before.

Five hundred yards farther and another two dozen corpses behind us, we encountered sentries of the more usual sort: cavalrymen close-spaced, with harquebus and sword, and eyes rolling at the dark around them. Behind them loomed the shadows of tents, and one of these was huge and complicated of shape, although it seemed half collapsed. Both Rudof and I recognized it as a command quarters. Perhaps the Sanaur Mynauzet was not within, but if he was not, I could not guess where he was.

At the king's signal we lay ourselves down among the dead and considered matters. "If we can cut through quietly, we can make it to the pavilion. Once we have the emperor, we can use him for protection."

King Rudof spoke as though he really believed this possible. I didn't. The Rezhmian sentries were standing no more than fifteen feet apart. I estimated we would have to kill a dozen to break through, and that was without any nonsense of secrecy. Once through, we would drag the entire line behind us, like a large fish in a small net.

Arlin crept up beside him. "Excuse me, sir," she said to the king and the grass. "But I have an odd thought."

"I expect no less of you, civilian," answered Rudof, with artificial formality. "Expound your eccentricity."

She rubbed her dirty face with two dirty hands. "The men I killed I could not see clearly, but they were carrying recurved bows and short arrows. They were not dressed in uniform."

He stared intently at her, and even under starlight I could see a touch of green in his eyes. "So?"

"So, remember the last Velonyan incursion. Remember that it was not Rezhmia that destroyed our heavy cavalry on the plains."

The king's whole frame jerked, silently. He shook his head. "You think it is the Red Whips? That have done this? All this to the second largest cavalry in the modern world?"

When she nodded, he stared again, and shook his head again. "It is almost impossible to get the tribes to unite, even against a large enemy. You know that."

"They did it before. Thirty-two years ago."

I suggested that if the assailants were Naiish, then there was a chance that the ruined cavalry might be approached peacefully. I had a chance to do it, with my resemblance to the family, and if the soldiers knew I had proved friend to my "grandfather."

Duke Leoue was at my side, still shivering. Now he sighed as well and ground his teeth. He put his hand over my mouth urgently, and I shut up. He crawled up to the other side of the king and said into his ear, "No, sir. I doubt it. I think it would be fatal to attempt a rapprochement with the Rezhmians now. I have another idea who has harried the enemy. I think it is the troops of Norwess Province. Of my own house."

Now King Rudof was not only incredulous but angry. As he could not shout, he shook the young man by the shoulder. "What possessed you to give orders to attack without my knowledge or permission? And why did you let us crawl out here on our bellies. . ."

"No, sir. No, sir, I did not order an attack. I did not even bring troops with me, except my personal guard." He dropped his face against the turf, hard enough to bruise. He did it again. "God! Oh God! It is only that I suspect. . . I suspect. . ."

He groaned and he waited to get his voice back.

"I suspect there are some of them who are not fully loyal to me. Who never accepted me as replacement to my father."

"And you let this continue? Year after year, you lived with mutiny!" The king scarcely bothered to keep his voice down. I thought we might get a dose of Rudof's famous temper, and that would surely see us into the next world at the swords or guns of those nervous sentries. But we were lucky.

"No, sire. Sir. I didn't know. I was at school, and with my teachers. And with you. Only recently have I suspected. . . They loved my father."

King Rudof's temper shut itself off like a water valve. "Was it your men who have been trying to murder Nazhuret? Who chased these two over the western plains like a beat of hunters after deer? Who attempted the life of his. . . of his wife and killed the baby in the womb?"

You must have told the king all this. I had not. Leoue grabbed the dead grass in both hands. "Not by my order, sir. In fact, when this man came to me this spring, I was confident it was some other enemy who was trying to kill him. It seemed to me that a fellow like him would have many enemies. I wanted to believe this."

"This isn't the time or place for this discussion," I said, but no one was listening to me. Arlin, with marvelous little respect for royalty, had leaned over the king's back. "Your troops have been burning Rezhmian cities, Leoue. Killing more children than just. . . Nazhuret's. Your troops have started this war."

As she said this, I realized it must be true. "We can't know that," said the young duke in misery. "We can't know it."

King Rudof, as is his custom when serving as judiciary, sighed and scratched his beard. "If not you, Leoue, who is it your father's men now obey?"

Leoue looked at the ground. "I don't know," he said. Then: "My mother," he said.

"She never accepted his death. Nor that he had done. . . what he did."
He did not look up, and we all crouched there on the chilly earth in the dark, wondering.

"Your accent is best, Zhurrie," said the king into my ear. "You do it. Back up a good hundred feet and call out. Cry for Garel: there's always a Garel in a Rezhmian company. Ask him to save you. Show pain. Be theatrical. And don't let them find you."

"You don't trust me to go in with you," I said. Oddly enough, I was not angry at this, nor hurt.

The king grunted and shook me by one shoulder. "Right, old friend, I don't trust you. Not between myself and this 'grandfather' of yours. You stay here."

It was almost silent on the plains now. No moon and a fog over the stars. I dropped my voice even further as I answered King Rudof. "I will stay if Arlin stays with me."

I heard the duke's anger in his throat. "You'll do what the king says, ingrate!" He spoke a bit too loudly.

"That would be a first," answered Rudof, more quietly.

Arlin tapped me on the head. "No. No, Zhurrie. One of us must go in with them or they'll never make it past the tent flap. Don't worry, Nazhuret. I doubt one of us will outlive the other by very long." She looked over to the king.

"But before we move, sir, remember that I am the one who killed the usurper, Reingish, and so saved the emperor's crown and his life. Do you still want me?"

Under his muffling hands, King Rudof laughed: a reckless, red-headed laugh. "We'll 'never make it past the tent flap' without you, correct? So we haven't much choice."

"You go back," said Arlin to me, as though speaking to a horse, or a dog, and by God I found myself obeying her. I felt her hand stroke my hair as I rose to leave, and I glanced back to see that it wasn't her lean face over me, but that of Dowln.

"It is hard for you," he said, not in Velonyie. His voice was filled with compassion.

I thought I was alone, but the young duke was still with me, trembling with human fear perhaps, or with the need to rush to the king's side. "I want you to know," he whispered, so loudly he spat into the air, ". . . that before I saw you this spring, I'd seen you before. All my life I've seen your goblin face out of the corner of my eye. In the house you think should have been yours."

I had forgotten—I, who was the image of the Minsanaur of Rezhmia—that I was also a ghost in the halls of Norwess. It was too much to accept, here in the dark, and at the edge of death, and I didn't answer him.

"Well, perhaps you will have it after all, as your father intended." He started to squirm away from me over the ground and I could think of only one thing to say, which was "I wouldn't take it, my lord. I don't want any of it. I have better."

And as he flinched away I knew I had been cruel.

I sneaked back among the dead and I cried out like a wounded man, as I had been commanded. I had no difficulty acting the part; I was weary and full of fear. The sentry line broke without resistance, and the night became lively with brave, blind men searching by touch among the corpses. I remember someone called out to me that Garel was dead, but that old Haimin would bring me in—that they had no opium but still some brandy. That there was a doctor somewhere in the line.

No one even asked my name.

I felt a huge respect for these Rezhmian sentries, who were such good men and such bad sentries. I was appalled that this game might end in my having to kill them, or them me. But they were soldiers and I was only a young tramp, used to nights without light. I avoided them for ten minutes and would have avoided them all night, except that the great bell was rung, and all the sentries flung themselves back to their positions.

I heard my name called by the Emperor of Rezhmia, and then the same awkward syllables from Rudof of Velonya. Before I could decide whether to respond, the two greatest rulers of the northern world shouted for me together, the aged treble and the young king's full tenor. The sentries spun in place, astonished, and in the distance I heard catcalls from the besieging army. I answered as respectfully as a man might answer two rulers at once, but as I was not confident of my welcome, I crawled through the sentry line on my belly and came in shadow to the door of the pavilion, where the height of King Rudof almost eclipsed the slight form of the Sanaur of Rezhmia.

"I am here, sir," I said. "I am here, Grandfather," and both men started. Their vision had been ruined by the lamplight within. Rudof grabbed me by the arm and pulled me through the door.

Dowln was drying his hair in a towel. Arlin was eating bread and gravy with a soldier's singlemindedness. The young duke sat on a stool in the corer of the pavilion, looking like a man who wished only to die. There was no one else in the room.

It was the 'naur who spoke to me first. He gestured to the tall blond, so recently his slave, and he hissed at me, "I thought I told you to take him to safety! I asked nothing else of you but that you take him to safety!"

Dowln answered without taking his face out of the towel. "How, master? What safety was there for them or for me, with your entire army descending upon Warvala? By the way; did you choose Warvala because I told you how entertaining it was? Because of my stories of the jewel-cutters and the jewel merchants and the jewel thieves? A poor reward to the place, and to my friends in the place."

I was astounded in the middle of my astonishment. I—who treated the King of Velonya with so little respect—could not believe Dowln's rudeness.

Sanaur Mynauzet was abusing me and would not be distracted by Dowln. "You could have put him on a horse and sent him north. It would have cost you little."

183

"How could any of us send the man north, south, or anywhere?" said Arlin, sounding much like you in your driest irony. "You freed him, didn't you? Whom the Sanaur of Rezhmia calls a free man, can any of us treat as a slave?"

King Rudof glanced from the tall woman to the short emperor, his green eyes gleaming, and inexhaustible energy and curiosity in his stance. I didn't want to fence with the old man, who was so clearly in pain about Dowln's danger. "Forgive me, 'Naur. Grandfather. He told me that many lives depended upon my bringing him with us."

"Rezhmian lives, or of your own kind? Or did he mean the tens of thousands of savages that have us trapped like bison?"

So Arlin had been right. I had not really believed it was Duke Leoue's men who had trampled the Rezhmian cavalry, but to hear that it was Naiish for certain was to hear us condemned to death. All of us. I was looking not at the emperor but at a wax candle sitting upon his map table, and the light of it dissolved and turned colorful in the prisms of the tears in my eyes.

"I did not ask whose lives, Grandfather," I answered him, and without invitation, I sat down beside Arlin and drank a long glass of the juice of the fresh harvest.

Rezhmia by the sea had been so beautiful.

King Rudof cleared his throat, and spoke in his clean but accented Rayzhia. "So. Velonya is safe—from this force, at least. And the land of Rezhmia is safe, too. The Red Whips will never extend their violence over the edge of the plains. It is only that all here are going to die."

He gazed calmly from one face to another. King Rudof was still full of spirit; that is his birth-gift. "Who is your heir, now, Emperor of Rezhmia, since Reingish proved disloyal?"

The old sanaur had one hand over the shoulder of his former slave. He had to raise that hand so far above his own shoulder, it was like a man comforting a horse. "I don't know, sir—that is the inadequate title they grant you, isn't it? 'Sir'? There are three or four of equal blood-standing. I have written my choice, but whether that holds after tonight I cannot tell. There will be a man ready to take the task, whatever."

King Rudof's bristly orange eyebrows rose. "You take the matter easily, Emperor."

The old man sighed. "I am eighty-two years old. I have outlived many heirs. What about you? If you are so careful of your line, why did you commit such idiocy as to break into our camp?"

Now the king laughed outright. "Well, you see, 'Naur, I expected you were about to overrun my city. And I had only two hundred soldiers under my command. Sometimes idiocy is an inspiration of genius."

184

The emperor put his hands upon his lap and worked to understand this. "But not this time. After what happened to your father's invasion, when I was a young man. . ." He sighed.

"Ah, but you see we have always believed the Naiish were loyal to you, Sanaur of Rezhmia. Loosely loyal."

The emperor's wrinkles retreated from his eyes, for just a moment. "What a barbaric thought! Is a mad dog loyal, even loosely? Besides, they are obviously more of your blood than ours."

Arlin made a rustling, to deflect national angers. "I suggest, sir, Sanaur, that those of us in this room exit the situation as we came, darkly and without noise. The riders' west line is weakest, and we have some chance of making it back to where we left the horses."

The old man snorted. "Leave my men to die and go as hostage? Why? My old life is worth nothing to my people if not as a figurehead."

King Rudof stood, and paced, and glared at the Emperor of Rezhmia. "No, 'Naur. Not as a hostage. Call off your infantry, which is probably murdering my people along the sea road even now, and ride with us as a free partner."

Now the old emperor laughed. "Of course. You have nothing to lose in that offer, have you? Call off the war you didn't want and can't resist and one old man can go free. Great thanks for your generosity!"

I was stung by the emperor's response, because I know my king's ridiculous generosity, and I knew the offer was Rudof at his best, not at his most politic. I thought the king would show his equally ridiculous temper, but he did not. I edged out the tent, hating arguments, but I heard him say, "Your war upon Velonya is over, Emperor, even if you are burning Morquenie now. There is nothing to win here but survival, or at least a quick death. The Naiish are not kind to captives. . ."

I remembered that the Velonyans had not been kind to a Naiish captive, once, but it did not seem the time to speak good of our common enemy. I let the tent flap down behind me.

In five minutes of listening outside, I knew that Arlin's plan was doomed. I came back in to more rancorous argument, this time about the attacks upon the eastern villages. I cut both monarchs short and told them that the Naiish had closed the southern aspect and we were fully surrounded.

"What then?" asked Arlin, as though we two were alone.

I sat down on the bench with the King of Velonya and the Emperor of Rezhmia. "I suggest, my lords, that the company gear up as quietly as possible and strike to make an opening. Use whatever powder weapons can be prepared quickly and leave no one behind. Strike as one, toward the West, where they have only now taken position."

185

The sanaur rubbed his old hands along his thighs. "We can be ready by dawn," he said.

"No. They expect that. Only the Naiish fight by night. This is their great advantage. We must surprise them with their own tactics."

Rudof stared at me intently, greenly. "And you think we have a hope of success, doing this?"

I was forced to honesty. "No," I told them all. "It is only the best thing."

For the first time since military school, I was dressed in armor, and for the first time in my life, in the light, silken Rezhmian armor, padded below with cotton pods. My arms felt slightly constrained in this gear, but after all what did a slight constraint matter? We were going out into hell.

Arlin wore her armor over her civilian clothing, remaining a secret always. The King of Velonya seemed to get a great enjoyment out of wearing the clothing of the people who had been his enemy until a few minutes ago. The duke refused to change.

The horses made the most noise, jingling in their harness. The men were by and large too frightened to talk.

It was a mad parade we prepared. Nothing like this had happened in the seven hundred years that Velonya and Rezhmia had been bad neighbors to one another. I saw the king and the emperor on matching gray horses, though the old man rode up behind his unfreeable servant, Dowln. The eunuch no longer cared about the impropriety of his riding a stallion.

The young duke rode in front of Rudof, and his face was whiter than the hide of the emperor's horses. In front of all, between the king and the emperor, rode Arlin and I. She held out her hand to me, and though our horses were confused and restive, I took it and held it. Behind us stretched a ghostly line of horses of all colors and men of all sorts upon them, and behind us all, those who had lost their mounts. Last of all came the wagons full of wounded—pitiful imitations of hope.

Our way was now utterly obscured by fog, and the wet air held the smell of death close to the ground. I could see the efficient little fires of the Naiish all around, and I imagined their voices.

"You're exuberant for a man going to slaughter," said the emperor to King Rudof. "Are you so sure of your little son and heir, then?"

"I'm sure he's my son," answered Rudof. "And my heir. What more can a man know?"

Old "Grandfather" wasn't finished with his teasing. "I've heard you don't get on with your queen, royal cousin. Is that why you are so eager to leave life behind?"

Rudof made an exaggerated gesture of outrage. "By God's faces, does the whole world know that story? Emperor, I tell you I do not leave life behind, and if it wants to be rid of me, it will have to leave me. Now let us do this thing, if we're going to do it!"

They both turned to me, as though I was to give the signal. I was willing. "Why wait?" I thought aloud. "The Naiish will only learn more of what we're planning."

"So," called the emperor. "The King of the Dead will lead us. So be it. Into the dark!"

But it was not I who spurred first into that solid fog. At least I don't think so. It was Arlin, still with my hand in hers. We sprang forward together on fresh horses, war-trained, leaping puddles and leaping the dead. I shouted a battle cry, and to my own amazement, it was neither that of Velonya nor of the East, but the treble scream of the Naiish themselves. Arlin did it better.

I did not see the archer who struck me first, and I felt only a light blow against my chest padding. The stuff was more effective than I had imagined. I heard other shouts behind me and the thud of a horse hitting the ground. I heard the bang of powder charges from the line behind us, spooking our horses left and right.

It seemed we were dead already, in one of the worst hells of Zaquashlan folk religion, for enemies came grimacing out of the white night and disappeared again, either dead or left behind. Something drummed me lightly on the back; it was another Naiish arrow. Beside me, close as parade drill, Arlin was using her dowhee. She cursed at something.

Behind me was the king, and a little arrow bobbed from the padding of his side. I saw this arrow had gone in, puckering the silk around it. The king was still full of life, however, and his saber was flickering against the obscurity of the night. I did not see the duke, but there was no time to ask; we floundered on over the corpses.

Arlin's horse hit mine, side-on, because she was assailed by two riders on barrel-ribbed ponies. I lost my objectivity and like any Velonyan I thought they looked inhuman. Like monkeys. Though I could see little enough of their faces or those of my friends. I could not help my lady, so I trusted to her blade and kept her back against the monkeys that came for me.

No one fights on horseback like the Naiish. I lost my dowhee and took another arrow in the padding of my thigh, and I heard my horse scream, though it did not go down.

Shoving between us was the white horse of the emperor, and upon it Dowln sat swaying and blinking, pricked as full of arrows as a thistle was full of thorns. He drove his beast between Arlin and me, and not by accident. The old emperor had a few arrows of his own in his armor, and was holding his slave upright with both hands. Again we found ourselves defending the

enemy of our native country, while behind us the king made a back gate no
Naiish warrior had the luck to open.

Even in the dim light I could see the stains spreading over Dowln's linen.
I wondered if some custom had forbidden him armor. The emperor, too, was
watching, and though he had no weapon, he kicked the horse forward
between us and shouted, in his old man's voice, "Rezhmia! Rezhmia! For the
pink city!"

The cry was picked up by a hundred men behind us, but then it was cut
and broken by a loud voice close behind my ear.

"Velonya!" cried the king. "For the swan, and the blue and white! Velonya!"
He charged to my left side, as though to show that the king himself was protecting this beggar.

Silence greeted this unexpected shout: silence from the men behind, and
silence from around us. A few more arrows sang past, and I heard a babble of
Naiish idiom, and then all movement stopped. I let my horse hang his head.

"Keep going," said Rudof, shaking me by the shoulder. It hurt. "They're
preparing something, but now we have a chance to break through."

I didn't want to tell him I wasn't sure we were breaking through. I distrusted the direction our wild charge had taken us, and besides, two torches
approached decorously through the fog. It looked like parley.

Dowln was at my other side, and he was drenched in blood. "One more
thing," he gasped, and even his mouth was bleeding. "One more thing I will
see. As I told you."

The old emperor was weeping, and I do not think it was from fear. The
wavering lights with their oil stink drew near, along with the clopping of
ponies' hooves. Two faces were so illumined. One was surrounded by feathers
and silk. The other wore Naiish dress, but wore it like a costume. He looked
at us—you looked at us—your damned eyes as expressionless as ever, and you
lifted one hand above your head, and all the Naiish cattle horns blew, one
starting another, until the round world was filled with them.

You trotted forward, and unless I misremember you said, "Sir, I think the
Rezhmian incursion is over."

The king came to meet you, his green eyes glassy and his breath hard in
his throat. "You did this, Powl? You got all the tribes to obey one rule?"

"Why not?" you said. "It was done before, as I have reason to know." He
bowed to the Naiish magician beside him—the one I had traveled with, eaten
with, and seen dressed as an old woman as well as an old man. "Even a
Velonyan nobleman can learn from his mistakes. Though of course I did not
expect to cause discourtesy to the Sanaur of Rezhmia himself. How could I
know? Besides, I have no real power among the dryland people." He bowed
in the same fashion to Sanaur Mynauzet.

In front of that old man sat Dowln, though whether anything other than the emperor's support held him in the saddle I do not know. He was conscious, however, and he said, "Earl of Daraln, I have waited to meet you. I am very glad it is now done."

"And I am honored to meet you, prophet of the emperor." You reached out your neatly groomed hand and touched Dowln, and then added, "Though I believe it is now too late."

I glanced again and you were right. The man was dead. The old man held tightly to the frame so much larger than his own, and he held it upright. The golden collar twinkled in the torchlight.

"Leoue is dead," said King Rudof. "He took a stroke in the neck, protecting me. He was scarcely more than a boy."

You must have looked as though you had something to say about Leoue, or about his house, for the king continued. "And anything else about him, we will discuss later. The emperor is my guest, or else I am his. The matter is disputable. We must send messengers to the South, to stop meaningless bloodshed."

Meanwhile, I remember, you were looking at me, with your mild concern. "And when is it not meaningless?" you said, but I think for my ears only. It was then you pulled at the loose silk covering over my chest padding and I felt the first fierce pain that told me the arrows had penetrated the armor. "Three of them," you said as you used the silk to pull them out. "You got away easy, lad." Ehpen, the great magician, was doing the same for Arlin's two wounds. I almost fainted.

All the rest, you know better than I.

I have no explanations, Powl. I do not know whether magic brought me to Rezhmia, whether it brewed that horrible and abortive war or whether it stopped it. I am enough your pupil that I dislike even the sound of magic. To me it feels like treachery, and I have known too much treachery. If I can, I will call my magical experiences drug poisoning, or deep philosophy, but all these names do not change the fact that I do not understand.

I understand that Dowln is dead, and that he was a good man and a haunted one, and that he was my friend, and that I envied him and treated him worse than he deserved. I doubt I shall ever have the chance to see whether our idea for building rubies would work.

I understand that young Leoue is dead, with my scorn on his lips, when in time I might have become *his* friend.

Further, whether what I endured was magic or no, and whether the rest my life is as peaceful as I plan it or no, I cannot look in a mirror, any mi without knowing myself as the King of the Dead.

189

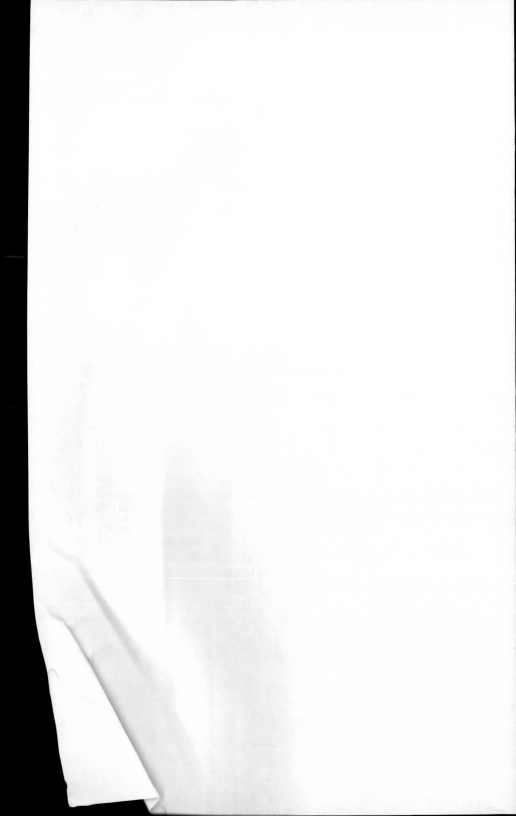

About the Author

R.A. MACAVOY is a highly acclaimed author, writing imaginative and original science fiction and fantasy novels. Her debut novel, TEA WITH THE BLACK DRAGON, won her the John W. Campbell Award for Best New Writer. She has also written the Damiano trilogy, the chronicles of a wizard's young son, set during the Italian Renaissance; THE BOOK OF KELLS, and TWISTING THE ROPE, the highly acclaimed sequel to TEA WITH THE BLACK DRAGON. She is also the author of the beloved and much-praised Lens of the World trilogy.

9 781585 869985